COURAGEOUS

ICONIC SONS MC: BOOK TWO

SHE

WILL NOT

LET FEAR

STOP

HER

KAHLANI B. STEELE

BOOKS BY
KAHLANI B. STEELE

ICONIC SONS MC SERIES:

Book One: Resilient

Book Two: Courageous

COMING 2026:

Book Three: Fearless

*"Those marks on your arms are a part of your past.
They represent what you've been through,
and that's some ugly shit.
Your scars are a part of you,
but they don't define your beauty."*
—Vin

lark used her key to unlock the door. It was four o'clock in the afternoon, and the house was shrouded in darkness. Her eyes swung toward the hallway, and she saw that her mom's bedroom door was closed. Knowing her mom didn't like being disturbed if her door was shut, Clark went into the kitchen to make herself a snack. She got out two stale pieces of bread, their dry texture crunching under her fingers, and layered several thin slices of savory ham between them. She sank into the worn cushions of the old, saggy couch, feeling the familiar dips and grooves beneath her. The faint scent of stale air lingered as she clicked the TV on with the remote control. The TV sound echoed in the silent house, even at a low volume, making Clark conscious of not disturbing her mom.

Since her daddy left, Clark's mom rarely spent time with her. She had no idea where her daddy had gone, leaving her with burning questions: *Where did he go? Why did he leave her? Didn't he love her anymore?* She realized he was truly gone when her mom told her Daddy wasn't coming home. He had a new family now. Clark was devastated when her mom said that he no longer loved her and chose to be with his other family. Her daddy's absence left a persistent ache in her heart, and she often cried herself to sleep, devastated at his rejection.

Her mom stopped doing the things she used to do when Daddy was around, like walking her to school, watching cartoons together, singing silly songs, and listening to her read. Clark often daydreamed about her daddy returning and everything going back to how it used to be. She remembered running barefoot outside, feeling the gravel crunch beneath her feet, to greet him when he arrived home from work. And when her daddy would scoop her up in his strong arms. He would lift her high above his head and twirl her around in joyful circles, her laughter echoing through the yard. Daddy would lovingly kiss her scraped knee, gently blowing to make the pain disappear. Clark remembered all this, but still, he never came home.

It was getting dark, and her mom was still asleep. Clark went into the kitchen to make herself some dinner. She rummaged through the pantry shelves, moving aside cans and boxes until she finally discovered a tin of spaghetti. She peeled back the lid, grabbed a fork, and started eating the spaghetti cold from the can. Her hand trembled as she raised the fork to her mouth, causing the tomato sauce to splatter onto her pale blue shirt in a messy, orange spray. Clark's heart raced, anticipating her mom's reaction. Panicked, she stripped off her shirt and frantically attempted to scrub the stain under the cold stream of the kitchen sink tap. She removed most of the orange stain after using a towel to rub the spot. Hoping Mom wouldn't notice the stain in the morning, she changed out of her school uniform, her mind already racing with excuses.

It was pitch-black outside, and while her mom stayed in her bedroom, Clark changed into her pajamas. She hopped into bed and snuggled under the blanket with her beloved teddy bear, Bugeye. She named him Bugeye because of his missing eye. Despite looking worn and slightly faded, Bugeye always comforted Clark, especially during her nightmares. She would squeeze him tight, and the feel and smell of him always chased away the monsters in the dark.

Clark anxiously waited to fall asleep, straining to hear any noises or movement from her mom's bedroom. She eventually drifted off to sleep, but it felt like mere moments had passed before it was morning again.

Jumping out of bed, Clark raced into the kitchen, expecting to see her mom sitting at the table, warming her hands around a hot mug of coffee. However, her mom was nowhere to be found, and a sense of unease crept over Clark as she gazed around the empty kitchen. Her mom had never slept this long. Maybe she was sick. A pang of worry gripped Clark's heart. Was it worth the risk to go in and check on her? Or would her mom's anger be worse than the worry gnawing at Clark's mind? She gently knocked on the door. When no one answered, she called out for her mom. She opened the door slowly, and to Clark's surprise, her mother was gone. Her ears perked, but she couldn't hear running water from the bathroom.

Clark wondered why her mom wasn't home. Her worry grew more intense with each passing moment. Troubled by her mom's absence, Clark felt desperate and immediately rushed next door to the house of her best friend, Damien.

Clark and Damien had been inseparable since they first met in kindergarten. Their bond was forged when Clark bravely intervened to protect Damien from a bully in the playground. She remembered the day vividly. Tears streaming down his face, Damien was huddled on the ground, his arms wrapped protectively around himself as a cruel circle of children taunted him. The nasty bully was shouting in Damien's face, calling him a wimp, a crybaby, and other mean names. Filled with anger that no one was helping the small boy, Clark charged forward and tried to push the bully with all her strength. Because of the bully's size, her shove had little impact, but at least it stopped the attack when he turned to confront Clark with a growl.

"Leave him alone!" Clark shouted.

"Get lost, girlie," the bully sneered, using his size to try and intimidate her.

Against the taunts and jeers, Clark extended a helping hand to the boy, lifting him from the ground. Mocking laughter filled the air as the bully and bystanders chanted insults. "Sissy! Sissy! Sissy!"

Discovering they were neighbors later was a remarkable twist of fate. One afternoon, while Clark was playing with her dolls in the backyard, she was drawn to the sound of laughter and shouting from some children next door. Climbing on a crate near the tall wooden fence, Clark gripped the rough edges with her hands, straining to peer over it. She spotted the boy from the playground with two older boys.

She called out, "Hello," amidst their raucous shouts.

Damien spun around, his face brightening with a wide grin, and dashed to her excitedly.

"Hey! You're the girl who helped me," he said.

The tallest boy came over and asked, "Helped you with what?"

"Simon was calling me names again, and she stopped him," Damien explained, pointing at Clark.

"Why didn't you tell me about Simon? I would have socked him!" the tall boy growled. Then he looked at Clark. "You want to come over and play?" Clark nodded eagerly, her red curls bouncing.

From that day onwards, Clark became a regular visitor, happy to have someone to play with, unknowingly stepping into a friendship that would bring unexpected adventures and lasting memories.

Clark's mom often scolded her for making too much noise, so going to Damien's house became a welcome escape. Mr. and Mrs. Halstead were very welcoming and frequently invited her for family meals, treating her like one of their own. Clark sometimes stayed at Damien's place, especially when her mom was in a bad mood or working late.

✳ ✳ ✳ ✳ ✳

CLARK KNOCKED ON THE solid door with a stained-glass panel. As she approached, she saw the silhouette of Mrs. Halstead, Damien's mom, through the glass.

"Hello, Clark," she greeted warmly. "Is everything okay?"

Feeling a lump in her throat, she whispered, "I can't find my mom." Her voice cracked with emotion as tears welled in her eyes, and she blinked rapidly, trying to hold them back.

"What do you mean, sweetie?" Mrs. Halstead gathered Clark up in a comforting hug when she saw that Clark was upset.

"Mom's not home. I thought she was sleeping, but she's not there." Overwhelmed, Clark broke into heaving sobs as Mrs. Halstead hugged her close, whispering soft words of sympathy.

"Come inside, Clark," Mrs. Halstead said with a welcoming smile, beckoning Clark to follow her into the homey living room filled with the aroma of freshly baked cookies. "Damien is out back playing basketball with Archer and Corey."

Following Mrs. Halstead through the sliding door, Clark spotted the brothers engaged in a basketball game. The ball bounced back and forth, and their cheers echoed in the driveway.

"Clark!" shouted Damien. "You can be on Corey's team."

Temporarily forgetting her worries, Clark joined twelve-year-old Corey, a big boy with curly hair, and began chasing the ball around the driveway. Whenever Clark caught the basketball, the boys playfully cheered her on, offering tips on shooting as she aimed for the hoop. Their encouragement fueled her determination.

As Clark sprinted after Damien, the police car pulling into the driveway caught her attention. Corey wrapped his arm around Clark protectively while Archer and Damien stood close, forming a protective circle around her.

A policewoman took Clark aside and started questioning her about when she last saw her mom, whether her mother had a history of disappearing, and where she might have gone. Clark felt confused and helpless. She could not offer much information. Her mom had never left her alone like this.

"I saw Mom yesterday before I went to school," Clark said, her mouth suddenly dry. Was that when her mom vanished? Why did she leave? Did she stop loving her, too? These questions swirled in Clark's mind, causing her to feel lonely and unloved.

Clark felt the urge to cry, but a sense of responsibility instilled in her by her daddy held back her tears. He would often tell her to be a brave girl. At almost nine years old, she knew she had to be strong, even when her world felt like it was falling apart.

When the policewoman mentioned involving the Department of Child Services, waves of anxiety crashed over Clark as she imagined the possibility of being separated from her mom and friends. Tears rolled down her face like raindrops, blurring her vision as she rushed over to Mrs. Halstead, her sobs echoing in the quiet surroundings. She couldn't be brave, not when the police were talking about taking her away.

"Please don't let them take me," she begged. Clark's heart thudded in her chest, the thunderous beats echoing in her ears as adrenaline rushed through her veins like a raging river.

Mrs. Halstead wrapped her arms around Clark, the sweet-smelling scent of jasmine calming her. "It's all right, Clark. Let me chat with the policewoman. We'll work something out," she reassured her.

Clark longed to be with her mom and stay with her friend. She found the thought of being separated too distressing. The idea of living among strangers, far from her home and friends, terrified her. The fear of being torn away from everything she knew cleaved at her heart with icy fingers.

Clark was extremely grateful when Mr. and Mrs. Halstead offered to look after her until her mom returned. Clark crumbled with relief as the police agreed to let her stay with Damien's family. A persistent, nagging worry troubled her, though, refusing to let go. Clark kept wondering when or if her mom would be coming home. What would happen if, like her daddy, she never came back?

ONE

"No!" Clark screamed, bolting upright as she tried to escape another haunting nightmare. She sank back onto the pillow, feeling the weight of the recurring torment and praying for the nightmares to stop finally.

The morning light cast a golden glow across the room. Clark closed her eyes, seeking just five more minutes of uninterrupted sleep. Yet, the moment her eyes shut, the image of Archer's lifeless body flooded her mind. She felt a sharp, stabbing pain in her chest, like a thousand needles piercing her heart. Clark wrapped her arms around herself, trying to stifle the gut-wrenching sobs that begged to escape, feeling the suffocating pressure of grief pressing down on her chest. She began rocking back and forth, the rhythmic motion comforting her. The visions hit her like a physical blow, knocking the air out of her lungs. The memories of their last conversation replayed in her mind, each word echoing the finality of his absence. Archer was gone.

Clark dragged herself out of bed, her stiff and heavy legs carrying her into the bathroom. Gazing at her reflection in the cracked mirror, a stark reality stared back at her, revealing the dark circles under her eyes and the unkempt tangle of hair framing her pale face. Her once vibrant eyes now resembled dull honey, devoid of their former sparkle. Her typically radiant complexion had faded into a ghostly pallor, sharply contrasting with her former healthy glow. Once again, Clark's heart seethed with curses towards Archer, blaming him for the excruciating pain he had caused her. Like a wilted flower in the frost, she had withered into a mere shadow of her former self over the past eleven agonizing months.

Confined to her bed, Clark never rose before midday. The rest of the day was spent moping around the flat she shared with Rachel. She would stare at the walls, lost in her thoughts, or sit by the window, watching the world go by without her, feeling a strange sense of detachment.

The sadness that Clark felt came and went in waves. She felt overwhelming sorrow over Archer's absence, devastated that he believed suicide was his only option. The constant ache in her gut, fueled by memories of Archer, made her cry incessantly. The memories replayed like a heartbreaking movie in her mind. Clark was heartbroken that she no longer had much contact with her family. She wished she could turn back time and undo the hurt that had been caused.

Tired of the pain, sadness, loneliness, and the inability to stop the memories, Clark hit the basin in frustration. She needed to take charge of her life and cease acting as a victim. This wasn't her. She wasn't a coward. Once upon a time, Clark had been strong, like a fierce warrior who faced challenges head-on, seemingly invincible to the adversity that came her way. Now look at her. What had become of the once tenacious and feisty woman?

A heavy weight settled in Clark's chest, an unsettling pressure that gnawed at her with increasing ferocity. She could feel the panic rising within her, warning her that if she didn't take action soon, she would be overtaken by one of her debilitating fainting spells. It was a sensation she knew all too well—the oppressive grasp of fear tightening around her, making her feel as though her very life was being drawn out.

The only way to make the feeling disappear was to distract herself by cutting. Not too deep, just enough to feel the sting of pain and a sense of relief. Afterward, she always felt drained, but a sense of calm washed over her, allowing her to breathe again.

Clark opened the cabinet and took out a fresh razor. As she sat on the edge of the bathtub, she rested her arm on her thigh and pressed the razor against her pale skin. Pressing the edge into her skin, a spot of blood appeared. As she pushed the blade deeper, a buzzing noise resonated inside her head like an insistent swarm of bees, growing louder with each passing second. The noise reached a deafening crescendo, and she trembled, fearing her brain would splinter under the relentless pressure. Clark quickly pulled the blade away from her fragile skin. That had never happened before.

Clark sat back on the edge of the bath, shaken by what had just occurred. If the buzzing was meant to stop her from harming herself, it worked as she carefully put the razor back in the cabinet. Afraid the unsettling noise would return, she refrained from attempting to cut herself again for now. Clark gazed at the scars that decorated her forearms. Each scar told a story: one of pain, another of anger, a third of fear, and the last of heartache. The scars bore witness to the inner turmoil that had tormented her since Archer's abrupt change in behavior. Lifting her gown, she smoothed a hand over her ribcage, feeling each bone. The reflection in the mirror revealed not just a physical transformation but also the striking manifestation of emotional distress, evident in her sunken eyes, hollow cheeks, and weariness etched into her features.

Archer's anger toward Clark often eclipsed his declarations of love. His hurtful words and manic episodes created a deep hole of anxiety in the center of her chest, a constant reminder of the toll Archer's illness was taking on her mental health.

Every time Archer came off the drugs that kept him doped up and out of it, his anger returned. He would unleash a barrage of obscenities, such as calling her demeaning names, hurling hurtful insults at her, and unjustly blaming her for trivial matters, like leaving a window open on hot days. With each instance, Clark retreated further into herself, grappling with the emotional turmoil caused by Archer's outbursts.

Clark mustered the courage to confront the situation head-on. She knew she needed to change her circumstances and find a new path. Rachel, her roommate, did her best to support Clark by encouraging her to go out and meet new people or letting her know that Clark could talk to her about anything.

Still, she hadn't been there to witness the impact of Archer's hurtful words or to help during his manic episodes, leaving Clark to face those challenges alone. It had been impossible to reason with Archer. Each attempt to calm him down or ease his pain proved unsuccessful. The madness would take over, lasting for hours and sometimes even days. Drugs and alcohol were the only things that could numb the agony raging inside his head. Archer had become a prisoner in his own mind.

Clark vividly remembered the time Archer repeatedly punched a brick wall in the dining room. His hand was bruised and bleeding, and it was later discovered at the hospital that he had broken his wrist.

Clark had asked, "What made you keep punching the wall?"

Archer replied that he felt an overwhelming need to rescue the people he believed were trapped inside the wall.

With a burst of renewed motivation, Clark spent the next hour grooming herself—something she hadn't done in a very long time. The citrusy smell of the shampoo delighted her senses as she lathered the foam into her hair. Clark couldn't believe the difference when she finished combing her newly shampooed hair. Her once dull hair now had a vibrant shine. Her teeth gleamed bright after she brushed them, the minty taste leaving a freshness in her mouth.

After months of feeling lost and stagnant, Clark felt a revived sense of purpose. Stepping outside, the brightness of the sunlight blinded her. A gentle, cool breeze carried the scent of sunshine and pine as it caressed her face. Clark felt liberated as she strode determinedly towards the bus stop at the foot of the hill.

Upon arriving at the bus stop, Clark passed by an elderly couple and politely smiled at them. She pulled out the book, which featured the beautiful yet ugly face of Dorian Gray on the cover, and recalled that it was Archer's favorite, a book he had read from cover-to-cover numerous times.

The Picture of Dorian Gray, she read softly, turning to the first page.

A fly landed on Clark's hand and, despite her brushing it off, it kept coming back. She eyed it warily as it whizzed around her head, a seemingly insignificant yet persistent presence.

"Gun! Vin!" a female voice yelled from the other side of the wall.

Clark looked up at the sound and realized she was standing outside a tattoo shop, "Blood Tattoos," with its neon sign glowing. The shop's windows were adorned with colorful tattoo designs, and buzzing tattoo machines could be heard from inside. Adjacent to the tattoo shop was a provocative sex shop, its windows displaying risqué mannequins dressed in lingerie. On the other side stood the lively "Brothers in Arms Bar and Grill," where clinking glasses and laughter spilled out onto the sidewalk.

Clark returned to her book, with the fly's buzzing still lingering in her ears. She shut out the street noise around her, immersing herself in the words on the page. When the fly returned, she swiped at it again, her annoyance growing with each failed attempt to maintain her focus. Frustration mounting, she growled at the persistent fly, adamant about not allowing it to disrupt her further.

"Go away!" With a swift motion, Clark tried to swat the pest with her book, only to watch it escape again.

A head popped around the corner. Clark gasped inwardly when she saw the resplendently gorgeous face of an incredibly tall man standing before her. His sudden and unexpected appearance sent a jolt of surprise barreling through her. Standing at a towering six feet, the man dwarfed Clark's petite frame of five feet, three inches. He was well-built, his biceps bulging like rugged boulders, exuding strength and power. Clark was certain he possessed the strength to overpower her with his bare hands easily. His arms were branded with colorful tattoos, including a massive serpent encircling one thick forearm and a tribal symbol on the other. His dark hair was swept back, flowing just past his shoulders in a mass of curls. The piercing gaze of his sky-blue eyes seemed to penetrate deep into her soul. Anyone—male or female—would envy his straight nose. The most compelling feature of his face was his lips, full and beckoning, ready-made for passionate kisses.

"Are you talking to me?" he asked, grinning.

"I'm talking to the fly. I mean … a fly is bothering me. It won't go away." At that moment, the fly landed on Clark's hand. "See?"

"Hold still," the man said and stealthily approached her.

Clark stood motionless, not a muscle twitching. Ever so slowly, he raised his hand. Just as the fly attempted to escape, the man's hand swooped down and snapped shut, capturing the fly. Opening his hand, he revealed the unconscious fly in his palm. Dropping the fly to the ground, he used the tip of his boot to squash it.

Locking eyes, Clark nervously chuckled, breaking the tension. "How did you do that?"

Just then, a rugged man appeared behind the bus shelter, interrupting the moment. Equally imposing, he sported a ponytail, a dense beard covering his jawline, and a plethora of tattoos decorating his entire body. He stood with his arms crossed, looking serious, while the definition of his large biceps hinted at his underlying strength.

His sharp gaze fell on her book, and he asked, "What are you reading?"

Clark had forgotten she was holding the book, so she held it up for him to see. A glimmer of a smile appeared, transforming his already intimidating appearance and sending a flutter through her heart.

"What's it about?" Mr. Fly Guy asked, his eyes lighting up with genuine interest.

Mr. Intimidating then laid out the storyline, astounding Clark with his brief synopsis of the story.

"Dorian has his portrait painted and wishes for the portrait to age instead of his body. The story turns dark, and his moral decay from his indulgent lifestyle is revealed in the painting."

"Have you read the book?" she asked, her voice tinged with disbelief and curiosity. Who would have thought that a deep appreciation for literature lay beneath all those tattoos and muscles?

"During the exuberance of my youth," Mr. Intimidating replied.

The roar of an engine revving caught Clark's attention. She watched as the bus rounded the corner and screeched to a stop before her. She courteously stepped aside and gestured for the elderly couple to board the bus ahead of her.

With a playful wink and a mischievous grin, Mr. Fly Guy affectionately said, "Bye, Shortcake," to Clark.

"Bye, Red," Mr. Intimidating added, one side of his mouth lifting briefly.

He was referring to her red hair. Despite receiving compliments on its unique color, she vehemently despised the term "carrot top," often used to describe her hair due to its reddish hue—a label she found far from flattering.

＊＊＊＊＊

THE BUS CAME TO a rumbling stop across the street from Jeb's Diner, an iconic spot where Rachel worked. At that moment, Clark felt a spark of apprehension, wondering how her friend and roommate would react to her spontaneous visit. She took a deep breath and heard the bell jingle as she pushed the door open, resonating through the diner. Rachel's eyes widened in surprise as she looked up from the cappuccino machine.

"Clark, what are you doing here?" Rachel exclaimed.

Clark's face lit up as she greeted her nonconformist friend. Rachel had always gone against the conventional image of young women. Her unconventional style, characterized by purple hair, dungarees, and studded boots, was just one aspect of her free-spirited nature.

"I've come to try that famous cappuccino you're always raving about."

"What I meant was, why are you here?" her friend clarified.

"I've decided it's time to make a change. I can't stay in bed forever; it's time to start moving on with my life."

"I understand your feelings, but what prompted this decision?"

Clark found it difficult to articulate her feelings. The depression sapped her strength, and it was time to let go of her sadness. "I'm sick of feeling sad," she sighed wearily.

Rachel nodded in understanding, her eyes reflecting compassion as she acknowledged Clark's desire for change. She indicated a table by the front window, offering an unobstructed view of the street outside. "I'm busy now, but I'll ask Charly to assist you."

Clark had encountered the friendly brunette a few times before. Rachel had a talent for reading people; her judgment of someone as "good people" was always accurate. In Charly's case, Rachel often mentioned that she could calm even the angriest person with her kindness.

"Hey Clark, it's great to see you again. Have you decided what to order or do you need more time?"

Clark looked up as Charly approached her table.

"I came to try one of Rachel's cappuccinos because I've heard they're the best."

Charly chuckled and nodded discreetly toward the flamboyant male server, Donny. "Donny fancies himself as the cappuccino king," she remarked.

Clark observed Donny flash a charming smile and engage in a flirtatious exchange with a young mother tending to her baby in a stroller.

"I'll bet on Rachel. Could I also sample one of your carrot and walnut slices?"

"Absolutely," Charly confirmed as she gathered the menu and placed her order.

Clark leisurely gazed out of the large bay window, and her attention was instantly ensnared by the sight of two men engaged in what seemed like a serious conversation on the opposite side of the busy street. They sported identical vests. She had noticed these vests on Mr. Fly Guy and Mr. Intimidating, waiting at the bus stop. Clark's focus sharpened as she read the prominent ICONIC SONS MC emblem on the back of the vests.

Clark had been surprised by her conversation with the bikers, mainly because of their unexpected friendliness and humor, which defied her preconceived stereotypes about them. These two men were also appealing: the tall, dark-skinned male with his ebony-colored hair and the slightly shorter one with a military-style hairdo. However, Clark doubted they would have the same charisma or impact on her as Mr. Fly Guy or Mr. Intimidating. Her pulse quickened with excitement as she recalled the encounter. She reasoned that perhaps she had been self-imprisoned for too long to explain her reaction to two strangers.

"Here's the cappuccino and slice," Charly announced. "What are you staring at?"

"Those men across the road. I met two guys earlier wearing the same vest."

"That's Gage and Pen."

Charly's casual revelation about the bikers across the road left Clark feeling unexpectedly connected to a world she had only encountered briefly. It was a small town, after all.

Her eyes widened in surprise as she asked, "You know them?"

"Yes, my boyfriends are also members of the MC," Charly said confidently.

The mention of boyfriends—as in plural—astonished Clark.

"Did you say boyfriends?"

Charly's radiant smile illuminated her face as she proudly stated, "Dom and Jax. I'm also stepmom to Dom's son, Jake."

Seeing the puzzled expression on Clark's face, Charly elaborated.

"Long story short, Dom was my boss at the Bar and Grill, and there was a connection. Later, I met Jax, his cousin, and sparks flew." Charly's laughter filled the room with unbridled joy.

"How did they react to feeling the same way about you?" Clark asked, her curiosity piqued.

"Well, they often shared women." Charly paused, her expression faltering, as Clark frowned.

"Sorry, this is all new for me. I understand this lifestyle is common, but your openness is refreshing," Clark explained.

"It's okay, Clark." Charly placed a reassuring hand over hers. "At first, I was hesitant about the idea of a ménage à trois, but over time, I found myself warming up to it. Dom and Jax can be very determined when the situation demands it."

"So, Jake is Dom's son?"

Charly's eyes lit up at the mention of Jake's name. "Yes. Jake was conceived before Dom and I began a relationship. Jake's mom and Dom didn't share a romantic connection; their relationship was purely physical."

Clark forced down the twinge of envy as she witnessed Charly's happiness.

"You looked sad, Clark. Is everything okay?"

Clark felt like something was stuck in her throat, and she tried to swallow it. "I'm all right, Charly. I had someone I loved very much, too. Sometimes it hurts to think about it," Clark explained, attempting to smile.

Charly sat down beside her, her eyes filled with concern for Clark. "I'm sorry, Clark. What happened?" She gently placed her hand on Clark's, offering comfort.

"He … died."

"That's terrible. Have you talked to anyone about it?"

"No, I don't need counseling. I need time. Time is the ultimate healer, isn't it?"

Charly's concern was palpable. "That's not true, Clark. It would help if you talked to someone about it," she urged, her voice filled with empathy.

"I won't waste my time on a pretentious therapist who's just going to spout psychological gibberish," Clark asserted. She saw no value in sharing her pain with someone who lacked personal experience.

"When I was twelve, my stepfather killed my baby brother," Charly shared, revealing a painful memory.

Clark's gaze locked with Charly's, and a profound understanding passed between them, transcending their sorrows.

"The pain and trauma lingered for many years. However, when I found the courage to open up to Dom and Jax about my experiences, I felt a tremendous burden had been lifted from my shoulders. I no longer felt isolated in my grief."

Clark made a mental note to have a conversation with Charly at a later time to learn about the strategies she uses to cope with her traumatic experiences.

✴ ✴ ✴ ✴ ✴

CHARLY'S WORDS ABOUT NO longer feeling alone with her grief strongly resonated with Clark on the bus ride home. The challenge lay in the fact that no one could fully understand the depth of pain she endured. Archer had abandoned his family when his mental illness had reached its peak, leaving her to navigate the upheavals alone in the months leading up to his tragic decision to end his life.

Clark had noticed a gradual change in Archer's behavior, including increased isolation and mood swings, several months after Damien's death. Naturally, he was dealing with grief and experiencing profound sadness that disrupted his daily routines and strained his relationships.

The whole family, including herself, was devastated and struggling to come to terms with Damien's overdose—the feeling of helplessness, anger, and guilt overwhelmed them all. Mom and Dad had sought counseling and tried to encourage Clark and Archer to get help. But Clark had been too worried about Archer to think about talking to someone.

Archer, aware of Damien's drug experimentation because of their strong bond, was devastated by his inability to stop his younger brother from using drugs. He believed it was a passing phase for Damien and was unaware of the extent of Damien's involvement with drugs.

Deep down, Clark knew that feeling depressed after losing someone you love was a typical response since he blamed himself for not intervening earlier. However, this realization coincided with Archer's initial experimentation with drugs as a coping mechanism for his grief. It started with heroin and later escalated to cocaine, the substance that ultimately led to his brother's fatal overdose.

Clark believed she had failed because Archer was no longer here. She couldn't shake off the guilt that her love hadn't been enough to make him want to live. Clark recalled the times she begged him to stay, but he couldn't resist the pull of his demons. This internal battle consumed her thoughts, leading to sleepless nights and emotional exhaustion, impacting every aspect of her life.

The bus rolled past the familiar stop, where she had met Mr. Fly Guy and Mr. Intimidating, two enigmatic strangers who had unexpectedly inspired a moment of profound insight.

It was time for her to stop grieving so hard and dwelling on the past. As Clark sat on the bus, the distant sounds of laughter and joy from outside reminded her of the vibrant life she was missing. The sun rose each morning, casting golden rays through the blinds, but she remained stuck in her cycle of pain and heartache.

Yet, deep within her, Clark yearned to feel the sun's warmth, enjoy the lively chatter of friends, and find joy in life's simple moments. She wanted to rediscover happiness and reconnect with the life awaiting her beyond her sorrow.

At that moment, Clark decided to confront her past bravely and hopefully find closure.

T W O

As Clark opened the door to the shop, a melodic chime echoed through the air, marking her punctual arrival at a quarter to nine. The warm glow of the early morning light spilled into the spacious room, creating a peaceful ambiance as she prepared for the day ahead. Clark shifted her gaze towards Gun's office. She noted the open door, confirming that he was present. Satisfied, Clark made her way to the rich, dark rosewood front desk of Blood Tattoos, which had a display of tattoo magazines and a vintage rotary phone. She took a moment to adjust her chair and then settled in to assume her role as receptionist.

Six months prior, she unexpectedly crossed paths with Gun and Vin at the downtown bus stop. She had nicknamed them Mr. Intimidating and Mr. Fly Guy at that time.

Little did she know, this encounter would lead her to the hidden gem on the town's main street. After facing repeated rejections in her job search, Charly's suggestion that Clark apply for the receptionist position at a tattoo parlor ignited a newfound hope within her.

Feeling like she was burdening Rachel, Clark eventually decided to call the shop. Following her call, she received an invitation to attend an interview. When Gun and Vin arrived half an hour late, their jaws dropped in disbelief as they laid eyes on her. Gun was so surprised that he impulsively decided to hire her immediately.

"Really? Don't you want to ask me about my experience first?" Clark wondered if her lack of experience might affect her chances of getting the job.

Gun indulged her by patiently asking, "Okay then. What experience have you had?"

"None," she replied, her dimples flashing.

"You want the job or not?" Gun asked brusquely.

"Is there a reason why the last girl left?"

"So, you don't want the job?"

Gun took his standard pose—arms folded, biceps bulging, intense stare.

"You know I do. Where's your sense of humor?" She hid a smile in case Gun changed his mind about hiring her.

Vin's eyes sparkled with amusement as Gun maintained his stony-faced expression. "He doesn't have one," Vin remarked with a chuckle.

"Absolutely, Gun, I would love the job! When can I start?"

Clark found great satisfaction in her role at the front desk, where she managed client appointments, handled administrative tasks, and ensured a welcoming environment for visitors. Her exceptional organizational skills and keen attention to detail consistently exceeded her bosses' expectations. This recognition brought her joy and motivated her to keep striving.

Clark quickly adjusted to the fact that Gun, who was aloof and analytical, stood in stark contrast to Vin, who was outgoing and spontaneous. As she observed their interactions, their differing personalities and approaches to life became increasingly apparent to Clark. Gun often maintained a stoic demeanor, yet his occasional flashes of humor and wit unveiled a hidden playful side beneath his reserved exterior.

One memorable incident was Gun's quick-witted response to an office prank, which had Clark struggling to contain her laughter. She would never tell Gun he had a sense of humor; he wouldn't believe her.

Given his dark blonde beard and the tattoos that essentially covered every part of his body save his face, his broodiness matched his appearance. He had an undeniable air of mystery surrounding him. Clark was unaware of what lay beneath his clothes, but she recognized tribal symbols on his legs, similar to Vin's arm.

Vin was an incorrigible flirt who never missed an opportunity to charm the ladies. He did this regardless of the woman's age or relationship status. The women always felt a sense of exclusivity and importance whenever Vin offered to do a small tattoo for free. However, they were unaware that he extended this offer to every client, regardless of gender. He did it as a gesture of good business rather than showing favoritism.

Clark was certain it was Vin's mesmerizing blue eyes, accentuated by his dark curly hair slicked back with gel, that captivated others. Or maybe even the intricate serpent tattoo on his right arm that appeared to come alive, seeming to coil with every flex of his biceps. Whatever the reason, Clark knew that he had a certain charm that drew people in.

Vin's laid-back demeanor and Gun's serious, no-nonsense attitude fulfilled different needs for Clark, making it difficult for her to decide which boss she liked more. Vin and Gun exhibited a strong sense of protection, especially toward the motorcycle club members and their tattoo shop employees. Clark found their protective nature and loyalty very appealing.

Over time, feeling overshadowed by the influx of attractive women who frequented the shop, Clark had to deal with keeping her secret crush on her bosses to herself, knowing it could compromise her job. Archer had been her only lover, so pursuing men, particularly bikers, wasn't in her nature. That could lead down a dangerous path—especially concerning matters of the heart.

She also knew she had little chance with either of them, given she was not at all like the women who traipsed through the shop.

Clark wasn't ugly by any means. However, she hated that her hair was bright orange. She didn't mind the freckles scattered across her cheeks and nose, although they weren't very noticeable. Being a redhead, it was fortunate that she didn't have freckles all over her body. However, her hazel eyes couldn't decide if they were more honey-colored or green.

Vin seemed to favor women with curvaceous hourglass figures and ample bosoms, contrasting with Clark's slender frame. Her dimples were considered a redeeming feature. Archer had always loved seeing Clark smile because of her dimples and had always tried to make her laugh.

Her dress style was the opposite of the sexy women in their revealing tops, tight skirts with legs for days, and immaculately applied make-up. Clark opted for a casual style at work, often choosing long-sleeved tops paired with jeans and sneakers. Occasionally, she wore a skirt but never above her knees. She firmly believed she didn't need to spend time on make-up. She preferred the natural, fresh-faced appearance.

✴ ✴ ✴ ✴ ✴

CLARK WALKED INTO THE kitchen to put the kettle on.

"You're early." Gun stood in the doorway of his office.

Clark's heart pounded against her chest, and a rush of warmth spread through her as she tried to catch her breath in response to Gun's presence; his proximity always stirred such intense reactions inside her.

"Yeah, I couldn't sleep," Clark replied, unaware of his approach, as she reached up to grab a mug. Gun got there before her. "Thanks."

"Bad dream?"

"Sort of."

"Tell me."

"Would you believe I can't remember?" She'd woken up screaming but couldn't recall the details of her dream, adding to the mystery of her nightmares.

"This happens often?"

Clark felt the energy radiating from Gun but consciously tried to suppress the tingling sensation it evoked.

"Not often," she fibbed. She had nightmares almost every night.

Gun's gaze bored into Clark as he commanded, "Look at me when you say that," his eyes probing for the truth behind her words.

Clark looked up at Gun. "Why?" she frowned.

"Because I want to know if you're lying." Clark could feel her cheeks burning up. He could read her like a book. It was embarrassing to realize how transparent she was to Gun.

"Why would it matter if I'm lying?" Clark's voice held a hint of defiance, masking her vulnerability under Gun's penetrating gaze.

"Now, that there tells me you're lying. Do you have nightmares often, Red?" Clark picked up on the authoritative undertone of his softly spoken question. The dominant alpha male was in the room.

"Would you rather I come to work late?"

"You're deflecting. I can hear the lie in your voice, you know."

Her eyes whizzed up to his. "How?"

"Your pitch goes up when you're not being truthful," Gun pointed out, his hard eyes softening slightly.

"I'll have to remember that," Clark said, dipping the teabag in the hot water.

"It won't make a difference. Your tells are too obvious. You can't help it."

⁕ ⁕ ⁕ ⁕ ⁕

IT WAS ALMOST LUNCHTIME before Gun left his office with Dom. Dom was the Vice President of the Iconic Sons MC and one of Charly's boyfriends. He was scary, but Gun scared Clark more.

"Charly says hi and sends her regards," Dom told her.

"Ditto," Clark grinned, revealing two deep dimples.

"See what you mean, bro," Dom whispered to Gun. "Good luck with that one," he added.

After Dom left, Clark refocused on Gun, intrigued by Dom's cryptic remark.

"Was Dom talking about me?"

"Yep," Gun replied.

"What did he mean? What did I do?"

Gun responded enigmatically, "It's those dimples."

"What's wrong with my dimples?" Clark asked, puzzled, touching her cheeks.

"Nothing," Gun said, checking his schedule.

Growing increasingly frustrated with Gun's lack of helpful responses, Clark remarked, "You're not making any sense, Gun."

"Not my problem."

Clark threw her hands up in resignation. "You're impossible."

At last, Gun flashed her a lopsided grin before strolling back into his office.

Vin dropped by as the shop neared closing time to check his schedule and talk to Gun. "Yo, Shortcake. What's up?"

She offered him a brief wave as she listened to the client on the other end. While she entered the new appointment, Vin stood beside her. He pulled up a chair and nudged Clark aside to check the appointment schedule for tomorrow. She started to get up to make room for him, but Vin stopped her with a gentle touch on her knee.

"Won't take a jiffy," Vin reassured, his tone casual and friendly.

Clark tapped the end of her pen on the table while Vin looked at the computer. Vin's lingering hand exuded an intense heat that seemed to melt her flesh. She pressed herself against the desk to hide her nipples, which were standing proudly because he was so close. Clark had difficulty swallowing the giant obstruction in her throat. She desperately wanted to pour herself a tall, refreshing glass of cold water to quench her parched mouth.

Gun emerged from his office and positioned himself directly behind her. Her chest constricted, making it difficult for her to breathe as the two men surrounded her.

"Do you need the computer?" Clark inquired, finding any excuse to get up.

Gun laid a hand on her shoulder, preventing her from moving. "No. You're good."

With one hand on her knee and the other on her shoulder, Clark felt a rush of arousal that sent shivers through her entire body. She longed to fan herself as a bead of sweat trickled between her breasts.

"Look," Clark blurted out. "I can move so you can see better."

Although being between Vin and Gun was her ultimate fantasy, the harsh reality overwhelmed Clark, and she couldn't bear the intensity. She looked at her watch.

"Would you look at that? It's time to clock off," she announced breathlessly before rushing off.

＊ ＊ ＊ ＊ ＊

THE FOLLOWING DAY, VIN diligently worked at his workstation. His focus was unwavering as he painstakingly created the outline of an intricate dragon tattoo. As an in-demand tattoo artist, Vin's expertise exceeded that of his colleagues Kim and Jacko, whose decent work did not match the level of skill displayed by Vin and Gun. Clark enjoyed watching him work, fascinated by the precision and artistry he displayed as he transformed his ideas into permanent designs on his client's skin. Drawing meticulously on someone's skin for hours demanded exceptional patience, endurance, and a steady hand to achieve flawless lines.

Clark had grown accustomed to the diverse clientele that frequented the shop. There were first-timers, old-timers, young and old, tough men who cried, and females covered in body art from neck to toe.

Gun and Vin were extremely conscientious about maintaining cleanliness and hygiene. They regularly sanitized their workstations, sterilized their equipment after each use, and ensured proper disposal of waste materials.

Clark was even more determined to uphold her hygiene habits and vowed never to revert to her former ways. Back then, she considered herself lucky if she bathed once a week, brushed her hair, or cleaned her teeth. During those dark days, all she could manage was sleep to escape the pain.

Since meeting Vin and Gun at the bus stop, Clark made a conscious choice to refrain from self-harm, marking a pivotal moment in her journey toward self-acceptance and healing. At times, she felt a strong urge to harm herself, particularly when haunted by memories of her past trauma. It required immense willpower to fend off the temptation triggered by those memories.

$$* * * * *$$

RACHEL LEARNED ABOUT HER cutting when her friend caught her in the bathroom with blood dripping down her arm. The poor woman mistakenly believed Clark was attempting suicide. Nothing could be further from the truth. She didn't have a death wish; she only wanted to release the firepit that consumed her. The grief and heartache would become so intense that the only way to let it out was to cut herself. Once the fireball was released, all her anxieties and pain would be temporarily numbed.

Clark hid her scars beneath long-sleeved tops to avoid judgment and scrutiny. They were unsightly, and she didn't want to see the pitiful looks or hear the cruel remarks. She grappled with shame, torn between the knowledge of the wrongness of her actions and the fear of being misunderstood by those around her.

Clark put on her welcoming smile when a client entered the shop. However, the smile vanished when the customer barged in aggressively and began scanning the room.

"Where's Vin?" the woman spat.

As Vin exited his station, Clark marched towards the angry woman, determined to keep her away.

"Stay," Vin ordered firmly.

Clark froze on Vin's command to avoid infuriating him but remained alert in case the situation escalated.

"You!" The woman pointed her long silver nails in Vin's face. "How could you, you bastard?"

"I don't know what you're talking about, Stephanie. You need to get out of here. Now."

Clark had never seen Vin upset. Now, she was witnessing a different side of him, and he was undeniably formidable.

The woman viciously lashed out at Vin, her nails leaving deep scratches on his face.

"Don't you tell me what to do, you bastard! I know you slept with my sister. I told you I hated her and that she would try to get with you. You promised me that wouldn't happen."

As she continued to attack him, all Vin could do was hold her back, further fueling Clark's protective instincts. Ignoring his earlier warning, she rushed towards the woman, who was now kicking Vin.

Moving around Vin, Clark pushed the abusive woman with all her might, propelling her backward. The screaming shrew fell on her backside with a loud cry. Stunned, she glared at Clark with shock and fury.

"You bitch! How dare you. I'm going to sue your ass for attacking me," she bellowed.

Vin forcefully grabbed Clark's elbow and pulled her behind the front desk. "Why did you do that, Clark? I specifically told you to stay put."

Clark felt intense anger emanating from Vin, causing her to tremble. "She was attacking you," she said breathlessly.

Vin's bright blue gaze locked onto hers. "I can take care of myself, Clark. You should have stayed out of it," he said, releasing her elbow and running a hand through his hair in frustration.

Stephanie declared, "I'm calling the police!" as she stood up, rubbing her behind. "Your new floozy's going to get arrested!" the she-devil threatened, her eyes burning with venomous fury.

"Shut it, Stephanie. You call the police, and you'll be the one arrested. All they need to do is see the red marks on my neck, and they'll haul your ass to jail. Nobody saw Clark do shit."

"Yes, they did. There are three witnesses," she stated.

"What witnesses?" Kim piped up. "I only saw you attacking Vin."

"Yeah, me too," Jacko said, a smirk playing on his lips as he looked at Stephanie. "Looks like you're outnumbered, sweetheart. Time to rethink your strategy, huh?"

"Fuck you, Jacko!"

"Been there, done that," Jacko cackled, his laughter dripping with sarcasm.

Stephanie fixed her gaze on the client, still reclining in the chair, and demanded, "What about you?"

Rocky retorted, "Me? Shouldn't hit a brother, you know what I'm saying?"

The furious woman screamed as she stormed out of the shop. She attempted to slam the door shut, but it was one of those self-closing doors.

Vin fixed Clark with a stern look. "You and I will talk later," he said before resuming work on Rocky's tattoo.

$$\ast\ast\ast\ast\ast$$

DURING CLOSING, CLARK STOWED the mop and bucket while her gaze returned to the closed office door. Ten minutes earlier, Gun had arrived, and the tension left her with no doubt that trouble was about to unfold.

Startled, she jumped at the sudden squeak of the door opening.

"Clark, in here, now!" Gun barked, summoning her into the office.

She exhaled shakily, feeling apprehension clinging to her like a suffocating shroud. "Oh dear," she muttered, her voice soft and shaky. Clark felt like she was on the brink of entering a daunting courtroom, her heart pounding like a drumroll of anticipation, a cold sweat breaking out on her skin as she awaited a verdict with bated breath, uncertain of what the future held for her.

Gun perched on the edge of his massive oak desk, his gaze piercing and displeasure palpable in the tense atmosphere. Vin scowled and leaned against the filing cabinet, clearly showing his disapproval.

Clark could no longer hold back, the words pouring out of her in an emotional rush. "I know I should've listened to you, Vin, and I'm sorry. But Stephanie was attacking you, and she didn't have the right to put her hands on you."

Clark gasped as Gun suddenly pulled her closer. Standing between Gun's thighs, Clark nervously swallowed. Her hands clutched his massive wrists as if she could prevent him from pulling her any closer.

"Remember this, Clark," Gun's voice was firm, "You never disobey an order under any circumstances. If Vin or I tell you to do something, you do it without question. You don't know these people or how they'll react to your interference."

Clark nodded solemnly, silently acknowledging her bosses' authority. It was a direct order, so she felt obliged to heed Gun's words.

"I know when you're lying, Red. You hesitated. I'm not letting go until I get the answer I want."

She fiercely protested, growling, "Wait a minute, Gun. Let go of me! You're crossing a line."

Though Clark silently willed him to release her, his grip remained unyielding. Instead, he jerked her closer until they were practically groin to groin, making her feel trapped.

"Stop it, Gun!" she exclaimed, her voice filled with frustration and arousal.

"Then don't lie to me."

Clark reached up and firmly grabbed his beard, her golden eyes flashing with determination. "If you don't release me, I won't let go. I won't stand for this invasion of my personal space."

After moments of strained silence, Gun slowly released her, his brown eyes softening and a grin spreading across his face. "Feisty."

Clark moved away from the fire, her pulse racing from the intense contact. Her blood rushed through her veins like a turbulent river. The warmth against her back hinted at Vin's presence. Once again, caught between the imposing duo, she felt extremely vulnerable.

Vin spun her around and stated firmly, "Listen, Clark, we don't want you putting yourself at risk defending us. We're capable of protecting ourselves. If anyone attacks, you stay put or get out."

"Yes, boss."

"Damn it! She's lying again." Gun's voice exuded a potent blend of anger and concern as he warned, "You disobey Vin or me again, and I'll personally put you over my knees. Now, do you get it?"

Clark's mouth opened and closed rapidly, resembling a fish out of water, gasping for air. "You can't say that. It's sexual harassment," she objected, her voice filled with shock and disbelief.

"And …?"

"It's illegal."

"So …?"

"Gun, you can't say that to an employee."

"I can if they don't listen."

✶ ✶ ✶ ✶ ✶

CLARK YEARNED FOR APPROVAL and recognition from her bosses as a valued team member. She was overwhelmed with deep remorse and regret for letting them down.

Arriving at her apartment, Clark felt anxious and on edge, as if her heart was about to explode. The searing fireball inside her was burning a hole in her chest. She reached for the familiarity of the razor's cold metal in the cabinet. Trembling, she lowered herself onto the edge of the bathtub, seeking respite against the cool porcelain. Her hand shook so violently that she had to take shallow breaths to steady herself. Running her fingers over the velvety skin of her forearm, she pressed the blade firmly, shuddering as it glided effortlessly across her flesh. Leaning against the icy tiles, Clark shut her eyes, feeling the tension ebbing away.

THREE

It was Friday night, and the shop was closed. Vin and Gun were about to go on one of their mysterious missions with the MC the following day. The tattooists and Clark would occasionally stick around for drinks, and tonight was one of those nights.

Kim was excited and nervous as she counted the hours to her much-anticipated date the following evening. Like Rachel, she didn't conform to the typical image of a modern woman. Kim's arms were decorated with full-sleeve tattoos depicting several Greek goddesses, reflecting her fascination with ancient mythology. Although it was uncertain if she had tattoos on other parts of her body aside from her arms, Kim boldly flaunted her unconventional style with confidence.

Jacko, at forty-three, with his leather jacket and mirrored aviators, exuded the aura of a rockstar ready to take on the world. His entire body was a canvas of intricate tattoo designs featuring roaring motorcycles symbolizing freedom and legendary beasts. The maxim "A man's paradise is freedom" summed up Jacko's life as a free spirit and single guy. Despite not being a patched member of the Iconic Sons MC, Jacko found kinship with the club members through their passion for motorcycles, often joining them on rides and sharing stories of their adventures.

"Vin, where are you going?" Clark inquired.

"Never mind, Shortcake. It's club business," Vin replied dismissively.

Clark rolled her eyes, and Gun's stormy mocha-brown eyes flared.

"Settle down, Gun," Vin cautioned quietly. "She doesn't know."

Gun pierced her with a wild look and said, "Red, don't roll your eyes at Vin or me. Understand?"

Clark sighed deeply and pursed her lips, reacting to Gun's demands. "Another rule?"

"Obey, or I take you over my knee. Your choice."

Clark raised her hands in surrender.

Gun turned to Vin and said, "The brothers from Bridgetown are coming down next weekend."

"Yeah, I know. Cork's bringing his old lady," Vin smirked.

"Aaahhh! Since our last visit to Bridgetown, she's been relentlessly stalking me, man!" groaned Gun, sweeping his hand across his head in exasperation.

Clark listened to their conversation, a smug smile playing on her lips. Gun had gotten himself into a pickle with some woman, she thought gleefully.

"Lady troubles?" she asked, amused.

Vin laughed, saying, "Portia is completely obsessed with him."

Gun threw Vin a dark look. "Go screw yourself, Vin. It was a drunken mistake at the Bridgetown races last summer, and I can't even remember what happened."

"Charming," Clark grimaced. Then, a thought occurred to her. "If you want to stop her stalking you, why don't you find someone to pretend to be your girlfriend? It will send a message that you're not interested or available."

This caught Gun and Vin's attention. "Perhaps you could pose as his fake girlfriend, Kim," Clark suggested, noting the need for someone who can stand up to Portia if she gets too close. "You have that edgy biker chick vibe and no romantic interest in Gun."

"I'm gay," Kim stated matter-of-factly, momentarily silencing Clark with her straightforwardness.

"Oh."

"What about you, Red?" Gun asked, his lips quirking.

"Huh?" Clark looked at him, dumbfounded.

"You could pretend to be my girlfriend. You'd be perfect. You stood up to Stephanie, so Portia should be a walk in the park."

"I'd be a disaster as a fake girlfriend. I'm not exactly your usual type," she joked self-deprecatingly.

Vin jokingly suggested, "Nothing that a bit of makeup and a sexy outfit won't fix."

"You didn't want my protection; now you want me as your bodyguard."

"I need you to be my pretend girlfriend. I've got Portia covered. There won't be any physical altercations with her, so get that out of your head. She'll take the hint when she sees I'm otherwise occupied."

"I'm not sure," Clark hesitated, her mind racing with scenarios. The mere thought of being Gun's girlfriend almost triggered a panic attack. Would they have to touch? Or kiss?

"Chicken?" Gun teased.

"Fine, I'll do it," she declared. "What do you need me to do specifically?"

It was a spur-of-the-moment decision to agree with Gun's suggestion. This could be her only chance to get close and personal with her secret crush.

Gun shrugged casually, seemingly unfazed by the question. "You know, girlfriend stuff."

Clark suppressed the urge to roll her eyes and commented, "You really don't have a clue, do you? That's so typical."

Gun proposed, "Let's go with the flow and be spontaneous. It'll make our act more convincing. Just follow my lead if you start feeling nervous."

"Since when are you ever spontaneous, Gun?"

"When I need to be."

"As long as you don't get too handsy, let's keep it PG," Clark quipped with a playful smile, her eyes dancing with mischief.

"I'll be the perfect gentleman," Gun promised.

✳ ✳ ✳ ✳ ✳

RIDING ON THE BACK of Gun's impressive motorcycle toward the lodge, Clark felt a surge of exhilaration. The rush of wind against her face and the comfort of Gun's solid frame made her feel incredibly alive.

Vin had suggested that she dress to impress, so she wore a cute purple long-sleeved crop top and white denim shorts. She paired the outfit with white sneakers for comfort and brought a denim jacket in case the weather cooled down later.

Clark decided to leave her hair flowing freely instead of pulling it back into her usual ponytail, relishing the freedom of the wind tousling her fiery red locks as they rode towards the lodge. Before starting the ride, she had carefully secured her hair with a few bobby pins to prevent it from getting blown in her face, ensuring it stayed in place while still enjoying the sensation of having it down.

Mesmerized by the vibrant dance of her fiery red locks, Gun's gaze lingered on her hair, captivated by the graceful flow of each strand in the wind. In that fleeting moment, she felt a tingle of anticipation, wondering if he would reach out to touch her hair. However, the moment vanished when he passed her a helmet.

Parking next to a line of Harley Davidsons, Gun shut off the engine, and Clark took in the view of the picturesque lake behind the two-story house. No fences separated the properties, allowing an unobstructed view of the open spaces. Down the hill, from where she stood, she spotted a charming gazebo and jetty, adding to the idyllic scene.

The area buzzed with activity as a diverse crowd mingled. Some engaged in lively conversations while others spread along the lake's edge. Men clad in distinctive biker gear filled the space; their camaraderie was apparent. Clark only managed to recognize a few familiar faces among the crowd.

Her tension melted away, and a smile spread across her face when she recognized Dom, Jax, and Vin relaxing with Charly and a young boy. She wondered if the boy was Jake. Among them was another biker accompanied by a lovely blonde woman and an older child who looked to be around seven or eight years old.

"Hey, Clark," Charly beamed at her, gesturing enthusiastically towards the blanket on the grass near the lake. "Come and sit here," she added, patting the spot beside her on the blanket. Beside Charly, a young boy with blond hair held his bug catcher with a cockroach inside. Clark shivered in disgust. She hated cockroaches. The way they scurried around and their crunchy sound when you stepped on them. But most disgusting of all, they carried diseases.

Charly laughed when she saw her reaction. "Don't worry. It has no chance of escaping. Jake will see to that, won't you buddy?"

He nodded eagerly, his eyes sparkling with excitement. "An' I'm gonna catch some more!" he declared with a broad grin. The boy's infectious enthusiasm captivated Clark, eliciting a warm smile from her. "I want to catch a hundred of them!"

The older boy with dark locks, engrossed in his book, looked up and confided, "I used to have that bug catcher, but now I'm too old for it. Mom said I should pass it on to Jake."

Clark replied conversationally, "That was very nice of you."

"Mom said it was a waste to throw it away," he said, pushing up his glasses.

Clark agreed, feeling more relaxed around the young boys.

Charly introduced her to Dom's son, Jake, and his nephew, Nolan, along with Nolan's parents, Sara and Chad. Sara was the sister of both Dom and Jax. Charly had previously shared that Dom was adopted by his aunt and uncle, Sara and Jax's parents.

"Care for a drink, Shortcake?" Vin offered, flourishing a sexy grin.

"Sure. What do you have in there?" she inquired, her eyes peering inside the cooler.

Vin checked the contents. "Beer, Jacks, Coke, or Solo," he listed.

"I'll get the drink. You stay put." Clark insisted on getting a drink and reached past Vin, seated in a fold-up chair.

She retrieved a cold can of Solo from the cooler, the condensation chilling her fingers, and deftly replaced the lid. Clark cracked open the can, releasing a satisfying hiss, unaware of the tension. She watched the bubbles form on the can's surface, then indulgently licked off the escaping bubbly liquid, enjoying the refreshing taste.

"Ah, Clark, could you pass me a beer?" Dom called out.

"Sure. Excuse me, Vin." Reaching over Vin again, she carefully grabbed a cold bottle from the cooler. As she passed it to Dom, he flashed a knowing smile. "What?" she asked, feeling like she had missed something.

"Nothing important," he said, smirking at the inside joke.

"I'd love a beer, too, Clark. Do you mind?" Jax requested.

As Clark leaned across Vin to retrieve another bottle, she noticed his tense expression and heard his labored breathing.

"Oh, sorry, Vin. Are you okay? Did I hurt you?" Clark recoiled.

"No," he croaked.

Her eyes inadvertently shifted, and she noticed a prominent bulge in his groin area. Realization dawned on Clark as she stared into Vin's eyes. Embarrassed, she averted her gaze and got up to fetch Jax's beer.

Vin swore. "Fuck you, fuckers!"

"Just helping out a brother," teased Jax, a knowing glint in his eye.

"Don't need your help," Vin grumbled.

"Let me know when you need that shoulder to cry on," Jax replied with a mysterious smirk.

Puzzled by their exchange, Clark turned to Charly for clarification, but Charly just shrugged.

A familiar face emerged from the crowd, and Clark's heart skipped a beat as she instantly recognized Gage, the handsome biker she had glimpsed outside Jeb's Diner.

"Cork's here. So is his woman," he warned.

Clark's gaze shifted to Gun, and she asked, "Is it Portia? What should I do?"

"Come sit here," Gun said, patting his knee. Clark cautiously sat down as he repositioned her across his thigh. He gestured, "Put your arm around my shoulder."

As her fingers brushed against Gun's broad shoulders, a shiver ran down Clark's spine, a mix of nervousness and excitement flooding her senses. Gun's body was firm, warm, and tempting.

They had a captivated audience.

Gun wrapped his arms around her waist, his hand moving along her exposed midriff. "Ah … maybe a little lower," she murmured, guiding his hand to her hip.

Clark felt a slight pressure between her thighs, making her muscles tense involuntarily. She shot Gun a disapproving look.

Gun firmly lowered her head and pressed his lips against the shell of her ear. "It's a natural reaction, Red. Don't take it personally. And stop moving; you're making it worse."

Clark felt completely out of her element, questioning why she had agreed to this charade in the first place.

As the newcomers, Cork and Portia, joined their group, Dom introduced them to the others. Portia's attention was focused solely on Gun, ignoring Clark's presence. Gun's hand gently squeezed her hip, making it unclear whether it was a gesture of support or something else. The absurdity of the moment prompted a giggle to escape. Clark covered her mouth to hide her amusement.

She was caught off guard when Gun's hand traveled back up to her abdomen. He told her to behave and play the part of the loving girlfriend in a hushed voice meant for her ears alone.

"Aw, come on, Gun," Clark teased, "You have to admit, it's a little funny. Portia's practically devouring you with her eyes."

"Can't help it if I have that effect on people. I guess I'm irresistible," he boasted.

"So, you do have a sense of humor. Good to know," she said jokingly.

A prickling sensation at the back of her head, like tiny needles poking her skin, made Clark aware of Portia's penetrating gaze drilling into her. Sensing Portia's hostility, Clark chose not to dignify it with a response.

"You're looking good, Gun," Portia purred.

"He does look great, doesn't he?" Clark affirmed casually.

"Thanks, babe," Gun shot back and smoothly pulled her head down to plant a wet smacker on her lips. She hadn't expected the kiss, and her mind instantly went blank. The great Gunnar McCoy had just kissed her!

Her lids closed briefly, and Vin was watching her when she opened them again. His lips were slightly parted, making Clark subconsciously lick her own. She saw him mouth the word "fuck" before turning away.

She looked back at Gun, who was brandishing one of his rare, seductive smiles. Clark mentally steeled herself to resist the allure of that captivating smile.

What kind of trouble had she unwittingly stumbled upon? Gun and Vin wielded an uncanny power over her, entangling her in their web. After six months of what seemed like a strictly professional employer/employee relationship, Clark found herself uncertain about navigating their sudden attention. She was torn between the desire for independence and the magnetic pull of Gun and Vin, who blurred the lines between professionalism and personal entanglement.

The urge to escape into the crowd intensified as the weight of her promise to help Gun bore down on her. Darn her bleeding heart!

"Can I have a word with you?" Portia whispered, her voice oozing with seductive sweetness.

Clark scowled at the persistent woman. She noticed that Cork was busy talking to Dom and Jax. No wonder Portia was aggressively pursuing Gun; her boyfriend was distracted.

"Speak your mind, Portia," Gun said nonchalantly.

"In private." Portia's demand sliced through the air with the precision of a surgeon's scalpel.

"No. Say whatever you want to here. Don't keep any secrets from my woman." Gun glanced at her briefly.

"Your woman?" she sputtered. "Since when did this tramp become your woman? I don't see her wearing your property patch."

"Mind your own damned business. Watch your language when referring to my woman," he said brusquely.

Portia's reaction was intense. Clark could see the fury simmering just beneath the surface, a testament to the fact that Gun had left an indelible mark.

✶ ✶ ✶ ✶ ✶

DESPITE KEEPING HER DISTANCE, Portia had the audacity to send hostile and malevolent daggers towards Clark and Gun. She was determined not to back down. Clark admired her tenacity, but she suspected Gun was just as relentless.

"She must be exhausted," Clark murmured to herself.

"What?" Gun looked at her.

"Portia. She hasn't stopped glaring at you. It must be exhausting, especially when you're not reciprocating. It doesn't seem to bother you at all."

"Why should it? I have you as my buffer," Gun explained matter-of-factly.

Clark couldn't help scoffing at his ridiculous explanation. "Sure, Portia is completely convinced I'm your girlfriend," she said with a touch of sarcasm.

Gun stared at her curiously. "You don't think she's buying it?" he asked.

"No way! Otherwise, she wouldn't still be fervently wishing for my untimely demise," Clark retorted, shooting Gun a skeptical look.

"Then let's make her believe it."

"I thought that's what we were doing."

"Not convincingly enough."

Clark didn't trust the twinkle in his eyes. "What do you suggest?"

"Let's kiss and show her we're crazy about each other," Gun proposed with a cheeky smirk, daring Clark to play along.

Clark's pulse raced at the mere suggestion; a surge of adrenaline ignited by vivid images of naked, writhing bodies sending her heartbeat skyrocketing. She had to swiftly shut them off before she keeled over from a heart-stopping shock.

Gun held out his hand and beckoned. "Come here."

Clark hesitated, torn between uncertainty and desire. She couldn't shake the fear that turning her fantasy of kissing Gun into reality might tarnish its beauty, relegating it to the mundane world instead of the realm of her dreams.

"I don't think it'll make any difference. Like you said, it won't matter to her," she argued, licking her suddenly dry lips.

"Are you scared?" Gun's eyes gleamed with amusement, his tone challenging Clark's bravado.

"No." Her immediate denial was a giveaway, and Gun chuckled at her obvious discomfort.

He rose to his feet, his movements fluid as he gently pulled her nearer. "Come here," he said, wrapping his arms around her. "Just a simple kiss, Red. It's no big deal."

Ignoring further protests, he deftly guided her back against the hard wall. Clark's breath caught as his lips met hers. He explored her lips, skillfully using his tongue to delve into her mouth. Clark welcomed his touch, glorying in the feel and taste of him. The man was good. Real good. Her hands unconsciously moved along his biceps to wrap around his shoulders. Pressing closer, Gun palmed her bottom and thrust gently.

The kiss went on and on until Clark needed to breathe. Gasping for breath, she reluctantly withdrew from the embrace, conflicted by a whirlwind of thoughts that refused to align.

"I think that should convince Portia," Clark said, trying to catch her breath.

Gun's gaze lingered on her parted lips. "I'm not done," he whispered, his eyes filled with hunger, before capturing her lips in another searing kiss.

Clark responded with an equal passion of her own. She forgot where they were and why they were doing what they were doing. Her head spun crazily, consumed by a single overwhelming desire: to be lost in this moment forever. She needed this. She wanted this. She craved this.

The distant sound of a bell clanging abruptly interrupted their passionate embrace. Gun gasped, his forehead pressing against Clark's, the unspoken emotions passing between them like a silent storm.

"Dammit," he murmured, his warm breath brushing against her face. "Dammit, Red," he repeated, his voice filled with longing.

Clark found herself speechless. It felt surreal to know that she had just shared a passionate kiss with the man who had been the object of her long-standing infatuation.

"Chow time!" someone called out.

The atmosphere shifted, jolting Clark out of her hypnotic state. For a split second, she was confused about her whereabouts. It wasn't until she turned back that she saw everyone circling the tables, carrying plates of food. While time had seemed to stand still for Clark during the kiss, life had carried on as usual for everyone else at the gathering.

"Hey, Red, you want to grab me a plate?"

Clark eyed him warily, her thoughts and body still reeling from the intensity of their incredible kiss. "Can't you get it yourself? I don't know what you like."

"A bit of everything will do. Heavy on the meat." Gun flashed a grin, and Clark couldn't shake the feeling that it was a calculated move on his part.

She marched over to the buffet table, determined to load Gun's plate with plenty of food before getting her own. As she proceeded back, she observed Portia approaching Gun. From a distance, it seemed the visibly upset woman was expressing her grievances. Placing her plate on a nearby chair, Clark sidled up to Gun and wrapped her arms around his waist, shooting Portia a scathing look. Gun instinctively put his arm around Clark protectively, keenly aware of the tension between him, Portia, and Clark.

"You okay, honey?" Clark added the endearment "honey," hoping the woman would back off.

"I'm good," Gun reassured her before planting another hard kiss on her surprised lips.

Aware that Portia was about to attack Gun, Clark moved aside to confront the woman directly. However, Gun forcefully shoved her behind him. Determined to protect Gun, Clark attempted to maneuver around him, but another pair of solid arms stopped her. Clark turned around in surprise to see Vin holding her back.

Vin leaned close to her and whispered, "Clark, stop. Let Gun handle it."

"If she wants to fight me, let her do it!"

Vin led Clark toward the house. She glanced back and saw Portia lashing out at Gun. He was attempting to subdue Portia when Cork intervened and forcibly pulled the screaming woman away.

Clark observed Cork pull a distraught Portia across the lawn from the kitchen window. His voice boomed across the yard as he shouted at her, his anger evident. He frantically gestured with his arms as they made their way to the front of the lodge, where the parked vehicles were waiting. Portia kept her head low, arms tightly folded, and hands clutching her chest in a defensive posture as she stumbled to keep up with her boyfriend.

Charly gave Clark a glass of water to help her calm down. Clark looked up and smiled gratefully at her friend, then took several deep gulps of the refreshing water, soothing her dry mouth.

Clark had a sinking feeling that Gun and Vin would give her an earful, especially after her confrontation with Portia. She had no business fighting the woman; she had undoubtedly worsened the situation.

Gun and Vin strode into the kitchen, and the atmosphere tensed up instantly.

"You asked me to protect you," she protested, her nerves stretched to the limit.

"That's not why you're here, so don't give me that shit excuse."

"I'm doing you a favor here, Gun. Don't direct your anger at me; blame Portia for causing this."

Gun took a deep, steadying breath to collect himself, his jaw clenched in frustration, before turning to address Vin. "Oh, I so want to put her over my knee."

When Vin refrained from making his usual light-hearted joke, Clark noticed Gun's expression turning from anger to a deep, simmering fury.

Clark leaped to her feet. "Why are you so angry with me, Gun? I haven't hurt you. I haven't been harassing you like Portia. I don't understand why you're treating me this way."

Clark stumbled back as Gun stalked towards her, her steps faltering until she collided with the wall. Gun towered over her, closing the distance until their faces were inches apart, their breaths intermingling in the charged atmosphere.

"Listen up real good, Red. I'll say this once more. You don't protect me. Not in front of my brothers, not at work, not ever."

"But you can protect me even when I don't need it?"

Gun straightened to his full six feet, three inches and nodded. "Now you're getting it, Red."

"That's so unfair!" she cried, her voice tinged with frustration.

"Too fucking bad. I told you not to get into a physical altercation with Portia, and what were you about to do?"

"I saw the look in her eyes. She wanted to fight me! I can defend myself, you know."

She caught a glimpse of Vin seated on a chair, his expression serious and unsmiling. She couldn't help but wonder why they were so upset with her.

Clark was infuriated when Gun ordered Charly to take her home. She sat gloomily in the passenger seat, staring out the window, while Jake and Nolan were belted up in the back seats. Clark pressed her trembling fists against her temples, trying to contain the violent tornado of emotions that engulfed her.

"Clark, what's on your mind?" asked Charly, her tone laced with concern.

"I'm upset because Gun and Vin have been constantly criticizing my actions lately. I'm genuinely trying to help, but their anger is hard to bear."

"One thing you must understand about the guys is that women don't fight their battles because it goes against their code of honor and is considered disrespectful."

"I'm simply staying true to myself by helping others as I always do because that's my nature. I protect those I care about; being female shouldn't change that."

"I get where you're coming from, Clark. I used to be unaware of their ways. Dom, Jax, and I have an agreement. I listen to them, and they accommodate me, so we're all happy."

"I don't see either of them making allowances for me; I'm a lowly receptionist," she said, staring out the window. "Why bother asking me to be your fake girlfriend if you don't want my help? Gun needs to make up his mind."

"You don't know why?"

Clark shook her head and explained, "No, it was initially my suggestion that Gun has a fake girlfriend, but I had someone like Kim in mind."

"Kim is gay!" Charly laughed.

"I know that now. Gun should have chosen someone from the club. The answer's a big fat no next time he asks for my help. I refuse to be taken for granted and used as a pawn in their games."

"Probably better that way," Charly agreed, nodding in understanding.

"Listen, Clark," Charly reached across and tapped her knee in support. "I understand your intentions. I went through a similar situation when Dom, Jax, and I were exploring our relationship dynamics. Dom strongly opposed my risking myself by getting involved in other people's problems, often reminding me of the potential dangers and consequences. Looking back, I now realize I took needless risks to safeguard the people I loved."

Charly peered over at Clark.

"I attempted to assist a friend with an abusive boyfriend by physically intervening, but I ended up getting injured too. He was significantly larger and stronger than me, nearly twice my size. I understand it might have seemed reckless, but the thought of watching my friend suffer without doing anything was unbearable."

"How did Dom and Jax take that?" Clark asked.

"At that stage, I hadn't met Jax, but Dom was so angry and worried about me that he ended up elbowing a police officer and spent the weekend in jail."

Despite the seriousness of the situation, a small smile flickered on Charly's face as if she remembered something amusing from that night at the clubhouse.

"What?" Clark inquired, curious.

"That night, my friend Jess and I were taken to the clubhouse for protection from her boyfriend because he had threatened us. And that's where I met Jax."

"Ah, I see," Clark nodded in understanding. "When sparks flew," she threw out cheekily.

Charly erupted into laughter, startling the two boys in the back seat.

"Clark," Charly said, now all serious, "the point is that the guys of the MC always protect their own. They feel it's their responsibility to make sure you're safe. They have this instinct to protect from the moment they are born, so don't attempt to change it."

"Then why did Gun ask me to pretend to be his girlfriend? He involved me directly in his problem, putting me right in the middle of it." Weary, Clark sighed as she crossed her arms in defiance.

Charly gave Clark a sly smile. "I don't want to embarrass you, Clark, but I did witness a pretty hot kiss between you and Gun."

Clark felt her cheeks turning red, easily noticeable due to her fair skin. "That was for show," she defended, palming her hot cheeks.

"Are you sure? Because you went in for seconds."

"Charly!" she cried, looking at her friend with a frown.

"Sorry. I couldn't help myself." After a moment of silence, Charly said, "I don't know what's inside your head, Clark, but Gun and Vin care about you very much and worry about your safety. It's the reason they get upset with you so easily. They're afraid you're going to get hurt, somehow."

"But that's simply not true, Charly. I know how to protect myself by being cautious and aware of my surroundings," she argued, sounding less sure now.

"I used to believe that as well, but experience has shown me otherwise. Without scaring you off, you need to know that Vin and Gun's lifestyle is dangerous," Charly warned.

"I'm beginning to see what you mean." She sent Charly a side-eye. "Are you attempting to get me to quit the shop?"

"No! Heavens, no! If I did that, they'd have my tail. I simply want you to be prepared."

"Well, now I am. Thanks, Charly," she said with a genuine smile. Clark felt immense gratitude for having such a loyal and caring friend by her side.

* * * * *

CHARLY WALKED OVER TO Vin and Gun, who were chatting up the barmaid. More accurately, the barmaid was openly flirting with them.

"Hey, guys," she said, standing between Vin and Gun.

"Yo, Charly!" Vin greeted with a wink. "What's up?"

Charly hesitated, feeling a knot of worry in her stomach as thoughts of Clark's well-being consumed her. She couldn't ignore the feeling that something was wrong.

"Listen, I don't exactly know how to say this …"

Gun cut her off. "Is it Dom or Jax?" Instantly, he and Vin became alert, scanning the room for the men. As Sergeant at Arms for the MC, they were responsible for Dom and Jax's safety.

Charly shook her head and said, "No, it's not them. It's Clark. I'm worried about her."

In an instant, two imposing figures had her cornered, their brows furrowed in deep concern and their bodies towering over her with an air of protectiveness. "What are you talking about?" Gun rumbled. "What happened to Clark?"

Charly raised her hands in a calming gesture, attempting to defuse the tension. "Guys, step back. Clark is fine. What happened at the lodge today? She was very distraught on the drive home."

"That's because she keeps stepping into the fray, potentially exposing herself to retaliation," Gun pointed out, his voice tinged with exasperation. "Clark doesn't fully comprehend the type of people she's dealing with."

"Gun, you need to tone down the macho posture."

"Don't tell me how to deal with Clark, Charly," Gun retorted.

Charly remained unfazed by his scowl, aware that Gun's bark was far more intimidating than his bite. He would never put his hands on a woman to harm them.

"Gun, I understand that you need to protect her, but something that happened today deeply disturbed Clark."

"Explain," Vin demanded.

Charly had never seen Vin behave this way. He'd never been interested in playing protector to any woman.

"She looked quite distressed, Vin," Charly said. "Her hands were shaking so badly she had to squeeze them."

"Did she say anything?" Gun's fists clenched at his sides, his jaw tight with restrained anger as he cursed under his breath.

"She doesn't understand the rules. To her, she's only trying to help. To you, she's interfering where she shouldn't. You must explain how things work and stop getting angry with her."

Charly's eyes glimmered with sympathy. She knew Gun didn't mean to take his anger out on Clark. Gun and Vin's behavior had been peculiar since the younger woman started working at the tattoo shop. Jax had jokingly said that Clark was their kryptonite. Charly suspected he was right because of how these two had been acting lately. They seemed to lose their usual cool and had become too over-protective of Clark.

"I'm calling Clark now," Vin said, retrieving his phone from the back pocket of his jeans.

"Wait! You can't let her know I said anything; she'll never trust me anymore. I like Clark, and I'm hoping we can become friends," Charly pleaded sincerely.

"Shoot!" Gun looked to his best friend, then back at Charly. "I need to know she's okay."

"There is someone I can call. Rachel." Charly pulled out her phone and looked up her contacts.

"Hi, Charly," Rachel answered.

"Hey, Rach. Listen, I have a favor to ask. Could you check on Clark for me?"

Charly activated the speakerphone.

"Um … Clark's been in her room since she got home. Why do you need me to check on her? What's going on?"

"Oh, nothing. I noticed she looked tired, so I wanted to check if she was okay," said Charly, fabricating a plausible excuse to appease Rachel.

"Yeah, she should be okay," Rachel said, hesitating.

"Rachel, it's Vin. I'm worried about Clark being in her room. Can you please go and make sure she's okay?" Vin asked Rachel.

"Hey, Vin. Of course, I'll go and check on her right away." They heard rustling, followed by a knock on the door and Rachel calling out to Clark.

Vin and Gun listened closely as Clark's voice responded, "What?"

"Is everything alright, Clark?" Rachel asked her.

Clark replied softly, "I'm fine … Why?"

"No reason. Sorry for interrupting." There was a click of the door closing. "Clark is fine, guys."

$$* * * * *$$

CLARK CAREFULLY COVERED THE fresh cut on her arm with her shirt sleeve to hide the small blood stain. She rested her head on the pillow, letting out a shaky sigh. The day's events replayed in her mind, each moment adding to the weight on her shoulders. As the tightness in her chest gradually eased, she felt the tension drain from her body, leaving a profound feeling of exhaustion and fragility.

<h1 style="text-align:center">FOUR</h1>

During the week, Clark managed her work responsibilities smoothly without any problems. It appeared as if the argument from the previous week had never happened. Yet, she found it unnerving to be under Vin and Gun's intense scrutiny, making her question how well they thought she was doing at her job.

Clark was preparing for her lunch break when an unexpected figure from the past, Stephanie, appeared at the shop's entrance. This time, she exhibited a noticeable departure from her prior erratic conduct. Clark watched Vin with anticipation. He emerged from his office and walked briskly towards Stephanie. After ensuring Clark stayed at her desk, Vin promptly escorted Stephanie out of the office.

Now Clark's curiosity was piqued. Eager to uncover the mystery, she rose, walked to the window, and peered out.

"Clark," Jacko cautioned sternly. "Mind your own business. Stay out of it."

"I am," she assured him. "I'm just keeping an eye on her to make sure she doesn't go after Vin again."

"You know he'll be furious if he finds out," warned Kim. "Remember what happened last time?"

"How could I forget? Don't worry, I won't interfere."

Stephanie and Vin were engaged in a friendly and animated

conversation, exchanging smiles and occasional laughter. Stephanie tentatively extended her hand, only to have Vin reject the gesture with a shake of his head.

Seeing Vin abruptly spin around and head back, Clark hurried back to her chair. Her heartbeat was like an orchestra building to a crescendo as he advanced towards her desk, his footsteps echoing in the room. Had she been discovered?

Vin bent down to softly whisper, "I'm alright, Clark. Stop worrying," and a wave of relief washed over her. The tension melted away as he kissed her cheek, letting her know he wasn't upset about her spying.

✶ ✶ ✶ ✶ ✶

GAGE HAD DROPPED BY Vin's office, and they appeared deeply engrossed in a serious discussion about an upcoming motorcycle event. Clark had noticed that Gage had been making regular visits over the past two weeks.

She found herself drawn to Gage's wry sense of humor. His knack for delivering witty one-liners was so hilarious that it often left her in fits of laughter. Clark discovered, to her amazement, that Gage had an IQ of 132 and held a law degree. When she asked Gage why he chose not to practice law, he shared that he craved the freedom and adventure of the open road lifestyle. He expressed a deep desire to carve out his own journey and explore new horizons instead of conforming to his father's expectations. Despite his affluent upbringing, Gage had been disowned by his father after opting for the motorcycle club over his family.

Lost in thought about the day's events, Clark absentmindedly chewed on the end of a pen at her desk. As Clark mulled over her thoughts, Gage casually strolled towards the door, waved farewell, then left the shop. With a wistful expression on her face, Clark observed Gage revving his motorcycle. The thunderous roar of the engine reverberated through the room as he accelerated down the road, the fading rumble echoing in the distance.

✶ ✶ ✶ ✶ ✶

VIN SCOWLED FROM HIS workstation as he noticed Clark's intense gaze on Gage. What on earth was she up to? Vin had noticed Clark looking at Gage with a soft expression on more than one occasion. This behavior made Vin hell-bent on finding out about the unspoken dynamics between them. If she had any romantic inclinations towards his brother, she could forget about it.

Vin pulled up a chair next to Clark, determined to set things straight about her feelings towards Gage. He wanted to protect her from potential misunderstandings.

Clark smiled at Vin, and his heart skipped a beat. No matter how hard he tried, he couldn't deny the powerful pull he felt towards Clark. Those dimples, as Gun had pointed out, were indeed lethal. Vin wondered how sweet her dimples would taste, maybe like freshly picked strawberries.

Vin leaned in, inhaling her strawberry scent, and asked, "Hey. What's up?"

"Nothing much," Clark replied, tapping the pen on the desk.

"You got a thing for Gage, Shortcake?" Vin teased, loving the way she blushed. Her innocence was a beacon in the room, and he couldn't help but feel protective of her.

"Ah …" She looked down at her notebook as if it was the most exciting thing she'd ever read before responding, "Of course not."

Vin detected the lie in the air, confirming Gun's insight. Clark's poker face was as transparent as glass. "Hey," he nudged her, his tone firm. "Don't even go there, babe. Gage's not your man."

"I didn't say he was," she spluttered.

"I mean it. If Gage knows what's good for him, he won't do shit."

"Vin!" she cried, her voice quivering with embarrassment. "You don't have to be mean. Stop twisting my words. Just go away. You're getting on my nerves."

Vin quickly returned her chair to its original position when Clark tried to swivel it away from him. "Look at me, Clark." He waited for her hazel eyes to dazzle him with their beauty. "Don't want to hurt your feelings, babe. Just need you to understand that the brothers are off limits."

"I've got it. Now go away." This time, when she spun around, he didn't stop her.

Clark brooded for the rest of the afternoon following the encounter. When Gun arrived, she barely acknowledged him. He frowned at Vin, who went straight into the office.

"What's going on with Red?"

"Talked to her this morning. She's sweet on Gage. Put a stop to that. She didn't like it."

"That's not fucking happening. He leading her on?" Vin knew his brother and best friend would knock the fucker out if he were.

"Nah."

Vin looked over at Gun, seeing in him a soul brother bound not by blood but by a lifetime of shared challenges and trust, solidified through their mutual dedication to the MC. Growing up in the MC world, a place of brotherhood and loyalty, Vin had built a strong bond with Gun that transcended friendship; their lives intertwined since childhood. He trusted Gun with his life.

Clark showed bravery and sensitivity, as seen in her defense of others while internally hiding her emotional fragility. She portrayed herself as a natural protector but was easily hurt despite her attempts to hide it. Her exterior demeanor exuded toughness, yet Clark harbored a gentle and sweet core beneath the surface.

After witnessing the relationship between Dom, Jax, and Charly thrive, Vin felt confident that he and Gun could start a romantic relationship with Clark or at least have a conversation about their shared feelings for her. Gun was the one holding back from moving forward. They would already be bedding the feisty beauty if it had been up to him. Gun was cautious and afraid Clark would run a mile if they proceeded too soon, fearing she might not be ready for their advances. Vin believed that Gun getting fired up over the kiss he and Clark had shared was a promising sign of Clark reciprocating Gun's feelings.

Vin was concerned about Clark's growing interest in other men, fearing it could jeopardize their potential relationship. He and Gun had staked their claim on her, but she seemed oblivious to their feelings. It was a situation that couldn't continue, and they were both determined to make her realize it—the time for action had come.

"It's time, Vin," Gun agreed but expressed hesitation about today's timing due to Clark's current mood.

Vin nudged Gun. "Clark's mopping the floor like she's got the devil in her," he chuckled softly.

"Whose fault is that?" Gun fixed him with a stern look.

"Oh? You think I should let her continue to daydream about loverboy, Gage," Vin said in a snarky voice.

"Not saying that."

Vin watched as Clark meticulously wiped the dusty benches, her movements echoing in the empty shop. She then shut down the computer with a decisive click and locked it securely. He could tell she was still upset with him.

He frowned, disappointed when she left the shop without saying goodbye, and got up to go after her. Gun intercepted him with a hand on his shoulder.

Gun advised, "Let her process it first, and then we can discuss our relationship. It's not the right time to talk to her yet."

Vin understood that it made sense to follow Gun's advice, but a mischievous part of him wanted to provoke a reaction from Clark to discover her true feelings.

✳ ✳ ✳ ✳ ✳

IT WAS A BEAUTIFUL sunny Saturday morning, and Clark sat at a table in the park, wholly engrossed in re-reading Archer's book. She blocked out the excited laughter of children playing, the high-pitched cries of infants, the incessant squawking of hungry birds, and the distant rumbling of passing motorcycles, fully immersing herself in Oscar Wilde's profound and dark tale.

She was unaware of the motorcycle club cruising down the main street. One of the riders signaled to the others, and two motorcycles turned a corner while the other three continued ahead.

Turning the page, Clark felt a rush of adrenaline as someone collided with the table.

"Hey, Shortcake," Vin greeted her as he plopped beside her, casually turning his back to the table.

"What's up, Red?" Gun leaned against the edge of the table, causing it to dip with his weight.

Their sudden appearance startled her, and a sharp gasp escaped.

She exclaimed, "Oh, my God. You nearly gave me a heart attack." Any resentment she harbored towards Vin was forgotten entirely.

"Sorry, babe. I didn't mean to scare you. What're you doing?" Vin bent over to see the book cover, grinning when he read the title.

"What does it look like? I'm reading."

Gun chuckled. "You still reading that book? Thought you would've finished it by now."

"I'm reading it again."

Vin gently tapped the dog-eared book with his index finger, his eyes narrowing with curiosity as he inquired, "What about this particular book that makes it so special?"

"It belonged to someone very special to me," Clark murmured. The thoughts of Archer pulled at her heartstrings, making her face contort in anguish.

"Red, what's the matter?" Gun placed his hand on her lower back and started gently rubbing to offer her comfort.

Clark surprised herself when she admitted, "It was my fiancé's book."

Vin choked, shocked at Clark's announcement. "You're engaged? Why didn't you mention it before?"

Clark noticed his gaze on her left hand, searching for a conspicuously absent ring. Archer's engagement ring, symbolizing their love and commitment, rested securely in her jewelry box. She couldn't bring herself to part with it; it was a tangible link to their past.

Gun, wide-eyed, added, "Engaged? For real?"

"I said that the book *used to* belong to my late fiancé. He passed away," she explained calmly, even though she was experiencing a storm of emotions inside.

The men immediately became more sympathetic. "We apologize, Red. When did he pass away?"

Clark swallowed hard, trying to shut down the pain, and softly responded, "It's been eighteen months."

Although Archer hadn't been fighting cancer, the burden of mental illness, including the overwhelming darkness of depression, the erratic highs and lows of bipolar disorder, and the disorienting effects of schizophrenia, had worn him down.

Vin reached for her hand, his eyes reflecting sincere sympathy, and said gently, "I'm sorry, babe. Come here."

"I'm fine," she protested, masking her true longing for the safe cocoon of his embrace.

Vin stubbornly said, "Don't care."

Ignoring her protests, he wrapped his strong arms around her. Clark's tense shoulders finally relaxed, and she released a long sigh of relief.

"Are you feeling cold?" Vin asked, looking down at her. She kept her head nestled against him, feeling slightly embarrassed by the guilty pleasure of being held by him.

"Have you eaten, Shortcake?"

When she shook her head, Vin suggested that all three of them go to the local bar and grill for a late lunch. Excited and nervous, Clark eagerly climbed onto the back of Vin's sleek black motorcycle. As they sped down the highway, Clark felt the gentle hum of the engine and the wind tousling her hair, creating a warm sense of belonging and freedom.

As soon as they were seated at the bar and grill, a striking server confidently approached their booth with a playful smile. Clark settled into the corner as Vin's large frame dominated most of the seat. Gun sat on the opposite side of the booth, directly facing her.

"Hi, Gun, Vin," the flirty blonde purred, fluttering her eyelashes.

Vin and Gun glanced at the young girl and nodded in acknowledgment. She handed out the menus.

Clark's eyes lit up as she saw the mouth-watering gnocchi with Neapolitan sauce on the menu, and she quickly gave her order.

Vin returned the menu to the server, who was still coyly eyeing both men, trying to catch their attention. Vin and Gun gave their orders, and then Gun sent the disappointed girl on her way. Clark's lips twitched at Gun's less-than-friendly dismissal of the server.

Shortly after their drinks arrived, Jax marched over to their booth. After exchanging greetings, he casually picked up a nearby chair, flipped it around, and straddled it, leaning in to join the conversation.

"Good to see you, Clark," he said warmly. "What're you doing here with these two?" Gun nailed him with a warning glare.

"They invited me for lunch. What girl says no to a free lunch?" she replied, tongue in cheek.

"Not you," he concurred, his bright blue eyes sparkling mischievously. "Is this a date?"

Amused by the question, Clark shook her head. "No. It's a free lunch," she said, quickly adding, "With friends, of course." Clark was under no assumption about this being a date.

Vin rudely interjected, "You going to leave us to have lunch with our friend?"

"Got it. I'll leave you to it. Enjoy your lunch, Clark," Jax said before excusing himself from the table.

"Thanks, Jax," Clark replied with a smile. Then she turned to Vin. "That was rude. Jax was only trying to make conversation."

"He was being nosy. It's none of his business what we do," Vin retorted a hint of possessiveness in his tone.

Clark wanted to roll her eyes at Vin's comment but stopped herself, aware of Gun's watchful gaze. She wasn't stupid.

"Tell us about your family, Clark. You don't talk about them," Gun said conversationally.

"You're not exactly forthcoming about your family either," Clark retorted, raising an eyebrow defiantly.

"I'll share after you tell me about your family first," Gun insisted.

Clark swallowed, unsure of how much she wanted to share with them. Ultimately, she decided that being open and honest would be best. If they flinched or showed any judgment towards her, she would stop.

"Well, my dad left when I was four, which was very confusing and devastating for me," she started, her voice tinged with sadness, memories of abandonment flickering in her eyes.

"After Dad left, Mom, who had always been so loving and strong, seemed to lose herself. She struggled to cope with his departure and turned to alcohol. I used to go home and find her passed out on the couch or locked inside her bedroom. Most of the time, I had to take care of myself.

I would often go next door to my neighbors. Damien and I had been friends since kindergarten, and his parents usually let me stay there.

One day, I came home from school and thought Mom was hiding in her room or asleep as usual. It wasn't until the following day that I found out she was gone. I went to Damien's house, and Mrs.

Halstead, his mom, called the police. The police were going to contact Children's Services, but thankfully, Mr. and Mrs. Halstead offered to take me in instead, providing me with a stable home." Clark bent her head, unable to hide her sadness.

"It's okay to feel sad, Clark," Gun reassured her, his eyes betraying a longing that mirrored her own.

"What happened to your mom?" Vin asked.

"Mom was killed in a car accident. Her car veered off the side of the road and plunged into a steep ditch. Mom was thrown through the window of the car and was killed instantly. Unfortunately, she had been drinking heavily and was in no shape to be driving."

The memory of her mother's recklessness still haunted Clark. The only consolation was that her mom was spared from any prolonged suffering.

"Did you move in with your dad after your mom's passing?" Clark closed her eyes briefly at Gun's softly spoken question.

The image of that sweltering July afternoon when her foster mom, Connie, somberly broke the news of her mom's car accident was etched in Clark's mind. Later, she discovered that her dad lived in another state with his new wife, who had a young son—Clark's half-brother. Clark could live with him, but that would require her to relocate thousands of miles away. The idea of parting with her best friend and his family, who had always been her pillars of support, filled her with terror—five long years had passed since she last had contact with her father. At nine years old, the prospect of venturing beyond the security of her home left her paralyzed.

"After losing my mom and having no contact with my dad for years, I chose to remain with Damien's family. They have become my parents, providing love and care for the past eighteen years."

Clark's golden honey eyes shifted to Gun. "Now it's your turn."

Gun waved at Vin. "You go first."

Clark's hearty laughter filled the entire restaurant, turning heads and spreading smiles across the diners' faces.

"What are you hiding, Gun? I just poured my heart out to you. The least you can do is reciprocate."

Out of the blue, Vin leaned in, his warm breath grazing her skin before he tenderly kissed her on the cheek. Clark instinctively recoiled, her eyes widening in bewilderment at his unexpected gesture.

Vin anticipated her unasked question and responded. "Wanted to taste them."

"What, my cheeks?"

"Your dimples."

She frowned. "It's not like I smear flavor on them; it's just skin."

Clark noticed Gun and Vin exchanging silent, knowing glances as if communicating through telepathy. They gracefully rose from their seats and effortlessly switched places at the booth without uttering a word.

Clark prompted, "Talk," when Gun settled beside her.

Gun indulged her. "We were born into the MC. Our fathers are members of the original Club. Like you, my biological mother abandoned me when I was very young. My father wasn't exactly faithful, so she left. I have little memory of her."

Vin explained, "Gun is two years older than me. We formed a strong bond when my mother disappeared when I was six, and he took me under his wing, becoming like an older brother to me."

Clark inquired, "What's it like growing up in the MC?"

"The MC holds immense importance for us. It represents a close-knit brotherhood. We are more than just individuals; we are a tightly bonded family," Vin explained, the passion in his voice highlighting his loyalty and love for the MC—his family.

"Our fathers were often on the road for weeks at a time, so we got used to life without them being around," Gun confessed.

"Who looked after you?"

"Whichever woman my father was with at the time. It changed frequently, so Vin and I learned to depend on each other."

"Did you ever try to get out of the MC?"

Both men looked at her incredulously. "Are you serious, Red? Why would we do that? The MC is our family, just like Archer's parents are your family."

"I was asking, that's all. I'm curious. No need to be offended."

"I'm not offended," Gun replied gruffly.

"Where is your dad now?" Clark inquired.

"Mine's locked up for murder," Gun said matter-of-factly.

"What about your dad, Vin?"

He grinned. "Same."

It was a coincidence that both Gun and Vin lost their mothers at a young age, just like her. They were lucky to have one caring parent still. Clark assumed Gun and Vin's fathers loved them, regardless of whether they were good role models.

"Shortcake, you need to know something. Our pops were just like us; they did everything together. It's a tradition," Vin explained, illustrating the deep connection between the generations. "We share, Clark. Do you understand what we're saying?" Searching intently for the answer, she looked into Vin's vivid blue eyes.

Clark nodded slowly. "I think so," she whispered.

Gun and Vin exchanged a glance laden with unspoken understanding. "She doesn't get it," Gun told Vin.

"Absolutely! You share, and you both watch out for each other. I get it," Clark argued.

"To be clear, we are open to sharing relationships with women, Red," Gun clarified, ensuring no misunderstandings.

Clarity dawned on her, illuminating her understanding like never before. "Why are you telling me this?" Gun typically valued his privacy.

"To help you understand and perhaps consider it."

"Consider what? In case I catch you two with a woman. You're always telling me to stay out of your business, right?"

Gun's behavior seemed out of character, as he rarely shared personal matters with others.

"Are you seriously planning to parade someone around the shop?" The idea completely repulsed her, summoning the ugly, jealous monster.

"Shortcake, what are we going to do with you?" Vin asked with a hint of amusement.

"Stop beating around the bush and tell me straight," Clark demanded.

"Look at me, Clark," Gun said, gesturing for her attention. "There are occasions when we mutually choose to be involved with the same women. Vin and I feel the same way about you. We're asking if you'd consider our proposition."

"What proposition are you referring to?"

"Of both of us sharing you."

Clark's eyes, the color of rich hazelnut, darted rapidly between the two men. "Sharing me? Is this a joke?" she exclaimed.

Gun's expression turned steely as he replied, "No, it's not."

Clark quickly retracted her accusation, her tone filled with apologetic regret. "I'm sorry, guys. I didn't mean to say that. You caught me off guard. I … I wasn't expecting you to proposition me."

"We understand, Red," Gun reassured her. "What's your decision?"

Clark replied, "I'm flattered by your offer, Gun, but I can't accept. You're my superiors, which complicates things," she said weakly.

The proposal left her reeling, her mind spinning as she tried to process it. She was unsure how to respond to their proposition. It was her sweetest dream and worst nightmare all rolled into one.

In the last six months, countless women have entered the shop searching for Gun and Vin, the two most sought-after men she knew. Clark heard tales from Kim and Jacko about the men and their wild parties at the clubhouse.

Her relationship with Archer had been intense and passionate from the beginning. Over time, the fierce passion mellowed into mild affection. She never stopped loving him, but as his illness progressed, their physical closeness became sporadic.

Clark longed for emotional closeness and connection. She hoped that one day, she would be ready to find a new partner and cultivate a deep and meaningful relationship. In the meantime, she remained resolute in her decision to avoid casual hook-ups for fleeting pleasure. Clark was determined to confine her vivid and elaborate fantasies about Gun and Vin to the sanctuary of her dreams, where they couldn't tarnish her idealized image of them as exceptional lovers.

"Don't like your answer, Red."

"Sorry?"

"I don't want your apology. I want your consent."

"Gun, I said I can't. It's not just about working for you; it's about my boundaries," Clark clarified.

Gun probed, "Why the hesitation, aside from working for us? What's holding you back?"

A tinge of exasperation crept into her voice. Clark trusted her instincts and made sure her feelings were crystal clear.

"Frankly, I have no interest in casual flings. I'm not seeking a relationship now as I'm still mourning the loss of Archer."

"We're not interested in just a one-night stand. We understand you don't want to forget Archer, but it's time to start living your life again," Vin pointed out, his words about living her life resonating with Clark.

"I know, Vin. I didn't plan to put everything on hold. I am actively working through my grief and taking gradual steps to move forward in my own time."

There was a sombreness about the way things ended after their conversation. She rode on the back of Vin's motorcycle, but a lingering sense of loss now overshadowed the sense of belonging and freedom she had enjoyed earlier. In its place, a dense darkness settled within her, dragging her spirit down like an anchor in her gut. Why did she suddenly feel like she was the cause of everyone's misery?

FIVE

In the dimly lit bar, Gun sat slumped on a stool, his hand gripping a cold beer bottle. He felt too drained to participate in small talk with anyone. Meanwhile, Vin had left with two women from the club, leaving Gun to wrestle with his inner struggles alone.

Gun turned his head as he sensed movement beside him. His VP, Dom, nodded in acknowledgment.

Dom inquired, "What's up, bro?"

Gun responded with a nonchalant grunt, showing his disinterest in talking.

"Heard you took Clark to lunch. How'd it go?" Dom probed further.

Gun replied tersely, "Not good. It was a disaster."

His stomach twisted at the memory. It still chafed Gun that Red wanted to deny the pull between them. He knew damn well she responded to him. Their kiss had been pure fire.

"That sucks. What do you plan to do?"

"Right now, I couldn't care less." Gun felt like a powder keg. Clark's feelings were beyond his control, and he didn't know how to rein in the mounting frustration.

"I've been in your position before. I understand the pain, but you need to keep moving forward."

Gun slammed his half-full glass, beer sloshing all over the bar mat. "I said I don't give a shit. She's only some fucking bitch. She means nothing to me!"

Dom stood up. "Let's take this outside, Gun."

Gun growled under his breath, the sound barely audible in the tense atmosphere.

"Hell!" He stood up and followed Dom outside the bar.

"This behavior is out of character for you, Gun. You're typically known as the cool, calm, collected guy among us. Ever since Clark came into your life, you've reacted irrationally, especially around her. You watch her every move, get angry if she's upset, and even go as far as threatening the brothers if they go near her. The way you threatened Gage to stay away is out of character for you, bro. We all know she belongs to you and Vin; you've made that abundantly clear."

Gun punched the chain link fence out of frustration and anger, the pent-up emotions boiling over. "I'm sorry, bro. I don't know why I'm acting this way. Clark's different, you know. Like Charly is to you. I got hot because she rejected us."

Dom firmly squeezed Gun's shoulder, his eyes gleaming with compassion. "I understand. Charly tested us in ways we never anticipated, but we refused to lose her without a fight. I'm so grateful we didn't give up because look at where we are now. The three of you could build a strong and successful relationship like ours. Are you serious about her, Gun?"

"Dom, I've never experienced anything like this before. How she affects me is indescribable."

"Have you had the opportunity to learn her story and background?"

"Yeah. She's had it tough. It started when her dad abandoned her when she was only four."

Gun shook his head, vaguely recalling the day when his mother had done the same thing. He still remembered the fights and arguments between his mom and pops. Gun couldn't remember much about his mother, only that she had been pretty with dark hair.

"Yeah, that can be rough."

Dom's father, who had a history of abuse, met a tragic end when he was murdered by another inmate while in prison. His mother had died of a drug overdose. Dom understood the ramifications of abandonment at a young age. Fortunately, his aunt Sharyn and uncle Declan opened their hearts and home to him.

"It doesn't end there. Her mom was killed in a car accident because she'd been driving drunk."

Dom whistled low and long. "Shit, man. I'm sorry."

"Thankfully, she didn't enter the foster system. The neighbors took her in. Cared for her. Loved her." Gun had been touched to learn that a family had genuinely loved Clark. She deserved it.

"Yeah. I get that," Dom nodded in understanding.

"Unfortunately, her fiancé took his own life."

"Her fiancé? Jesus. How long ago did this happen?"

"A year and a half."

"Since this is still a sensitive topic for Clark, it might be best to proceed slowly and carefully."

"Considering we've been taking it slow for six months, isn't that enough time?"

Gun had held off pursuing Clark, fearing he might scare her away. He was concerned that rushing things could jeopardize the chance to establish a deep connection with her. Vin had always been the impatient one.

"Do you know why she rejected you?"

"She's still mourning the loss of her fiancé and is not seeking a casual fling."

"I believe your intention is for her to be more than just a short-term fling," Dom observed.

"She had me hooked from the get-go, man. The instant I saw her at the bus stop, her vibrant red hair mesmerized me, drawing me in."

Dom chuckled softly. "Red," he said.

"Not only is she feisty, but she's also incredibly courageous and funny. Half the time, I want to put her over my knee. The other half, I want to crush her to me and kiss the life out of her."

Gun couldn't forget the electrifying way she had responded to his kiss at the lodge. It was a powerful and unforgettable moment that had etched a lasting memory in his mind.

"I get it," Dom chuckled. "Given the situation, have you considered how you will approach your relationship with Clark moving forward?"

"I haven't figured it out yet."

"Do you recall when Sara gave us that pep talk back when Jax and I thought we had no chance with Charly?"

Gun shook his head. "She suggested that we should make an effort to woo her. It would be a good idea for you to do the same. Take the time to find out what Clark is passionate about and what she enjoys doing in her free time. Try to surprise her with spontaneous gestures."

"Damn! I had completely forgotten about that. We decided to take Clark out for an impromptu lunch at the bar and grill," he admitted.

Dom agreed with a nod. "However, you propositioned her. Keep the focus away from sex for now," he advised.

"You're asking the impossible, Dom!" Gun grumbled. "Sex is practically all I think about when it comes to Red."

"I never said you couldn't consider it. Just make sure to avoid bringing it up too soon. Give your relationship time to simmer." Dom clapped him on the shoulder and left.

Gun spotted Vin coming out of the games room, hastily zipping up his pants. Two women confidently strolled out behind him, clearly pleased with themselves. Vin marched over, his expression a mix of annoyance and regret as he dealt with the aftermath of his actions.

"We're not giving up, Vin. We believe in what we feel for Clark. It's time we let her know."

Vin's face lit up. "Hell yeah, I'm ready, bro. Let's do this."

* * * * *

CLARK HUNG UP THE phone and quickly typed the appointment into the calendar. The buzzer sounded, and her stomach tightened anxiously as Vin entered the shop. Offering him a smile, she was grateful when he reciprocated. Gun had been quiet all morning, not saying much to Clark since their awkward goodbyes on Saturday.

She had been wrestling with her conscience, coming to grips with the fear of being manipulated by Vin and Gun into something she didn't feel ready for—or ever would be. Clark regretted turning down their offer, yet her gut instinct told her she'd made the right choice.

The thought of being exploited by them and then discarded without a second thought had caused her sleepless nights. She was haunted by the fear of being abandoned like Stephanie and Portia. Clark had witnessed firsthand the way they treated women. Stephanie and Portia were vivid reminders of the consequences she could face if she went down that road.

The buzzer sounded again, and this time, Cork, Portia's boyfriend, entered the shop with two other men. He disregarded her completely, and Cork and the other two men proceeded directly towards Gun's office.

Vin and Gun quickly stepped out of the office, their fierce expressions alarming Clark. This was not good.

Gun immediately approached her, his eyes narrowed as he physically blocked her path. "Clark, I need you to leave now. Go home. It's for your safety," he said, gently but firmly nudging her towards the door.

"Hang on, Gun. I think we've got a situation. I should hang around and make sure they don't cause any problems," Clark responded, trying to peer around Gun's large body to eyeball the men.

Clark gasped softly when Gun cupped her cheeks, guiding her to meet his gaze. "I said go home, Clark. I won't repeat it. Don't piss me off," Gun warned, his tone leaving no room for argument.

"But ..."

"Clark," he growled softly. "Go home. Now." This time, he shoved her out the door none too gently.

A few seconds later, Jacko, Kim, and their clients, who witnessed the escalating tension, also stepped outside. The tense scene involving Gun, Vin, and the three intruders did not require an audience.

Jacko grabbed Clark's elbow and forced her to keep moving forward. "Clark, don't be reckless. Let Gun and Vin deal with it. Come on."

"Fine," she relented. "I'll go home." Clark walked ahead in the direction of her apartment. She glanced over her shoulder to check that Jacko and Kim were out of sight. Jacko was still watching, so she kept walking.

She turned the corner and, when out of sight, backtracked down an alleyway towards the shop. Careful to avoid being seen by her workmates, she snuck around the side of the shop. Peering around the wall, Clark's tense muscles relaxed, and she breathed a sigh of relief when she saw their vehicles were gone.

Silently tiptoeing towards the front door, Clark's eyes widened as she noticed one of Cork's men hurriedly closing the blinds. Fortunately, the security shutters were still up. Clark's heart sank as she watched Cork attacking Gun and Vin lying unconscious on the shop floor, prompting a horrified cry to escape her lips.

Knowing it would be futile to call the police, she carefully tried the door to find another way to help. It was locked. Panic rising, Clark's eyes darted frantically, searching for any object that could break the window and provide a distraction. The sunlight reflecting off the shiny metal of three motorcycles caught her attention.

Impulsively, she ran to one of the motorcycles and kicked it without thinking. It set off the shock sensor alarm, and a loud, piercing sound blasted the air. Dashing behind the wall, Clark's heart raced as she heard the door swing open, followed by the angry voices of three men pounding the pavement and hurling curses into the air.

The three men straddled their motorcycles and rode off, hurtling down the street. Out of sheer relief, Clark wept tears of joy. Fearful of the repercussions from her bosses, who would not tolerate her interference in such a dangerous situation, she hesitated to step inside the shop. But she couldn't leave without knowing that Gun and Vin were okay.

She cautiously approached the door and peered inside. Gun extended a hand to Vin, offering support as Vin struggled to stand. Satisfied that they were safe now, Clark hurried down the street and went home before she got into any strife.

✶ ✶ ✶ ✶ ✶

VIN MOANED IN PAIN, rubbing the spot on his head where he had been struck, and asked, "What the hell happened?"

Groaning in pain from the injury he sustained, Gun said, "You were knocked out cold."

"The fucker! Is it because of Portia?" Vin suspected that Cork might have been aware of something between Gun and his woman at the lodge get-together.

"Yeah," admitted Gun. "I thought something would go down since Portia's outburst at the lodge on Saturday."

"Shit, man. What are you going to do?" Vin rubbed the back of his head and found blood on his hand.

Gun went to get the first aid kit. "Don't know. Hopefully, Cork got it out of his system. My ribs are killing me," he groaned as he touched the tender spot.

"I'm surprised they stopped when they did," Vin said, eyeing Gun's swollen eye and lip. "The damage seems minimal."

"Cork's alarm went off, so they bolted."

"What triggered the alarm to go off?"

"I need to check something out on the security cameras," Gun said before heading to the computer. After viewing the footage, it confirmed his suspicions. "Dammit, Clark!"

Vin watched the video in which Clark was caught sneaking around the shop. He swore when it showed her marching up to Cork's motorcycle and unleashing a swift, powerful kick.

"Jesus Christ!" he grumbled. "Will she ever listen to us?"

"Not in her nature. She's protective," Gun replied, absentmindedly tapping his fingers on the table.

Vin's voice was tense as he asked Gun, "What do we do next?"

Gun explained the plan. "First, she needs to learn her place. Then, she will belong to us." Clark was their reward; they needed to claim her and end her foolishness.

✶ ✶ ✶ ✶ ✶

CLARK RECLINED ON HER bed, reading Archer's book. All afternoon, she'd been freaked out by the incident at the shop and worried that Gun would find out she'd disobeyed his direct order to go home.

Clark's stomach dropped when she heard Gun's deep voice. Then, another voice joined in—Vin was here, too. Setting the book on the bedside table, she braced for the inevitable confrontation.

A chilling blast of cool air swept through the room, heralding the arrival of Gun and Vin, who barged in without knocking. Anticipating their fury, she wasn't surprised by their lack of formalities.

"I told you to go home." Clark could almost visualize the steam billowing out of Gun's ears.

"I couldn't. Those guys didn't come by for a friendly chat."

Gun struck the wall next to her head with a resounding thud, causing her to jump in alarm. "Don't assume your actions were heroic. They were reckless, not brave!"

"Gun ..." Clark gasped for air at his fury, her chest tight with emotion.

"No, Clark. Listen to me. When I give you an order, you follow it. Do you understand? There will be no more foolish behavior from you."

"I was only trying to—"

"I don't bloody care what you were trying to do! You don't understand our world, Red. It's dangerous. Every time you intervene, you put yourself at risk."

"They didn't see me, Gun. I swear."

"But we did."

"How?"

"Security cameras caught it. We've deleted the footage."

"I'm sorry. I was only trying to help."

"Did I ask for your help, Clark?" Gun shook her softly when she didn't reply immediately. "Answer me."

Clark's throat tightened as she swallowed hard, her head shaking in silent admission of her mistake.

"This is your last chance, Clark. If you defy me again, you will be fired."

"What did you expect me to do, Gun? Let them beat you up?" Clark released a series of muffled cries, clearly exhausted.

"Gun, don't you realize? I've already lost my mom to a car accident, my dad has another family, and my fiancé and brother to suicide. Losing another person I care about is too much to bear."

Clark buried her face in her hands, overwhelmed by a torrent of deep, agonizing sobs that she couldn't control.

"Come here," Gun demanded, crushing her against his chest. "Red, I know why you do what you do," he murmured. "But the people we deal with, they're dangerous. They won't hesitate to retaliate. If they ever found out what you did, it would kill me. I never want anything to happen to you."

It was bliss to be in his arms, free from the usual shouting, to feel his warmth, and to hear his gentle words.

"I struggle, Gun. It's just difficult for me to stand by without doing anything. What if I had followed your orders, and you were in mortal danger while Vin lay unconscious, unable to assist you, but I could? I had no choice but to intervene."

"I've managed to stay alive for thirty-five years, Clark. I know how to defend myself." Gun lifted her chin, forcing Clark to meet his gaze. "I mean it, Red. If you keep interfering, I'll fire your butt!"

Drowning in the chocolate swirls of his eyes, it took a second for his words to register.

"That's unfair, Gun!" she gasped.

"Perhaps, but if it ensures your safety, then so be it."

When the men departed, Clark sank onto the bed, her mind filled with thoughts of Gun's warning.

Suddenly, the door opened.

"Are you all right, Clark?" Rachel's voice was filled with concern as she cautiously entered the room.

"Yes. I'm okay."

Rachel stood there a little longer, her concern deepening at Clark's defeated expression.

"Would you like to talk about what happened?"

"No, thank you. I just need some time alone."

S I X

Vin had been worried about Clark since their conversation the previous night. He repeatedly asked if Clark had arrived at work, but the answer was the same each time. No.

"What the fuck is keeping her?" Frustrated, he reached for his phone and dialed Clark's number. When the call went unanswered and straight to voicemail, he hung up. He then called Jeb's Diner. Jeb answered the phone, so Vin asked to speak to Charly.

"Hey Vin, how's it going?" Charly greeted with her usual warmth and enthusiasm.

"Have you heard from Clark? She hasn't shown up for work today."

"I'm sorry, but I haven't. Is she unwell?"

"I don't know. She's not answering her phone."

Vin ended the call upon seeing Gun's bemused expression. Before hanging up, Charly instructed Vin to call when he heard from Clark.

Vin demanded to know, "What's happening with Clark? Is she okay?"

Gun passed his phone to Vin, who read the message from Clark.

I need time to think. I'll be back at work next week.

"Think about what? Damn, Gun!"

As Vin's phone rang, he checked the caller ID, thinking it might be Clark, but it was Charly. "What?"

"I just spoke with Rachel. Clark left last night. Rachel is unsure of where she went, though."

Vin thanked Charly and updated Gun about Clark's sudden departure. Gun collapsed into a chair, groaning. "I blame myself. I was too tough on her."

"No, Gun. This is *our* fault. We're in this together."

"We must find Clark, Vin. Losing her is not an option."

"I'll call Cole and ask him to help find Clark's whereabouts."

* * * * *

CLARK SAT AT THE rustic farmhouse table in the house she had called home for many years. The faint smell of lavender lingered in the air, reminding Clark of her mom. Connie Halstead, a graceful woman with silver hair and kind eyes, placed a delicate China cup brimming with fragrant chamomile tea in front of her, its steam swirling gently.

"Thanks, Mom," Clark said, cupping her hands and inhaling the herbal infusion.

"I'm overjoyed to have you back home, sweetheart. I've truly missed you." Connie looked beautiful at fifty-five years old despite the hardships she had endured in recent years, including the tragic deaths of her two sons.

Clark's dad, Lawson Halstead, was in the shed under the hood of his car, working on his 1966 Alfa Romeo convertible. Ever since Archer passed away, Lawson sought solace in the shed, immersing himself in car repairs to ease the pain of his son's absence. Archer and Lawson used to spend hours together in the garage, covered in grease and laughter, bonding over their shared passion for fixing cars.

"You are welcome to stay for as long as you need. Your bedroom is just how you left it when you entered the big, wide world. Your favorite books are neatly arranged on the shelves, and the old quilt your Aunt Irene made is still on the bed. Bugeye is there too," the older woman said with a fond smile.

The thought of her cherished teddy bear, Bugeye, warmed Clark's heart. She had entrusted Bugeye with all her secrets, and he had never let her down or judged her; he only offered comfort and security.

"I won't overstay my welcome. I need to process everything that has happened before I can return to work."

The previous night, after several years apart, Clark and Connie had had a heart-to-heart conversation when Clark showed up at her parents' doorstep. Connie's eyes filled with tears of overwhelming happiness as Lawson, with a gruff exterior, tenderly enveloped her in a long, tight embrace, reluctant to let her go. They talked until the wee hours of the morning.

She had been a lost, nine-year-old girl when they took her in after her mom went missing, treating her as if she were their own flesh and blood. Clark felt a deep sense of gratitude for everything they had done for her, and she was weighed down by an intense feeling of remorse for not being present with them, especially after Archer's suicide.

"What have you been up to lately?"

Clark paused, hesitating to bring up Archer's name. "You know, the first year after Archer's passing was tough," she finally admitted, her voice tinged with sorrow.

"I met Rachel through a mutual friend who mentioned that she needed a new roommate after her previous one left unexpectedly. The timing worked out perfectly, and we hit it off. Since then, we've become firm friends.

One morning, I decided to reclaim my life, and as part of that journey, I came across an opportunity to work as a receptionist at a tattoo shop, a place that felt like a new beginning."

"A tattoo shop?" Connie's surprise made Clark grin.

"Initially, I had some reservations about working in a tattoo shop, but my perspective changed completely after getting to know the people who worked there," she said, thinking about her coworkers and their friendships.

"Honey, I can see you're troubled. Did something happen with the people you work for? You can talk to me about it." Clark appreciated her mom's concern.

"No, we have different expectations when it comes to situations in the workplace. You know what I'm like, Mom. I have this strong urge to save people."

"What do you mean?" A former schoolteacher, Connie had an exceptional knack for getting straight to the heart of a problem.

"My bosses are a little … shall we say, protective. And so am I. So, we tend to clash on that aspect."

The distinct rumble of Harley-Davidson motorcycles outside made Clark's heart skip a beat. She gazed out the living room window and was astonished at the sight of Gun and Vin pulling into the driveway. Their engines hummed softly before they dismounted the motorcycles.

Clark hurried outside to intercept them, taken aback by their sudden appearance. The whereabouts of her parents were not widely known, so she waited for them at the top of the porch steps.

"What are you doing here?"

"We came to check on you and make sure everything is okay," Vin said.

"You can stop worrying. I'll be back next week. I need some time to think about what you said yesterday."

"What did I say yesterday?" Vin almost shouted, which was unusual for him.

"It's what Gun said, but you both implied. That you'll fire me if I keep interfering in your business."

"Then don't interfere." Vin made it sound like she could easily suppress her feelings and the need to protect others at will, but deep down, she knew it was a constant battle. "Never pegged you for a quitter, Red."

"I'm not quitting, Gun. I'm taking a break to clear my head."

"I realize my communication may be lacking, but I'm prepared to have an honest conversation and tackle our issues directly if you're open to it," Vin proposed, his usual charm replaced by earnestness.

"I know I came down on you a bit heavy. It was out of concern for you that I got angry. I'm working on it, though. I'm sorry for hurting your feelings. I'll make a conscious effort to rein in my temper and control my reactions better," promised Gun, to which Clark nodded in understanding.

Concerned that Connie might overhear their conversation, Clark gestured for Vin and Gun to walk over to the garden for privacy.

"I understand that your reaction comes from a place of concern, and I appreciate that. We need to set boundaries so that we don't continue to have these run-ins."

Sensing a breakthrough in the conversation, Vin cautiously took a step closer to Clark, and Gun subtly mirrored the gesture, gradually encroaching on her personal space.

Maintaining eye contact with Gun, Clark opened up with raw honesty. She wanted him and Vin to understand where her need to save others came from.

"The things I've seen are indescribable. They've shaped my purpose—to protect and rescue others like a guardian angel in a broken world."

"Clark, we've got this. Vin and I are more than capable of taking care of ourselves."

"I will always look out for the people who matter to me."

"You care about us?" Gun smirked.

Clark hesitated, then responded softly, "As a friend, sure, but there's more to it."

"Your pitch went up, Red."

Her cheeks flushed crimson, and Clark became defensive. "I'm telling the truth."

"We care about you, too, Shortcake," Vin interjected. "What did you see that impacted you so deeply?"

Aware that Gun's keen intuition would detect any falsehood or omission, Clark revealed the truth. "I was the one who discovered both Damien and Archer after they had tragically taken their own lives."

Both men froze at her disclosure, realizing Clark's emotional fragility was akin to a tightly wound wire on the brink of snapping at any moment.

"Damien got into the wrong crowd when he was a teenager. He started hanging around friends who were into drugs, alcohol, shoplifting, and engaging in reckless behavior. His actions frequently resulted in clashes with the police."

Clark paused to take a breath, but really, she needed a moment to stem the pain in her chest. Damien had been her best friend even after Mom and Dad adopted her.

"Mom and Dad did everything to change his behavior. They grounded him, confiscated his phone, and blocked his friends' numbers to prevent contact by restricting access to our home. They weren't allowed to come to our house. But it didn't matter because Damien always found a way to sneak out, whether by climbing down the trellis outside his window, picking the lock on the back door, or even using a hidden spare key. Once, Dad boarded up his bedroom window, but Damien still got out by kicking out the board."

Clark's hands were shaking so badly that she tucked them into the pocket of her jeans, trying to steady her nerves. She mentally prepared herself to reveal the worst part of the story: the tragic discovery of Damien.

"When Damien was seventeen, he was grounded for a week for stealing Dad's car and taking it for a joyride. Instead of calling the police, they grounded him.

One afternoon, I quickly stopped by to drop off some dishes Mom had lent me. By now, Archer and I were living together in our tiny flat around the corner. I inquired about Damien's progress with his grounding. She seemed pleased to report that he had stayed in his bedroom all morning without any attempts to escape. I told her

I would go in and say hello before leaving. I knocked, but he didn't answer. I remember looking at Mom; she was frowning. I knocked again, but still no answer. Feeling worried, I opened the door and called his name again. That's when I saw him face down on the floor next to his bed."

Clark abruptly halted, turned away, and started to sob quietly, with big, gulping breaths. She sensed the air move behind her and raised her hand to stop whoever was going to approach her.

The silence was initially a welcomed respite, allowing Clark to dam the looming emotional flood. However, as moments stretched in silence, the once comforting atmosphere morphed into an unsettling awkwardness.

"I'm so sorry, Clark," Vin said, his voice laced with regret. He fisted his hands, his knuckles turning white from the pressure. Gun's jaw was clenched so tightly that it seemed his teeth might shatter under the force.

"Thank you," Clark replied sincerely. "Now you might better understand me and my motivations for behaving like I do."

"You fear losing the people you care about," Gun clarified. "It's understandable that you want to protect others, Clark."

"That's why I need this time away. I need to step back and sort things out to find some clarity."

Gun accepted her reasons and assured Clark that her job would await her when she returned.

The awkward silence made Clark nervous. "So, I'll see you on Monday?"

Vin paused before speaking. "Sure, Shortcake. How about we hang out before then? What do you enjoy doing?"

"As in hobbies, you mean?" Clark frowned at Vin's unusual question.

"What are your hobbies and interests? What do you enjoy doing for fun? That kind of stuff," he elaborated.

"Why do you want to know that?"

"Well, Gun and me thought we could take you out for the day. Do something together."

"You're not talking about a date, are you?" Clark's eyes narrowed, her suspicions growing.

"If you want to call it that," Vin replied smoothly.

"I'm not looking for a relationship, Vin. I explained this to you before."

"What's troubling you, Clark? Are you uncomfortable with the idea of being involved with two men?" Gun persisted.

"That's just part of it, Gun. I've witnessed your treatment of women, and it's far from kind."

"It will be different with you, Red," Gun vowed. "We want to explore this with you."

"I'm … I'm a little too messed up to be in a relationship."

"What do you mean by "messed up?""

Clark let out an anxious breath. "There are things about me that I haven't been able to share. It's a personal issue I'm dealing with, so I'm uncomfortable getting close to anyone now."

✶ ✶ ✶ ✶ ✶

A FEW DAYS HAD passed since Clark had confessed she wasn't ready for a relationship due to her past trauma.

Her refusal to pursue a relationship with him left Gun feeling powerless. He felt defeated by his lack of control over the unfolding situation. Clark was too damned headstrong.

Gun had assigned Pen to watch over Clark because he couldn't risk leaving her unprotected. Pen gave him regular updates. So far, there have been no significant developments. Clark mainly stayed in the house.

Gun's phone chimed. Looking at it, his pulse accelerated. Clark had sent him a message, warning him to release Pen from his babysitting duties. Invigorated, he immediately texted her back.

Not happening.

His pulse was pounding so hard in his chest that he could only stare at the moving dots while waiting for her response.

Why are you doing this?

Need to know you're safe.

Safety was paramount to him. Clark had taken careless risks, including provoking Cork by kicking his motorcycle.

I'm safe.

Good. Want it to stay that way.

Not happy.

A slow grin crept across Gun's face, shattering the emotional dry spell he had been experiencing recently. Even if she was unhappy, the relief of seeing her response filled him with joy. He'd take her being unhappy over being hurt any day.

Too bad.

Stop it, Gun. I mean it.

Let's talk about it.

Gun waited for her response but was disappointed. She had hung up. Regardless of how their communication ended, a tiny seed of hope sprung. Clark could have ignored Pen and kept the lines of communication locked down. Instead, she'd opened them up. Gun took this as a positive sign and resolved to keep them open. He felt it was crucial to maintain regular communication with Clark, knowing that by keeping this connection alive, he aimed to sway her opinion gradually and ultimately gain a chance for himself and Vin.

Their conversation had to be postponed because the Club needed to address internal issues among the brothers in Bridgetown. According to Achilles, a growing dispute among a few brothers had led to a rift. Ensuring unity among the members of the Iconic Sons MC was essential to upholding their strength and solidarity within the Club. To restore peace and harmony, the MC needed to uncover why there was disagreement among its members.

SEVEN

Clark hurried through the corridors of the hospital, feeling her heart pound in her chest. She asked the desk clerk for directions to Gun's ward. Her fears escalated with each passing second as she waited for the clerk to check the computer.

Upon entering Gun's ward, she noticed Vin, Jax, Dom, and Achilles, the Club President, gathered with tense expressions and hushed voices discussing the situation. Vin's gaze locked onto her, and his eyes narrowed with determination as he strode towards her, purposefully blocking her path.

"Clark, you need to go."

"No!" she cried. "Gun's been shot. I need to see him!"

Charly had called Clark and informed her that Gun had been shot but couldn't provide any additional information about his condition. Devastated by the dreadful news, Clark's world shattered into pieces, and she fled from her parents' home, with her only thought being to reach the hospital as fast as she could.

"Clark, you made your choice. He doesn't want to see you because he's not ready to face you in his current condition," Vin said.

Clark gasped in utter disbelief, her eyes widening in shock at Vin's unexpected and harsh words. "Did he say that?" she asked, eyes searching Vin's face for confirmation.

She tried to duck under his arms as he nodded, refusing to accept Vin's words. "Babe, if you don't leave, I'll throw you out myself," Vin threatened, his expression hardening into a stubborn scowl.

"Please, just for a minute. I need to see that he's all right, then I'll go, I promise," she begged, her voice cracking with emotion.

Vin's expression softened slightly as he opened the door to a nearby disabled toilet, motioning for Clark to step inside. He locked them in with a loud click echoing in the confined space to give them privacy.

"Why are you here, Clark? This is Club business. It shouldn't be your concern."

"Gun is hurt, Vin. I'm worried about him. What happened?"

"The doctors assured me he's going to be fine. He got shot, and that's all I'm saying."

She pleaded, asking, "Can I see for myself?"

"No." Clark had never known Vin to be stubborn and cold. "I'm going to escort you out now. Don't make a scene," he warned.

Clark complied, but she planned to hang around until the others left and then sneak back inside. Her primary concern was to see for herself that Gun was safe and well.

* * * * *

VIN COULDN'T HELP CHUCKLING when he noticed that instead of heading for the bus stop, Clark turned a corner and hung around, unwilling to say goodbye. He decided to text Gun immediately to inform him.

What the little vixen didn't know was that Pen was tailing her. Pen had been the one to give Vin the heads-up about Clark's arrival. Her first reaction would likely be to try and save them if either of them were hurt. He'd suspected once she found out about Gun being shot, she would hightail her cute little ass here.

He believed Clark's reaction further reinforced the possibility of a relationship between them. While Vin disliked seeing her upset, it also sparked hope that Gun's health scare might ignite their relationship. He understood that Clark's tragic past was the main reason holding her back; therefore, it would take time to earn her trust. Impatience had always been Vin's weakness, evident in his quick temper and restless demeanor. Considering the circumstances, Vin had no other choice but to have patience.

After the brothers left, Vin entered Gun's room and sat on the chair next to the bed.

Vin smiled as he said, "Clark's here."

Gun chuckled, then winced, putting his hand on his injured shoulder. "I heard. What did she say?"

"She wants to know you're okay," Vin explained. "I told her you didn't want to see her. She got upset and tried to get past me. I walked her out and told her to go home."

"Did she?"

Vin smirked and replied, "What do you think?"

"Good," Gun nodded, relieved that Clark didn't leave. "We can't tell her what happened, Vin. Only that I got shot, you hear?"

"I know," Vin agreed. "But what about Cork, Farmer, and Binge? They're still on the loose. And for some messed-up reason, Cork thinks you're why he and the other two lost their colors. What's that about?"

"Portia," Gun said.

"They were selling drugs for the Bratzvic Brothers. You know we've had an ongoing rivalry with them because we don't do that shit anymore. That's a betrayal to the Club. They deserved to be kicked out."

"I get it, Vin, but this is not over yet. Cork's angry, and Farmer and Binge are just plain greedy. My gut tells me they'll be back."

"If Clark ever found out about this, we'd have another problem on our hands," Vin said, worry evident as he combed his fingers through his hair.

"True, brother. That's why she can't ever know the truth about what happened here."

✳✳✳✳✳

WHEN THE COAST WAS clear, Clark quietly slipped past the sliding doors to check on Gun. Remaining vigilant in case any of the guys were lurking in the shadows, she scanned the area closely, her senses on high alert. She moved slowly and softly into the dimly lit room, relieved that no one was nearby. The air was thick with the clinical scent of disinfectant, stinging Clark's nostrils as she inhaled.

Gingerly sitting on the edge of the chair, Clark couldn't resist reaching out to touch Gun. She placed her hand on top of his, feeling emotionally centered for the first time since learning of his close call. Her gaze followed the rhythmic rise and fall of his chest.

His arm was in a sling, and a bandage wrapped his right shoulder. As her eyes roamed over Gun's face, she was startled when his brown eyes met hers, a silent exchange of unspoken emotions passing between them.

"What are you doing here, Red?" There was no trace of anger or disappointment in Gun's question, giving Clark hope that he might allow her to stay.

"I came to see how you were doing after what happened."

"I thought Vin told you to go home," he said with a hint of amusement.

Clark cast her eyes downward, shielding her emotions. She didn't want him to see the lie that popped into her head. "When do I ever listen to you and Vin?"

"Fair enough," he agreed with a nod. "Now that you see I'm fine, you can leave."

Her eyes shot up to meet his. "But I'm not sure if I should leave yet …"

"No need for you to stay."

"I don't want to leave yet, Gun. Can I stay a little longer? I need to be here with you."

"Why?"

"Because … I don't want to leave you when you're hurt," Clark confessed.

"You made your choice." Gun's statement reminded her of what Vin had said earlier.

Clark stood up, feeling the impact of those words. "I know, but I feel much better when I'm close to you."

Gun patted the bed, inviting Clark to sit beside him. "Come here and sit with me."

Clark wriggled onto the bed before he had a chance to change his mind. Gun slipped his good arm around her shoulder, and she happily snuggled against him.

"Can we finally have that conversation? Are you ready to talk to me now?" Gun's eyes bore into hers, searching for honesty and a glimpse of her true feelings.

"Yes."

Gun gently placed a finger under her chin and lifted it so she had to look at him. "This is what I know. I know when we kissed, there was a spark, a fire. I haven't forgotten that kiss, Red. It's ingrained in my memory." He kissed the tip of her nose. "I can see that you care deeply for Vin and me. Your actions show genuine concern and feelings that go beyond friendship."

Clark felt a lump in her throat at the truth of Gun's statement. Their kiss had ignited a fire within her, and her emotions for Gun and Vin transcended mere friendship. They occupied her thoughts constantly, day and night.

"Given this, do you still deny the attraction between us? If so, leave this bed, walk out, and don't return."

Clark stayed where she was, feeling brave for the first time. She was ready to take a chance with Gun and Vin, even though inside, she was shaking like a leaf.

Clark's first thought upon hearing that Gun had been shot was that he was dead. It was a brutal reminder of the fragility of life that we expect people to live, but in reality, we could die tomorrow.

Panic gripped her, and the foremost thought in her mind was to rush to Gun, to feel his pulse and reassure herself that he was alive. Never before had she felt such overwhelming terror. After Gun narrowly escaped death, Clark resolved to overcome her fear of loss and live in the present moment.

Gun's close call made Clark realize that life is fleeting, and she wanted to spend it with Gun and Vin. She was prepared to take a chance, aware that it could be short-lived. Clark was prepared to face any outcome, accepting the risks in exchange for a relationship with the two men she adored.

"Red." It was a warning that he was about to kiss her, a gesture she was fully prepared to welcome.

The softness of the kiss threw Clark. Gun's lips delivered quick kisses, leaving a glistening trail on Clark's skin. Yearning for his lips' soft yet firm touch, she eagerly sought more, chasing the fleeting sensation. Her unspoken desire was answered when Gun turned those fleeting kisses into long, slow ones. With his strong arm securing her in position, Gun delicately and unhurriedly explored her mouth. When they finally pulled away from each other, both were left breathless.

"Stay," he whispered.

Clark spent the night cradled next to Gun on the narrow hospital bed, feeling the warmth of his body against hers. Throughout the night, she would wake to find them entwined together in the same position, their bodies intimately close, Gun's good arm protectively around Clark. Being with Gun during his time of need gave Clark a deep sense of satisfaction—she could protect someone very dear to her.

In the stillness of the morning, she woke to the gentle murmur of voices drifting from the hallway outside the room. Overcome with sudden shyness at the prospect of encountering Gun and Vin, she swiftly conjured up excuses to make her exit.

Vin appeared cheerful, his eyes alight with mischief as he greeted Clark with a flirtatious smile. "Where are you off to, babe? We got plans to make."

Clark, in wrinkled clothes with disheveled hair and unbrushed teeth, had no desire to make plans with them.

"Some other time," Clark said with a forced smile, quickly straightening her top. She needed time to collect her thoughts before discussing further plans.

"Whoa! Shortcake, stop. Hold on a minute. I just got here. We need to talk."

Clark nodded. "I know. Can we do it later? I have to go."

Vin agreed. "I'll pick you up at one in front of your place, and we'll drive to Peekapine Lake. It's secluded, and we can be alone."

Clark's eyes darted towards Gun. "You're getting out?"

"Yep. Been given the all clear."

"Peekapine Lake? I've never been there."

"Get ready for an unforgettable experience," Vin promised with a sparkle in his eyes.

After making plans, Clark dashed out the door to get ready.

✳ ✳ ✳ ✳ ✳

VIN AND GUN SHARED a conspiratorial grin, their eyes alight with anticipation, ready for the upcoming adventure. "It's happening," Vin declared with confidence.

Gun nodded in agreement. "It's time to show Clark how we feel."

Vin smirked when he observed Clark dozing off on the hospital bed earlier, her limbs dangling over the side. She liked taking up the whole space, which gave him dirty ideas. She looked beautiful and peaceful, resembling a serene dove gracefully resting in the moonlight. He had to tear his gaze away from her and step outside to the hospital corridor to discuss the previous night's incident with Gun. The news that Clark was ready to give them a chance after weeks of uncertainty was heartwarming.

With his pulse quickening, Vin eagerly anticipated practicing all the moves he had imagined doing with Clark in private.

* * * * *

CLARK GASPED IN DISBELIEF, feeling a rush of wonder as she took in the breathtaking panoramic views of the Peekapine Mountains spread out before her.

Vin and Gun had arrived in their Toyota Land Cruiser to whisk her away on an adventurous journey that took them over an hour through winding roads and scenic landscapes to reach their destination for the day. Gazing out of the window, her eyes widened in awe at the beauty of the surrounding landscape. The serene, pristine waters of Peekapine Lake perfectly reflected the majestic mountains.

Vin spread a large, soft blanket on the lush, emerald-green grass, its gentle texture inviting Clark to relax and unwind. In this serene setting, the area was deserted except for a few blue herons.

Clark felt like she had stepped into a dream, an otherworldly realm plucked from her wildest fantasies. The fresh scent of pine trees filled her nostrils, and a gentle breeze caressed her skin, carrying the soft murmur of the nearby stream.

Gun told her to sit down and relax. Relax? Clark was aware that her relationship with Vin and Gun had changed. In that pivotal moment, a bead of sweat formed on her brow, her palms growing clammy with nerves as she grasped the gravity of what was about to unfold. Clark's mind raced with worry as she faced the prospect of disclosing her hidden secret to Vin and Gun, unsure how they would react.

As she settled onto the blanket, two strapping figures surrounded her. Having permitted them to delve into their connection, they enthusiastically seized the opportunity. She knew she would have to disclose her secret at some point and hoped to delay that moment for as long as possible.

Clark's scars were unsightly. They marred her skin like stitches of intersecting patterns. She often traced their jagged ridges with trembling fingers, studying the colors, convinced that any onlooker would recoil in disgust. Then, there was the reason for her self-harm. Naturally, people would be curious about her motives. She knew why—because of the fireball in her stomach—but didn't understand her choice. Why did she choose to self-harm rather than consult a doctor and potentially receive medication for her anxiety? It all made sense, except she feared falling into the same pill addiction that had trapped Archer.

Vin asked, "Are you hungry, babe?" as he opened the picnic hamper and laid out a delightful spread of sandwiches, a fruit platter, refreshing drinks, and a plate of tempting brownies.

"Wow. You packed enough for an army," Clark joked as she accepted the sandwich. "Did you make all this?" she asked, sweeping a hand over the abundant food spread before her.

"No, Sara made them."

They engaged in light-hearted banter as they savored the food, washing it down with beer and champagne. After a while, Clark felt a warm, fuzzy glow from the champagne, alleviating some tension from the fear of having to expose her secret.

"What led to your injury?"

"I got shot."

Clark, being careful not to roll her eyes, asked, "I know you got shot, but why did it happen? Who shot you?"

"Shortcake," Vin warned. "You know Gun can't tell you."

"I know it's Club business, Vin. You don't have to explain," she said before Vin could respond further.

✳ ✳ ✳ ✳ ✳

GUN KNEW IT WOULD upset Clark to know that Cork had been the one to shoot him. The incident occurred during a dispute with Cork and three other club members. They'd been engaging in drug deals with a rival club in which the Iconic Sons MC no longer participated. The disloyalty deeply affected the Club, leading to internal conflicts and betrayal among the brothers, who did not take their expulsion kindly. The shootout resulted in the death of one Bridgetown Club member and Gun's injury, further escalating the tension. Cork and the two remaining traitors had escaped.

"Are you ready to discuss our relationship now?" Gun asked as he packed away the last of the food.

"Sure," Clark said. Gun sensed her initial apprehension returning.

"So, are we doing this?"

Gun's ambiguous question made Clark laugh. "If you're talking about a sexual relationship, then yes, we agree," she replied.

"Good."

When he leaned forward, Clark held up a hand. "I have some questions first."

A flicker of a frown appeared, then just as quickly disappeared. "Okay. Shoot."

"What will this be?"

"I can't say right now, Red. Let's wait and find out."

Clark sighed. "Gun, I need some boundaries to know what I'm getting myself into."

"What specific boundaries are you thinking of?"

"I need to know how this will work. You know, with the three of us."

Gun's eyes crinkled. "The sex? You had your ass taken, Red?"

"Yes," Clark whispered. "However, not two men at the same time."

Gun said, "We'll take care of you, Red. You'll enjoy it."

"Our girl's blushing, Gun," Vin teased, chuckling.

"Are we in an exclusive relationship, committed only to each other?"

Gun recalled what happened between Dom, Jax, and Charly. A jealous clubwhore, Angel, had shown Charly a video of Dom and Jax in bed with two women. Understandably, Charly was devastated and heartbroken and ended the relationship. Dom and Jax were furious and threw Angel out of the Club. The situation weighed heavily on his brothers, who were consumed with guilt over their colossal mistake. This realization marked a pivotal moment for Dom and Jax, as they comprehended that Charly held greater importance than anyone else. Yet, they grappled with the pain they inflicted on the woman they cared about.

Charly, in her forgiving nature, granted them a second chance. Although a bit of groveling didn't hurt, Dom and Jax were determined to show Charly they wouldn't betray her trust again. Unfortunately, people tried to sabotage Charly's relationship by accusing her of stealing. Charly disappeared after learning that there had been a hit out on her, which forced her to go into hiding for her safety. Thankfully, through persistence and encouragement from Sara, their sister, Dom and Jax found Charly and worked even harder to regain her trust.

Gun knew how crucial trust was in relationships. The only way their relationship would work between him, Clark, and Vin was for them to be open and honest.

Gun made sure there was no confusion this time.

"We are exclusive, Clark. There won't be another man for you. Got that?" Addressing Vin, he added, "And no other woman for us."

This was no hardship because his cock only wanted Clark. The club whores didn't do it for him nowadays—not since he'd met Clark. His heart raced with adrenaline and lust once again. He was impatient to get down and dirty with his woman.

"Lie down," Gun instructed authoritatively.

Gun deftly unbuckled his belt with his good hand, then forcefully shoved his jeans down to reveal his hardened cock.

Clark's hands clenched at her sides as Vin eased his body down, careful not to crush her.

Gun felt a flash of jealousy as Vin and Clark's tongues intertwined in a dance of strangers—exploring, tasting, and battling each other. His lips tingled, and he distinctly recalled the sweetness of Clark's lips.

Gun's fingers caressed Clark's silky skin, drawn to its softness. He needed to touch her. As he leaned in closer, his hand slipped under her top. He found the front clasp of her bra and skillfully unhooked it. He firmly cupped her breast, gently massaging it, as his thumb caressed her nipple, feeling it harden.

Vin helped lift her top, revealing Clark's pert breasts. Gun then lowered his head, taking the other nipple into his warm mouth, flicking the erect bud vigorously. Wanting more skin privileges, he rose.

"Remove your top, Red," Gun demanded, tension evident in every muscle of his body. He'd waited so long for this moment that he found it difficult to slow down.

"Um … I'd rather not. It's a bit nippy."

"I'll warm you up. Don't worry." They engaged in a tug-of-war—Gun attempting to take her top off while Clark tried to pull away. "Red? What's the matter?" he growled. "Take your top off."

"I'm cold," she said.

"Are you going to take anything off?"

"My bra's off." Her hands went to the buttons of her jeans. "I'll take my pants off."

"But not your top?"

Clark chewed her bottom lip.

"It's not that cold." Gun moved closer to her, entering her personal space. "You're always in long sleeves. What are you hiding, Red?"

"Here's the thing," she started, her voice trembling. "I … um … I don't … well, I …" Clark stuttered.

The atmosphere grew tense as he took charge of the situation. "Show us your arms, Clark," Gun demanded.

"I'm … well …" Clark dipped her head and blurted everything out. "I should warn you, they're not very appealing."

"You got burn scars?" Clark shook her head. "Scars from an accident?" Gun persisted.

"No," she whispered, her voice trembling. "I … I have scars from cutting myself." Gun watched as Clark swayed slightly, her eyes avoiding his gaze. The only sound breaking the silence was the shrill squawk of the herons. Clark raised her head, and his deep brown eyes clashed with a pair of golden honey.

"Let me see." Gun's grip tightened as he seized her hand, his eyes widening in shock as he pulled up one of her sleeves. "Jesus Christ!" he growled.

* * * * *

CLARK STARED AT HER arm, seeing the healed lines: some scars were white and raised, while others appeared as fine slithers of white, with the most recent cuts being dark pink and scabby. Many were crisscrossed, varying in size from a few centimeters to several inches. She never made cuts too deep, always just enough to divert her attention from the fireball in the depths of her stomach.

"Fuck, Clark. What the fuck?" Vin whispered, looking heartbroken at seeing her scars.

"Why?" Gun rolled up her other sleeve and closed his eyes. "Why do you do this to yourself?"

Feeling embarrassed and exposed, Clark quickly covered her arms to shield her scars, feeling the need to protect herself.

"Explain."

It was a complex subject to understand, let alone talk about. Rather than seeking help from a professional or using medication for her anxiety, Clark had made the unconventional decision to resort to self-harm. There was no rhyme or reason why; she just did.

"I'm not sure, Gun. I do it when I feel as if I can't breathe. It helps relieve the tightness in my chest."

"What causes you to feel like you can't breathe?"

"I have panic attacks."

"Do you have to cut yourself? Have you tried taking deep breaths or other coping strategies instead?"

Clark tried to stand up, but Gun quickly reached out and grabbed her hand to prevent her from doing so.

"What?" Clark's voice cracked as the urge to flee gripped her.

"Come on, Clark, talk to us. Help us understand."

"You can't understand, Gun. I feel like I'm suffocating, trapped in my mind with no escape in sight."

"Clark, you need help," Vin suggested softly.

Clark glared at Vin, insisting, "I may need help, but I want to try handling this on my own first. I understand my body's needs."

"Clark, Vin is right. Let's look into arranging counseling for you."

Disregarding Gun's advice, Clark abruptly stood up. Her need for solitude kicked in, and she insisted on being taken home. A sinking sensation in her heart, accompanied by a pang of sadness and regret, engulfed Clark as she realized their budding relationship was crumbling before it could fully blossom.

Throughout the journey home, Clark sat hunched in the back seat, consumed by a profound sense of misery. She stared out of the window, her distant gaze lost in thought, her mind trapped in a relentless loop, replaying the distressing moment when the men had first seen her scars. Their shock and repulsion had been unmistakable, which perhaps explained why they had offered no resistance when she had asked to leave.

Clark noticed Vin and Gun were absorbed in their phones while she wallowed in self-pity. It felt like they had already forgotten her. She couldn't shake the feeling that her scars grossed them out. Clark regretted Gun's insistence on removing her top, wishing the situation had been different.

Questioning the future of her relationship with Vin and Gun, Clark closed her eyes, seeking solitude and shutting out the world.

The sudden movement of the car stopping jolted Clark awake from her daydreams. Looking around, she realized they had arrived at the clubhouse. Bewildered and disoriented, she questioned, "Why have we come here? I thought you were driving me home."

Both men exited the car, and Gun went to the passenger door. "Get out, Red," he said, unfastening her seatbelt.

"What's going on? What's happening?" Clark scanned the area, her eyes locking onto clusters of men deep in conversation.

"We have plans, remember?"

Was Gun referring to their sexual relationship when he mentioned plans? "You still want to do this, considering everything that has just happened?" she asked hesitantly, not moving.

Vin positioned himself in the doorway. "Didn't say otherwise, did we? Get out, Clark," he commanded.

As Clark stepped out of the vehicle, Vin reached for her hand and firmly led her inside, his grip solid and comforting.

Dim light shrouded the bar, casting long shadows across the crowded room. The only illumination sources were the faint glow from the windows and the buzzing fluorescent lights suspended over the pool tables. Half-naked women stood nearby, watching the men play pool.

Vin and Gun skillfully navigated through the lively crowd, strategically making their way to a secluded exit at the far end of the room. Aware of the probing stares directed at them, Clark kept her head down, not wanting to attract any attention.

Once they entered the bedroom, Vin quickly secured the door with a decisive click. "Trust me, we won't be disturbed," he said with a sly smile.

"Red, help me out with these boots." Clark knelt in front of Gun to untie his laces. She shivered as a warm hand skimmed along her neck, slipped under the top's neckline, and caressed her shoulders.

Clark tugged at his boots, struggling to remove them.

"Do you need help with your shirt?"

"Yeah."

Clark started unbuttoning his shirt, aware that Gun hadn't taken his eyes off her. Vin instructed her to assist him in unzipping his jeans and sliding them off. Clark secretly enjoyed being controlled by Gun and Vin because it took the pressure off her.

Clark had spent many years worrying about others. She sometimes yearned for someone else to take over and relieve her of any responsibility, seeking a moment of respite. This was the perfect opportunity to be guided by Gun and Vin, considering they had a lot more experience. Clark couldn't explain her certainty, but she trusted they would never push her beyond her limits. Although they might attempt to test her limits, she was prepared to assert her boundaries and explore her comfort zone.

Now that she was in this vulnerable position, half undressed and having seen her scars, they still desired her. Clark felt empowered to submit to them without reservation.

After shedding the last of their clothes, Gun told her to undress completely. He ordered her to remove her top as though he could read her mind.

"My scars?"

"Top off, babe. Then we'll talk about your scars."

After fully undressing, Gun slid a gentle hand down her forearm, tracing the raised ridges of her scars with a tender touch. Then he grasped her wrist firmly and tugged her closer.

"This ends now. You will not cut yourself anymore."

Stunned by his sudden ruling, Clark tried to object. "I'm not sure."

"You don't have a say, Red. We won't allow you to hurt yourself."

Clark persisted, her voice tinged with frustration. "You don't understand, Gun."

"Maybe not, but I want to. That doesn't mean I'll let you continue to self-harm. Your safety is our priority. No more cutting."

"But …"

"Enough!" barked Gun. "Lie down."

Clark was torn between asserting her autonomy and yielding to their commands to satisfy her desires. Her desires won out, and she rationalized that she could argue with them later.

Lying on the bed, Clark felt the cold air make her nipples pucker. Vin instinctively moved his hands to cup her breasts while Gun's hand ventured between her thighs.

Clark's thighs slammed shut. "That feels good," she gasped.

"It's meant to. Open." Gun thrust a hand between her knees, spreading them wide. He inserted a finger inside her warm, wet channel. "Fuck! She's dripping, Vin." His thumb found her clitoris and began rubbing it in small, circular motions.

Clark's fingers clenched the quilt tightly as she arched off the bed, soft moans escaping.

"Not yet, Red." Gun looked at Vin. "Pull her to the edge of the bed. I need to taste her."

Vin got up and dragged her by the ankles. Clark burst into nervous laughter, but Gun's tongue quickly silenced her. While one man suckled on a nipple like a baby and teased the other like a toy, the second man explored between her legs with a mix of poking, prodding, and tasting. Clark didn't care what she looked like or how she sounded—only that the incredible sensation inside her was building, building, until she was ready to explode. She was swallowed up by a torrential storm, launching her into ecstasy.

Clark's eyelids fluttered shut, and a blissful sigh slipped from her parted lips, basking in the afterglow of her climax.

"She liked that, bro." Despite Vin's smug tone, Clark kept her eyes closed, the heavy thumping of her heartbeat gently rocking her to sleep.

✶ ✶ ✶ ✶ ✶

WHILE HE CRAWLED ONTO the bed next to Clark, Vin lay on the other side of her. Gun smiled happily as he observed her resting peacefully. He felt pleased with himself, knowing he was responsible for her euphoric state. Her tired smile, combined with the way her hand gently caressed his arm, sparked arousal in him.

"Red, straddle me," he ordered, pulling on his cock.

Her mouth formed an "O" as she watched him pleasure himself, his good hand sliding up and down his erect penis.

Licking her lips, she asked, "Do you have a condom?"

It was proof she had him so twisted that he had forgotten about using protection.

Vin got up from the bed and headed to the bathroom. He threw a small packet to Gun. Clark picked it up, tore open the foil, and easily rolled the condom onto Gun.

Gun frowned and inquired, "Have you had a lot of practice, Red?"

"Well … I was in a long-term relationship for seven years, so I have some experience."

Gun watched her, his eyes glowing with desire, as Clark mounted him. She carefully lowered herself onto him, sheathing him in her tight pussy.

"Jesus, Gun. You're big," Clark gasped.

"Thanks," he said with a smirk.

"All right for you to say. It's been a while for me."

Gun felt a sense of narcissistic satisfaction knowing that Clark had only been in a relationship with one person.

Behind her, Vin eased himself inside her. Clark bent her head and sighed.

"Take it easy, Vin," warned Gun, afraid Vin would hurt her.

"I know what I'm fucking doing," Vin groaned, his breathing uneven.

Clark almost collapsed on top of him, but she stopped herself at the last minute, mindful of his injury. Her moans echoed like thunder in his ears, a symphony of desire that drenched him in a cold sweat of anticipation and longing. A harmonious rhythm began, each thrust synchronized in a passionate dance, with Vin and him taking turns in deep, primal movements. Gun wasn't sure how long he could last—the tightness enveloping him was heavenly. Her inner muscles clenched in response as Vin leaned in, taking control of the pace.

Gun wanted his first time with Clark to last. He needed to muster self-control and deliberately slow down his movements. It didn't help that her pert breasts were inches from his eyes.

Gun leaned forward to lick the sweat dripping down her neck. He found every detail of her exquisite: the salty sweetness of her perspiration, the smoothness of her velvety skin, and the gentle heat of her breath caressing his face.

Finally, Gun caught the slight hitch in her cries, a telltale sign of her impending climax—feeling her body tense under his touch. Clark's body started shaking as her orgasm began to build. He was transfixed, unable to look away, as he watched her mouth part in a silent, muffled scream of ecstasy. Her head was thrown back, and her eyes were shut tightly in rapture. Cursing softly, Vin withdrew carefully and rolled to the side to avoid squashing Clark. Gun started powering up again, wanting to join Clark when they soared high together. It didn't take long before they flew into the abyss of pleasure.

This time, she wasn't as careful when she collapsed on top of him, her breath hot against his skin, a mix of exhaustion and satisfaction in her movements. Gun grunted in discomfort but held her tightly, feeling a twinge of pain shoot through his shoulder as she tried to shift.

"Gun, your shoulder," Clark gasped, trying to move off him.

Gun wanted to hold on to the deep emotional connection they experienced while slowly recovering.

✱ ✱ ✱ ✱ ✱

CLARK FELT TERRIBLE FOR hurting Gun's shoulder, but he held her firmly against him anyway. She sighed in contentment, a soft, relieved exhale that filled the room. The initial discomfort as Gun entered her, his size stretching her, quickly gave way to a mix of pain and pleasure. She was already aroused from the most intense foreplay of her life. Gun had been careful, guiding her with a gentle touch as he slowly, deliberately entered her.

When Vin entered her from behind, his prodding shocked her, and it must have shown on her face. Clark almost laughed because

Vin didn't hurt her; he was gentle. But she felt a deep sense of intimacy and a hint of apprehension with both of them inside her. Once they found a comfortable rhythm, she could let go of her worries.

Double penetration was everything she'd heard about but didn't believe. The fullness was present, but the sensation of two cocks moving within her hit her G spot precisely. Clark was amazed by the strength of the two intense climaxes that swept through her one after the other.

It had been exhilarating to watch Gun from above. She felt a surge of euphoria as she realized she was responsible for his erratic breathing. She also noticed the glistening perspiration on his skin, the tight grip on her thigh, and the satisfying sounds of his groans.

She heard the mattress squeak and felt it dip a little as she was still recovering from a high in the warm comfort of Gun's arms. Turning her head to the side, she chuckled when she noticed Vin's cheeky grin.

Clark was surprised when Vin pulled out early. Seeing the spark in his bright blue eyes and the subtle smile, she felt grateful that he still desired her.

$$* * * * *$$

AS THEY LAY CUDDLING on the bed, they both turned their heads when they felt the mattress shift beneath them.

"My turn," Vin drawled lazily, a slow smile spreading across his handsome face.

His palms instinctively glided up her forearms, and he felt the bumpy ridges and uneven texture beneath his fingertips. Clark pulled her arms back, her face contorting in a grimace.

"What's wrong?"

"I don't like you touching my arms. They're ugly."

In one fluid motion, Vin rolled over, effortlessly bringing Clark along with him. With Clark pinned beneath him, he commanded her full attention.

"I'm only going to say this once, babe. Those marks on your arms are a part of your past. They represent what you've been through, and that's some ugly shit. Your scars are a part of you, but they don't define your beauty. Don't say they're ugly again. Got it?"

"Can I disagree with you?" she asked, raising an eyebrow.

"No."

Clark's dimples surfaced, eliciting a surge of excitement that coursed through him. Vin did not resist, spellbound by her beauty and the depth of her gaze. He lowered his head, sampling the sweet taste of her lips as they engaged in a long, wet, unhurried kiss that stole his breath.

Vin's hand delicately traced the outline of her small but pert breasts, feeling their shape with a gentle touch. He relished the musical sound of her moan as he tenderly teased her nipples, eliciting a subtle shiver of pleasure. Sensing her invitation, he gently kissed one nipple, cherishing the moment as she responded with a sigh of contentment. Clark's fingers glided through his hair, giving a soothing scalp massage and urging him to keep going.

His other hand trailed down, slowly caressing her inner thigh with just the feather-light touch of his fingertips, evoking a soft gasp. With a single touch, he explored her wet and warm center, gauging her response to his tender ministrations.

Suddenly, Clark's breathing changed, and she frantically started tugging his hair. Despite the sharp pain, he focused on Clark's reactions. Vin continued to rub her swollen clitoris, knowing she was close. He felt the stiffness of her body, a clear indication that she was on the brink of climaxing. Vin watched intently as her body lifted off the bed in a tense arch, her breaths growing erratic. Vin saw Gun coming out of the bathroom in his peripheral vision. He heard the bed creak as Gun settled in to watch. His gaze remained fixed on Clark as he absorbed the melody of her soft moans, unable to tear his eyes away. His fingers were coated in warm secretions.

"Oh, my God," Clark cried, rolling to her side and curling into a ball. "Oh, my God," she repeated, breathless. She started rocking back and forth, her thighs tightly clenched, as soft moans fell from her lips.

Vin watched silently, his heart pounding with curiosity and concern. Experiencing a woman in the throes of a powerful climax was a profound and enlightening moment for him. He was captivated by the raw display of emotions and vulnerability. Turning to Gun, he saw the reflection of his astonishment mirrored back at him.

The women he bedded knew how to moan, sigh, cry, shout, and scream in response to his foreplay, but it was a practiced move. The women at the Club strategically tailored their responses to feed the egos of the men they were with. Their calculated responses lacked authenticity. In contrast, Clark's raw and unfiltered response was unmistakable in the flush of her face, the ragged rhythm of her breath, and the tremors rocking her body.

Clark stilled, and her body visibly sagged as she let out a final sigh.

"Hey," he murmured against her cheek. "How are you feeling?"

She mumbled something in response, clearly exhausted and unable to speak. Vin chuckled softly and tenderly kissed her slack mouth.

"You ready for me, babe?" he whispered, trailing a series of kisses along her collarbone, loving the feel of the heat radiating off her skin.

At last, Clark's eyes fluttered open, mesmerizing him again with their golden depths. Pausing briefly, he retrieved a condom from the side drawer and carefully tore the packet open with his teeth.

Missionary wasn't his usual sexual position; he often took the club women from behind, but with Clark, he wanted to look into her eyes and inhale every real gasp and moan from her luscious lips. As he eased inside her, he heard her first gasp slip out. She felt amazing, like the stroking of a warm hand slowly tightening around him, restricting his blood flow. Vin never wanted this moment to end; it was a rare instance of pure bliss that he wished could last forever.

Groaning, he felt the urgency rise within him. "I'm sorry, babe, but this will be quick," he confessed, his thrusts increasing.

"You don't have to hold back for me," she murmured.

"Yeah, I do, babe. I want to feel you squeezing my cock."

Clark chuckled softly, her eyes dancing with amusement and desire. "I love the way you talk dirty," she admitted, a playful grin on her lips.

Encouraged by her words, Vin kissed her passionately. His fingers found her clitoris, and he began gentle, circular movements, mindful of not applying too much pressure or speed. He knew she would be sensitive because of her previous orgasms. Then he felt the tightening of her inner muscles around him, a sensation that sent electric shivers down his spine. Vin let out a primal cry as he reached the zenith of pleasure, his body quivering with release.

Vin luxuriated in the warmth of their bodies pressed together, craving intimate skin-to-skin contact. *Just until she recovers*, Vin thought drowsily. He felt a sense of contentment as Clark wrapped her arms around him, willingly supporting his weight. The only sounds that filled his ears were the ragged symphony of their breathing, accompanied by the rhythmic thumping of their hearts.

$* * * * *$

CLARK REVELED IN THE feel of Vin's weight on top of her. He was heavy, but she could tell he wasn't putting all his weight on her.

She felt as though she was in a dreamlike state. She had never known such divine pleasure, especially from two confident men who felt entitled to women without exerting effort. Clark was immensely relieved by the sexual chemistry that she, Vin, and Gun shared, as well as the sexual prowess they possessed in bed. Vin and Gun were also attuned to a woman's needs so she could experience pleasure, too. If she were truthful, she'd harbored doubts about their ability to satisfy a woman sexually because of their casual attitude toward sex.

Clark, Gun, and Vin spent the rest of the night exploring each other and learning about each other's bodies. During their intimate exploration, they delved into discovering her desires, explored her erogenous zones, and playfully experimented with various positions. Clark was pleasantly surprised to find out that it *was possible* to have multiple orgasms.

EIGHT

After two days, Clark was still at the clubhouse. Vin and Gun suggested that since it was a long weekend, she could relax at the clubhouse with Charly, Sara, and their friend, Carrie. She suspected they kept her around for easy access to sex. Clark didn't mind because it was the best sex she'd ever had. The intense passion and deep emotional connection during their encounters were compelling reasons for her to remain at the clubhouse.

The morning after, she woke up to find her arm draped across Vin's shoulder and her leg intertwined with Gun's in a somewhat awkward position. She initially felt embarrassed when she opened her eyes and saw Vin's sparkling blue eyes filled with laughter directed at her. Now, Clark was completely at ease with their nudity and the fact that she invariably occupied most of the bed, a situation her lovers didn't seem to mind.

Clark had always had trouble sleeping peacefully and without interruptions, frequently waking up at night and struggling to fall asleep. This led to a constant feeling of fatigue and frustration during the day. For the past two consecutive nights, Clark had finally experienced profound and restful sleep, untroubled by any nightmares or the debilitating sense of loneliness that used to accompany her insomnia.

Gun and Vin were the reason for Clark's improved sleep. Driven by insatiable desires, they often whisked her away for passionate marathons of lovemaking or spontaneous, fiery sex. She slowly picked up on the subtle changes in their behavior that indicated their sexual intentions. Gun would hug her tightly, thrusting his erection against her and whisper sweet nothings in her ear, sending shivers down her spine. Vin had a confident, sexy swagger, almost like a peacock strutting about, its iridescent feathers moving with a captivating grace to draw attention.

Once, Sara laughed and whispered conspiratorially, "Here comes your peacock."

Gun and Vin were on a business trip somewhere, but they wouldn't tell her where or why. When she suggested to Vin that she should go home, he promptly dismissed the idea.

"I've left Rachel by herself," she'd argued.

"Rachel's a big girl. She can look after herself," said Vin.

"I need a change of clothes. I can't keep wearing Sara's clothes."

"Tell Pen what you need; he can collect it for you."

"Are you trying to keep me here for some reason, Vin?"

"Well, isn't it obvious?"

"Let me gather my belongings, and I'll return before you come back."

"Shortcake, let Pen do it for you. The girls like having you there. So do we."

Vin's silver-tongued charm and calculated gestures—his persuasive compliments and subtle manipulations, made Clark uneasy, fueling her belief that they were orchestrating her stay against her will. A dreadful thought crossed her mind: were they concerned she might harm herself or bring in a razor surreptitiously?

The idea of keeping a razor as a precaution haunted Clark. Eventually, a triggering event was bound to cause a panic attack. The fear of harm befalling Gun or Vin, losing control, or feeling trapped, particularly when they demand she remain at the clubhouse in their absence, could easily trigger a panic attack. She had to be prepared for potential emergencies or unforeseen circumstances. Choosing to ignore the issue for the time being, she mentally reminded herself to look for a razor in the bathroom later.

* * * * *

FEELING INCREASINGLY FRUSTRATED, CLARK muttered to herself while rummaging through the bathroom cabinet, desperately searching for a razor. She was frantically looking for a shaver or men's razor, but all she found were tubes of creams, hair accessories, packets of condoms, and toothbrushes. She found an electric shaver among the items in the cabinet, but her search for razors proved fruitless.

Clark tried to think of other possible locations where she might find razors. She considered the possibility of another bathroom in the clubhouse, which she might have overlooked. If not, Clark considered getting a knife from the kitchen.

Cautiously making her way towards the kitchen, Clark listened for any sounds. Peeking around the corner, she saw that the kitchen was strangely quiet, devoid of any signs of life. She furiously rummaged through the drawers, only to find a collection of useless butter knives that did not meet her immediate needs. Scanning the benchtop, she saw no knife block or knife rack. That seemed odd. Every kitchen had a knife rack. Opening the second drawer, Clark's frustration mounted as she found only plastic tongs and spatulas but no knives.

Where had all the sharp knives gone? It was as if someone had deliberately removed all the sharp objects. Did Gun and Vin deliberately remove them?

Clark felt a tightness in her chest, a growing pressure building within her. She sat on the floor and took deep, slow breaths until the dizziness passed. Realizing she had no other viable options, Clark knew heading home immediately to retrieve one was her best course of action. The desolate surroundings created an eerie calmness, allowing Clark to slip away unnoticed without encountering any obstacles. Sara was busy in the office next to the garage, and she doubted Carrie could stop her from leaving.

She grabbed her handbag and walked towards the front entrance. Her stomach dropped when she saw Pen leisurely smoking a cigarette by the chain-link fence.

She waved briefly at the taciturn biker and said, "Catch you later, Pen."

Pen asked, "Hold on. Where are you going, Clark?"

"I'm going home to pick up a few things. I'll return shortly. Goodbye."

Pen blocked her exit using deliberate steps, stating, "Can't let you leave, sweetheart. I promised Vin and Gun that I'd keep an eye on you."

At six feet, four inches tall, Pen was a mountain of a man and not someone you could easily wrestle with. It seemed unlikely that Clark would be able to leave at this point.

She frowned and asked, "Why? I'll be back soon."

"I'll go with you then," he said as he dug out his keys, firmly grasped her elbow, and escorted her towards the Jeep, ordering brusquely, "Hop in and belt up."

Resigned to being chaperoned, Clark got into the vehicle without further resistance. She planned to make him wait in the lounge room while she gathered a few belongings, including her razors. It irked her to know that Vin and Gun distrusted her.

Unfortunately, her plans didn't quite pan out. Instead of waiting, Pen asked her what she needed and went to retrieve them.

"Is there anything else you need?" he asked as he quickly and haphazardly stuffed her clothes and underwear from the drawers into a bag.

Clark stood in the doorway and said, "I just need to grab some personal items from the bathroom."

When Pen started following her into the bathroom, she cried, "Pen! I need some privacy. I need to get some female stuff."

Clark's failed attempts to stop him physically were in vain. His towering frame and iron grip effortlessly subdued her, leaving her feeling helpless and trapped. Pen randomly gathered her toiletries and cosmetics, tossing them carelessly into her small travel bag.

Fuming at Pen's actions, Clark stormed into her bedroom, the door slamming echoing through the apartment. Clark had had enough of Pen's high-handedness. She ignored his loud knocking and orders to open.

"Go away, Pen. I've changed my mind. I'm staying here," she shouted through the door.

"Can't do that, Clark," Pen said. "Gun and Vin expect you to be at the clubhouse when they return."

"I'll be there tomorrow," she promised.

Clark's heart raced with uncertainty, each passing second feeling like an eternity, as she questioned if Pen had left the apartment. It wasn't until she heard a sharp, piercing metal-on-metal sound that she realized he was attempting to break in. What on earth was he doing? She listened anxiously as he continued to jiggle the door handle. Abruptly, the handle detached with a loud clatter. He had skillfully inserted a flathead screwdriver into the lock, deftly removing the locking mechanism. Twisting the screwdriver, the door opened. Where had the screwdriver come from? There certainly hadn't been one in the apartment.

Clark's body was frozen on the edge of the bed, and a gasp escaped her lips in sheer astonishment. Pen demonstrated impressive lockpicking skills.

"Pen, this is absurd. I refuse to go with you."

"I don't want to have to force you, sweetheart. But I will if necessary."

"Please, allow me this one night. I beg of you," Clark implored, her hands pressed together as if praying. "I swear I'll be at the clubhouse first thing tomorrow." As Pen continued denying her request, tears welled in Clark's eyes. "Why, Pen? Why do I feel like none of you trust me?"

"I know," he replied solemnly.

"Know what?"

Pen indicated her arms, referencing the scars. His eyes hinted at a deeper understanding of her hidden pain as he softly said, "I know you're hurting, Clark. You don't have to face it alone."

"You … you know?"

At his nod, the realization of his knowledge caused Clark to crumble in humiliation, her cheeks burning with shame and her heart sinking in despair. How could Vin and Gun betray her by sharing her secret with Pen and the rest of the group as if her issues weren't distressing enough?

Her stomach roiled, and she began dry retching, the acidic taste of bile rising in her throat.

"Clark! What's wrong?" Pen urgently flipped her over, his eyes widening at her pallor. "Damn it! Clark, are you with me?"

Clark could hear Pen, but he sounded far away. She curled into a tight ball and began rocking to ease the ache in her chest. Sweat slid down her face and neck, soaking into the duvet.

Pen disappeared but returned, placing a wet, cold washcloth on Clark's hot face. He gently wiped her face and neck. Gradually, the pounding headache and intense throbbing sensation lessened.

"Clark? Can you hear me?"

Clark's eyes fluttered open as the attack subsided, meeting Pen's worried, dark brown gaze filled with concern.

Returning with a glass of water, he carefully sat her up and brought the cold glass to her dry lips. Clark eagerly gulped down several mouthfuls before Pen took away the tumbler.

"Take it easy, Clark. Small sips only," he advised. Weakly nodding, she swallowed several more sips before pushing the glass away.

"I'm okay," Clark said. She tried to get up, but Pen insisted that she stay put.

"You're coming back with me, and I don't want any of your bullshit, Clark," Pen firmly stated. Too weak to resist, she acquiesced and allowed him to guide her outside to the Jeep.

Pen tossed the screwdriver with a clatter into the toolbox inside the Jeep's boot compartment.

Clark needed to see Sara, but Pen tried to convince her to rest instead. The pretty blonde was speaking to one of the mechanics in the garage. The concerned look on her face told Clark that Mr. Blabbermouth Pen had gossiped about her panic attack. Who else had he shared the news with? Vin and Gun? They were not expected back until tomorrow.

"Clark! How are you feeling?" Sara asked, her face etched with worry.

"I'm all right, Sara," Clark reassured, holding up a hand.

"Here," she said, stacking the cushions to one side of the cane lounge, "Sit down." Sara sat in her swivel chair and asked, "What happened?"

"It was a panic attack, nothing major." Clark tried to minimize its importance.

"What brought it on?"

Clark leaned forward, her voice barely above a whisper, and asked Sara, "Have Vin or Gun mentioned anything about … you know?"

"About you cutting yourself? Yes, they told me."

"I thought I could trust them, but I was wrong," she griped, crossing her arms defensively.

"They want to protect you, Clark, not hurt you."

"Were all the sharp objects removed?"

"Does that mean you've been looking for something to cut yourself with?"

"Not exactly," she lied. "Listen, Sara, I need a razor, just in case," she pleaded, her voice tinged with desperation. "You know what happens when I have a panic attack? Having a razor nearby is for my safety, not just for cutting, but to calm myself. I can control the urge."

"I hope you're not seriously asking me to get you one, Clark?" the petite woman said sternly. "Because I won't do it. What you need is help, not a razor."

Clark felt cornered. "I've made it clear multiple times that I don't need any of that psychological nonsense. You're just like the guys."

Clark's heart sank when the familiar rumble of motorcycles arrived. She hadn't expected Gun and Vin back so soon.

Clark sat on the lounge chair and waited for Gun and Vin. The sound of boots crunching on pebbles signaled their approach. Their silhouettes darkened the doorway, and she glared defiantly.

"Hey, Sar," Vin said somberly. "Mind if we have a moment with Clark?"

Once Sara left, Clark curled up on the lounge, hugging her knees tightly. Gun wheeled the chair closer and studied her. "What happened that led to the panic attack?"

"I was upset that Pen wouldn't leave me alone. And angry that you told everyone!"

"It was necessary to protect you. Not everyone knows."

"Should I be grateful?"

"Cut the sarcasm, Red. You need help, but you won't admit that you do. So, we took measures to prevent you from hurting yourself. Don't be mad at us for caring; be angry that you're hurting yourself."

"Stop acting as if you know what I need, Gun!" Her voice grew louder with each word. "You can't possibly understand what I'm going through because you're not in my shoes! I resent that you want to control how I live, dictating what's best for me without considering my perspective. If you can't take me for who I am, then there's no point in continuing this."

"You're misunderstanding, babe," Vin interjected, "we're trying to protect you because we care about you and only want what's best for you."

"Vin, what if cutting myself is best for me?" she argued.

"How can hurting yourself be beneficial? Just look at your arms. The scars make you feel ashamed. Is that making you feel better?"

In the past, Clark had been able to navigate challenges confidently. She had a knack for charming her way out of trouble with a cheeky smile or sweet compliments to help smooth things over. Everything shifted when Archer's mental health issues became apparent to Clark.

Gun extended his hand, speaking softly, "Come on." Although his sling had been removed the day before, Clark could tell his shoulder was still tender. Tough man Gunnar McCoy refused to let a bullet defeat him. Noticing Clark's indecision, he decided to take control of the situation.

"Gun!" she squealed. "Your shoulder!" He slapped her bottom as she dangled over his good shoulder like a sack of potatoes. Clark demanded, "Put me down now, Gun!" Gun ignored her outburst. "Gun! Stop! You're embarrassing me!"

With purpose, he strode across the courtyard toward the main house. Clark squeezed her eyes shut to drown out the wolf whistles and cheers.

Gun dumped her unceremoniously onto the bed. Scrambling away, Clark stood determinedly. "What the heck, Gun? Our arrangement doesn't include you controlling my life."

"Being under our protection gives us the responsibility to make decisions for you, especially when your choices may not be in your best interest."

"That's ridiculous, Gun! I'm twenty-six years old. I can make my own decisions."

"You need to understand how things work here. We have strict rules and responsibilities that we take seriously," Vin explained.

"Vin, I'm not your responsibility! That's the part you both seem to miss. Listen, I don't think this is going to work."

"I'm going to stop you right there, Red," Gun declared, forming a barrier with Vin that made it clear: the only way past them was through them. "You may disagree with how we do things, but quitting just because you're uncomfortable isn't an option. This is where we focus on your needs and find solutions."

"Oh, really? You're suddenly open to my input? I must have been speaking a different language all this time."

"Cut the attitude," Gun admonished. "We know what you think you need, but there are better solutions."

"Like what?"

"Talking to a professional. Help you get to the root of your problems. Find a different way to deal with your panic attacks," Gun suggested.

"Dealing with panic attacks is like trying to navigate through a maze blindfolded."

"Know that. Didn't say it was going to be easy."

She asked casually, "Can I take some time to think about it?" Allowing her to go home and think about their idea would bring her one step closer to freedom.

"Yes, take all the time you need, but remember, your safety is our priority. Leaving is not an option."

"You're aware that kidnapping is a serious crime, correct?"

Gun graced her with an exclusive smile that always set her belly alight. If his charming smile was meant to distract her, it worked like a spell, making her forget her worries momentarily.

✳ ✳ ✳ ✳ ✳

AFTER SARA FINISHED FOR the day, Clark hid in Sara's office. The knowledge that several people were aware of her self-harm still stung with shame. Clark refrained from searching for sharp implements, knowing she wouldn't find any. She'd already tried the door to the garage, but it was locked up like Fort Knox.

Approaching midnight, Vin entered quietly, breaking the silence with, "Time to come to bed, babe."

Clark replied stubbornly, "No thanks. I'll sleep here tonight."

Vin suppressed a smile as he offered, "Be happy to carry you to bed. What'll it be?"

"You said you would give me some space!"

"We did. Now it's time for bed."

"You can try to keep me here to 'help me,' but I'm done with our arrangement."

Vin calmly asked, "Are you planning to walk on your own, or shall I carry you?"

"Fine. I'll walk. So, where am I supposed to sleep then?"

"In our bed."

Clark angrily brushed past Vin, huffing and puffing. She stormed down the hallway to the bedroom, marching past Gun. Clark chose a pair of comfortable shorts and an oversized T-shirt and went into the bathroom to change into her sleepwear. After exiting the room and noticing it was empty, she pulled back the covers and climbed into bed. Exhausted and emotionally drained, she succumbed to sleep within minutes.

✳ ✳ ✳ ✳ ✳

WHEN CLARK BROACHED THE subject of going home the next day, she again encountered resistance from the men.

Vin reassured Clark, "We won't give up. It's important to work on your issues to overcome your panic attacks. You're not alone in this." While Vin's advice was valid, the undeniable truth remained—she wasn't ready to face her demons.

"I'm not ready yet. I have to work through this by myself. I understand the truth in your words, Vin, and acknowledge my mistakes. The problem is that you're not allowing me the freedom and time to handle this alone."

"We don't want you to face this alone, Red. You deserve support from those who truly care about you," Gun consoled, his eyes darkening with concern.

Gun's gentle words made Clark want to surrender everything to his total control, but surrendering to Vin and Gun would threaten her last fragment of independence—something she was unwilling to give up.

"Why keep me here? I feel like a prisoner. I need my freedom."

This prompted Vin to react: "If we let you go, you'll go right back to cutting yourself. You're in a vulnerable state right now."

Clark glared at Vin, saying, "I wish I had never confided in you!"

Glancing at the alarm clock, the red numbers told her it was just after eight a.m. As both men got up, the bed springs bounced and creaked with each movement. They closed the door with a soft click behind them.

Clark felt twitchy with anxiety. She felt her stomach muscles tensing like coiled springs and her heart pounding against her ribcage. Clark knew if she failed to address the issue promptly, it could lead to another panic attack. Vin and Gun's persistent habit of making decisions on her behalf and disregarding her desires left Clark feeling stripped of her autonomy, exacerbating her anxiety. She should be free to choose how to manage her physical health and tackle her challenges independently.

Feeling trapped and desperate, Clark grabbed her phone to call the police for help. Calling the police was her only means of escape from this situation. Clark knew that the MC preferred to handle problems internally without involving the police. However, this was *her* predicament, and she needed their assistance.

Clark turned down the volume of her phone and dialed the number for the police to avoid being overheard. Despite feeling relieved when she hung up the phone, Clark was perplexed by the overwhelming sense of guilt that followed.

She quickly put on her clothes, collected her things, and quietly slipped out the door. In the front room, the sight of several naked bodies sprawled unconscious on the sofas and the floor added to the quiet of the morning. No one noticed as she tiptoed past them. She scanned the area for Gun and Vin, wondering where they'd gone.

As Clark managed to make it outside, her heart pounded with adrenaline as she searched for the best hiding place until the police arrived. There was plenty of cover behind the shed, which the guys had converted into a makeshift gym for their workouts. Even now, Clark could hear the grunts of the men inside the gym as they pounded the punching bag, letting all their aggression out. Clark listened closely, her ears filled with the rhythmic clanking of weights being assembled as the gym-goers continued their quest to build muscle mass. This rigorous workout routine explained the bikers' muscular builds and extraordinary strength.

Startled by raised voices, Clark ducked low behind the gym, straining to listen for a police car. The heated exchange the previous night with Gun and Vin had intensified her need to act quickly. Clark heard Gun calling her name. They were looking for her!

Clark cried with relief as a police car arrived at the locked gate. Two officers emerged from their vehicle to speak to the prospect patrolling the grounds.

To become a patched member, a prospect must demonstrate loyalty and commitment to the Club. Vin once explained to her that it was important that prospects observe sacred Club rituals and do whatever was necessary to prove their allegiance. It was no surprise to Clark that one was stationed at the gates as part of his initiation process.

She remained hidden when Vin, Gun, and Achilles exited the house.

"What's up, officers?" Achilles politely inquired, "Is there a problem?"

"We received a call from someone in distress. A woman says you're keeping her here against her will," the older officer replied sternly while the younger man surveyed the area intently.

Clark popped out from behind the shed and practically ran towards her saviors.

"It was me! I called you. Please get me out of here."

"Clark!" shouted Gun. "Don't do this."

Gun clutched Clark's hand to stop her, and the officers immediately drew their guns. "Let her go!" the senior officer shouted. He glanced over at the prospect. "Open the gates now! Release the woman."

Vin stepped in front of her, blocking her view of the policemen. He grasped her wrists. "Clark, listen to me," he spoke softly. One hand cupped her cheek. "Let us help you, babe. Tell the guys to leave. We'll work this out. I promise you everything will be okay."

Clark pulled away, her mind racing. "No, Vin. Please, officer, get me out of here."

As they were held at gunpoint, more police cars arrived at the scene. The men were forced to the ground by the police officers. After the gate slid open, at least a dozen men from outside converged on the bikers. More members exited the building, but Achilles told them to stay back.

Clark desperately pleaded with the officers, tears threatening to spill, begging them not to arrest Vin, Gun, and Achilles as they were handcuffed and led away to the patrol cars. She assured the boys in blue that they hadn't hurt her, but her efforts were in vain.

Guilt flooded her, and Clark fought to suppress the all-too-familiar pang of regret that clawed at her heart. She felt responsible for the guys going to jail, believing that her actions had inadvertently led to their arrest. Unfortunately, there was nothing else she could have done. They weren't going to let her go voluntarily. The policemen drove her home.

She told Rachel she had to leave to take care of some personal matters and assured her that she would return when ready. Clark promised to help with the rent while she was away, knowing it would be tough for Rachel financially as they had agreed to split expenses evenly. Since she couldn't return to the tattoo shop, finding another job became her priority. This was particularly important in light of the events at the clubhouse.

NINE

SIX MONTHS LATER

Shortly after the police incident, Clark sought refuge at her parents' house. Initially, Clark refused to talk, unwilling to revisit the unfortunate incident that weighed heavily on her conscience. Through Charly, Clark learned that Vin, Gun, and Achilles were released later that evening, but she still felt responsible for their arrest.

Not long after arriving home, Clark was undressing in her bedroom when Connie entered the room with an armful of washed and ironed clothes. On seeing her scars, her foster mother let out a loud, piercing cry. Clark could only imagine what Connie must have been thinking, having already lost two sons to suicide, a tragedy that still deeply affected her.

★ ★ ★ ★ ★

CONNIE AND LAWSON URGED Clark to undergo therapy to address the emotional trauma from the loss of Damien and Archer to suicide, mirroring the support given by Vin and Gun. Following this, Connie showed a proactive approach by taking the initiative to schedule an appointment with Dr. Martinez, the same psychiatrist who had supported Connie and Lawson through the loss of their sons.

"How are you feeling today, Clark?" asked Dr. Martinez.

"Good. I haven't had a panic attack since our visit last week."

"That's great. What is it now?" Dr. Martinez looked at her notes. "Twenty-two days have passed, and you're making progress."

"I know. Last Friday, I got some bad news, so I used the deep breathing and relaxation techniques you showed me. It worked."

"What happened that required you to use the technique?"

"My brother, Corey, was in a car accident. He's currently staying with us while he recuperates. He fractured his leg."

"That's terrible. How did it happen?"

"A drunk driver T-boned him. He hit Corey's front driver's side, causing it to spin out of control and hit a tree. Thankfully, the worst that came of it was the leg injury. He got other minor cuts and bruises, but they'll heal with time."

The memory of Gun being in the hospital after being shot caused Clark to wince, vividly recalling the fear and anxiety she felt during that time.

"What is it, Clark? What just flashed inside your head?"

Clark often joked that Dr. Martinez must have a hidden crystal ball in the room, given her uncanny ability to anticipate her thoughts.

"I was remembering when a friend got shot," Clark explained.

"This friend means a lot to you because of your strong reaction."

Clark nodded.

"An ex-boyfriend?"

"No."

Dr. Martinez pressed Clark, "Was it a romantic partner then?"

"How did you know?"

"You have that look of reminiscence," she explained. "And … perhaps of someone in love?"

"No! Not after Archer." Clark had been deeply in love once before, but the tragic death of her fiancé had shattered her to pieces, leaving her heartbroken and lost. She couldn't go through that again.

"Who was it, Gun or Vin?"

"Gun."

Clark had spent the first few months courageously reliving the horrible, painful memories of Damien, Archer, and her mother. Dr. Martinez had miraculously managed to elicit every harrowing detail of their deaths. During her sessions, Dr. Martinez used her soft, calm, melodic voice to guide Clark through the memories, teaching her relaxation techniques. Clark wondered if the doctor had used hypnosis to help her cope with the panic attacks more effectively.

"Tell me about the time you found Archer," Dr. Martinez asked while Clark rested on the couch.

They had been discussing the circumstances leading to Archer's death, but now the gruesome image of him suspended from a noose assaulted her thoughts.

Clark's breath quivered deeply before she could muster a response.

"I had just arrived home from work. The apartment was unusually quiet, and I remember calling Archer's name, but he didn't reply. So, I went into the bedroom to change into my regular clothes and discovered Archer there. He had fashioned a noose from the bedsheets and attached it to the curtain rod. I vividly remember that Archer's feet dangled above the floor, his body suspended by the makeshift noose. His face was pale like the sheet around his neck, and his eyes were closed like he was sleeping peacefully.

I remember stumbling towards him and brushing my fingers against his cold cheek. It felt icy cold. I must have screamed because the next thing I knew my neighbors were banging on the door."

Dr. Martinez had explained that due to overwhelming guilt, Clark, being highly sensitive and perceptive to the emotions of people around her, felt an undue sense of responsibility. Her empathetic nature led her to experience guilt even when she hadn't done anything wrong. In her sessions, Clark learned to express herself more clearly through self-talk, journaling, and practicing with a trusted friend. Dr. Martinez taught her to set limits and assertively prevent others from overstepping them to maintain her well-being. Finally, Clark learned techniques such as visualization, where she imagined positive outcomes, and positive affirmations, where she reassured herself, to shield herself from others' disapproval or criticism.

Each morning, Clark would stand before the mirror after her shower, engaging in a ritual of empowering self-affirmations to set a positive tone for the day. She encouraged herself by setting specific goals and intentions for the day and spoke words of affirmation to boost her confidence. This practice helped her start each day with a positive mindset. She mastered relaxation techniques and began facing her deepest fears, like the fear of losing loved ones. This process helped reduce her fear of experiencing panic attacks.

✶ ✶ ✶ ✶ ✶

THE FOLLOWING DAY, UNDER the bright morning sun, Clark stepped off the bus and walked towards the familiar cream brick building where she worked. As she stepped through the heavy glass doors of the local library, the familiar scent of aged paper and the gentle hum of the air conditioning enveloped her.

"Hi, Mrs. Prentiss," Clark greeted her supervisor as she walked in.

Mrs. Prentiss, a sixty-something woman, reveled in overseeing her charges and creating a quiet, organized, and efficient library. She had no tolerance for disrespect.

Sophie, a stunning twenty-two-year-old with luscious dark hair and an attractive figure, was one of Clark's colleagues. Unfortunately, she sometimes exhibited a sense of entitlement, such as expecting special treatment, which often led to conflicts in her interactions with others, particularly Mrs. Prentiss. Due to her rebellious tendencies, Sophie's bold and outspoken nature often led to clashes with her strict supervisor. She received most of Mrs. Prentiss's scowls of disapproval for her constant infractions, such as talking back during meetings, speaking too loudly in the library, or engaging in inappropriate interactions with male patrons.

Teresa, known for her reserved and efficient manner, worked

diligently under Mrs. Prentiss's management, earning her praise for her consistent dedication. Teresa was a colleague whom Clark was quite fond of. She was a mother who always went out of her way to help others, displaying exceptional professionalism and courtesy, qualities that Clark greatly admired. In her mid-forties, Teresa carried herself with an air of elegance and focused demeanor. Occasionally, Clark found Sophie's antics amusing, appreciating the light-hearted entertainment they added to her otherwise sedate existence. She heard the muffled giggles of three teenage girls who should have been studying as she pushed the book trolley down the fiction aisle. Clark grinned in response to Mrs. Prentiss telling the girls to shush. Having efficiently shelved the last two books alphabetically, she then pushed the trolley to collect the next pile of books.

Clark was surprised to see Vin standing at the end of the aisle, watching her guardedly.

"Hi, Shortcake."

Clark remained speechless until Vin spoke again. "You're looking well."

"Thanks," she whispered, still stunned that he was standing beside her. "What are you doing here?"

"I came to see you and find out what you've been up to," Vin explained, breaking the silence.

"Shhh," Mrs. Prentiss interrupted sternly, her eyes narrowing as she gave Vin a warning glare.

Vin responded with a charming smile. "Sorry," he said, reading her name tag. "Patricia, a beautiful name. I hope you don't mind if I talk to Clark. I haven't seen her in a while."

"Do it during her lunch break," the prim librarian retorted, unaffected by his charm.

"Only need a few minutes, Patricia, to ask Clark for a date. You wouldn't be opposed to that now, would you?"

Taken aback by his audacity, Clark chose not to apologize for Vin's boldness. This wasn't her fight. Vin could deal with the consequences if he wanted to disrespect Mrs. Prentiss. Feeling proud of herself for standing her ground, Clark folded her arms and observed the encounter between her formidable supervisor and her equally formidable ex-lover. She had to admit she was surprised when Mrs. Prentiss backed down.

"Don't take all day." She peered over her spectacles at Clark. "Clark, be a dear and accept his invitation, then return to work and focus on your tasks."

On that note, the stern woman disappeared around the corner.

Vin was mistaken if he thought he could easily sweet-talk her into having dinner with him. Clark was not one to be swayed by his charm.

"Why? Do you have other plans tonight?"

"No, Vin. It's not a good idea. I'm seeing a psychiatrist, as you and Gun wanted me to. I need to spend time working on myself." She lowered her voice so the patrons couldn't listen to her private conversation.

"That's good, babe," he said. He didn't know it, but hearing his approval gave her immense pleasure. Her heart jolted as he leaned forward and whispered discreetly, "We stayed away so that you could have the space and independence you wanted."

Despite Dr. Martinez's advice to avoid complications, Clark found it comforting that Gun and Vin hadn't completely vanished from her life. However, upon seeing Vin, she was torn between joy and uncertainty, unsure about her next steps.

"Come on, Shortcake—one dinner. The pleasure of your company for a couple of hours," he persisted.

Clark looked past Vin to see Sophie gawking at her from the front desk. The girl mouthed, *What the fuck?* She caught Mrs. Prentiss glowering at her but refused to be manipulated, turning down Vin's invitation.

✳ ✳ ✳ ✳ ✳

A SLEEK SILVER SUV pulled into the driveway, and Clark waved enthusiastically to Connie and Corey. Connie carefully passed the crutches to Corey as he gingerly hopped out of the vehicle, trying to avoid putting any weight on his injured leg. Skipping down the steps, Clark hurried over to lend a hand to Corey. She wrapped her arms around her brother, embracing him with affection. Clark caught sight of Connie, who was struggling to carry multiple bags filled with clothes from Corey's house, so she stepped in to assist.

As the oldest sibling, Corey has always been the most stable, reliable, and fiercely protective of his little sister. Unfortunately, after Archer fell ill and passed away, Clark chose to stay away, consumed by feelings of shame over the events that had unfolded.

However, over the three weeks following his unfortunate accident, Corey and Clark have actively worked on rebuilding their strained relationship. Their heartfelt conversations had cleared any misunderstandings from the past and resolved conflicts that stemmed from Archer's illness.

Clark stepped onto the porch to join Corey after assisting Connie with carrying his luggage into the house. Corey settled himself comfortably into the porch swing, letting out a contented sigh, and Clark joined him, sitting closely by his side.

With a grin, Corey looked at Clark and asked, "How are you doing Sparky?" Clark felt a rush of nostalgia and warmth at the familiar nickname in honor of her fiery and spirited nature and was grateful for the bond they had rekindled.

Clark responded, "I'm good, Chubs," playfully nudging Corey's side.

When Corey was younger, he had grappled with weight issues, but his unwavering dedication to fitness and healthy living led to a remarkable transformation. At thirty-one, he was in peak physical condition, with six-pack abs from rigorous workouts and a marathon completion.

His career as a loan manager at a local bank was equally impressive. He exceeded sales targets for five consecutive quarters and earned the "Employee of the Year" award for his exceptional financial acumen, a testament to his professional success. Clark had always admired her brother and felt an overwhelming pride in his achievements.

Despite numerous romantic opportunities, Corey remained dedicated to his career. He'd mentioned his hope to become a senior executive one day.

"How's your job at the bank?"

"I've accumulated six months' worth of leave, so I've decided to take a break," Corey shared a rare departure from his usual work-focused mindset.

Clark chuckled and teasingly commented, "You're such a workaholic!"

"What about you? How have you been?"

"I'm okay." Clark bowed her head to hide the anxiety shimmering in her eyes.

"How are your sessions with Dr. Martinez? Is she helping?" Corey pressed further. "Yes. She's given me some great techniques when I feel like I'm about to have a panic attack."

"What kind of techniques?" Corey rested his arm on the back of the porch swing, and Clark settled back against the headrest. She felt the porch swing's gentle sway and the warmth of the afternoon sun on her skin.

"One technique she shared is deep breathing exercises. It involves breathing in through your nose, holding, and exhaling through your mouth. That's been helpful. Another technique Dr. Martinez introduced is positive self-talk, which involves consciously replacing negative thoughts with positive affirmations.

One of the main challenges I faced was being overly critical of myself, constantly fixating on my flaws and mistakes. Dr. Martinez explained that the first step in overcoming negative self-talk is becoming aware of it. I used to despise my scars, feeling ashamed and repulsed by the reminders of my past." Clark admitted, unconsciously pulling her sleeve down. "I couldn't bear the thought of people seeing my scars, afraid of being judged and rejected for my imperfections. I hated looking at them. Now I view them as a part of my identity."

Clark's eyes misted over as she remembered Vin's words about her scars when she told him they were ugly.

Those marks on your arms are a part of your past. They represent what you've been through, and that's some ugly shit. Your scars are a part of you, but they don't define your beauty.

Corey and Clark spent the afternoon reconnecting and exchanging stories to catch up on each other's lives. Clark shared details about her work at the library and tattoo shop but avoided discussing her connections with Vin and Gun or her romantic feelings for them. Corey confided in Clark about his deep-seated concerns about the long-term effects of his leg injury on his physical and mental well-being. He was apprehensive about how he would cope with the sedentary weeks ahead, unable to let go and relax because of his relentless drive to excel.

TEN

"Hey, Clark!" Sophie called out from the back room to Clark, who was about to leave for the day. The soft afternoon light filtered through the window, creating a golden halo around Sophie's figure as she leaned against the doorframe, her hand resting on the polished wood. The tall, elegant brunette approached Clark, her chestnut hair swaying gently with each graceful step.

Her eyes held a glint of curiosity and mischief as she paused and inquired, "Who was the hot guy you were chatting with yesterday?"

"Just a friend," Clark hesitated, torn between the urge to maintain her privacy and the growing guilt of hiding the truth from Sophie. She wasn't with Vin anymore, so he couldn't be called a friend, could he?

"Come on, Clark! He's so good-looking that there's no way I could consider him just a friend. If he were my friend, we'd be more than friends."

Despite Sophie's youthful enthusiasm, she would soon find herself outmatched by Vin, who possessed over a decade more experience. Clark imagined he'd eat her up in seconds.

"Listen, Sophie, I have to finish putting these books back onto the shelves. The library is busy, and I need to finish my work. I promise we'll have a chat later."

Clark immediately pushed the cart, its wheels rattling, in the opposite direction, grateful for a small reprieve from the persistent woman. She felt depressed whenever the topic of Vin came up.

Clark caught sight of a weathered book resting on the arm of a chair. Crossing the room, she reached for the book, intending to return it to its place on the shelf. She cradled the book, her gaze fixed on the embossed title: *The Picture of Dorian Gray*.

Whenever she thought of Archer, bittersweet sorrow flooded her heart. His presence lingered in every corner of her mind. Lately, her thoughts about him had become less frequent, sparking feelings of guilt as she contemplated moving forward. Clark was torn between the desire to hold onto memories of Archer and working on her mental health.

The pain of Archer's loss still haunted her, making the thought of facing another loss unfathomable. The fear of an unimaginable fate befalling Vin or Gun—a fate worse than she could imagine—was like a constant, sinister presence that filled her with paralyzing dread. It was a feeling that she needed to work on to maintain her sanity.

During lunchtime, Clark sat with Teresa in the staff room, filled with subdued conversations and the tantalizing aroma of freshly brewed coffee. Teresa vented about the challenges of raising twin teenage daughters. Clark burst into laughter while marveling at the capricious nature of the mischievous thirteen-year-olds. She was thoroughly entertained as Teresa regaled her with accounts of their secretive pranks and adventurous exploits.

Clark remembered the trouble she had caused her family during her teenage years. Luckily, she had avoided any serious consequences. She felt incredibly fortunate to have Connie and Lawson as her parents.

Clark looked up at the sound of heels clacking on the tiled floor. Sophie entered the staff room and sat at the table where Clark and Teresa were seated.

"What's so amusing?" Sophie inquired, leaning in to join their conversation.

"Trudy and Tina," Teresa replied, referring to her teenage daughters.

Sophie expressed her frustration, "You allow those two to escape consequences too easily. If they were my daughters, I would send them to a boot camp for troubled teens," she remarked while clicking her tongue disapprovingly.

Teresa replied irately, her tone laced with annoyance. "It's a good thing they're not your daughters, then." She rose from her seat, crumpled the remnants of her untouched lunch, and discarded it in the nearby bin before leaving.

Clark scowled and said, "That wasn't a kind thing to say. Her daughters act like most teenagers."

Sophie retorted sarcastically, "Oh, suddenly you're an expert on teenagers, huh? You barely know the first thing about parenting."

Without a word, feeling a rush of indignation, Clark stood up abruptly. The chair's legs scraped against the tiles as she pushed it back to follow Teresa.

Sophie instinctively reached out, her fingertips lightly brushing Clark's arm. "I'm sorry, Clark. I didn't mean for it to come out like that," she said, her voice tinged with remorse.

Clark remained unconvinced, her skepticism deepening as she observed the disingenuousness of Sophie's smile.

Later that day, in the quiet of the late afternoon, Clark noticed an elderly woman struggling to open an email attachment on the computer and graciously offered to help troubleshoot the issue. She patiently guided her through downloading files, taking the time to explain each step. The elderly lady's face lit up with gratitude as she thanked Clark, her words filled with heartfelt appreciation. Clark headed back to the front desk to assist the waiting customers with their inquiries and loans.

"Is your friend picking you up today?" Sophie asked, her playful smile lighting up her face.

Clark was startled by Sophie's sudden question. She had been sitting alone, lost in thought, and she couldn't help but let her mind wander to Gun and Vin. Clark found herself pondering their whereabouts, imagining what they could be doing. Did they miss her? Were they thinking about her?

Clark halted the brakes on her negative spiral of thoughts. She consciously tried to stay in the present and think positively about her progress and the steps she took to get her life back on track.

The sound of Sophie's voice had snapped Clark out of her reverie, and she turned to see her standing there, her expression expectant. She hadn't even realized she was nearby, so immersed was she in her thoughts.

Clark sighed, tired of the lies and half-truths she told. Eventually, her deception would backfire. For a moment, she considered disclosing the truth to Sophie.

Until Mrs. Prentiss caught Sophie and Clark talking.

"Sophie! Clark! Why aren't you working? Get back to your stations." Sophie let out a frustrated groan, her eyes reflecting exasperation as she glanced back at Mrs. Prentiss. "Oh, my God," she muttered, "I must be the highlight of the old cow's life, the way she picks on me."

"She's like that with everyone, Soph," Clark reminded her, annoyed at Sophie's attitude.

"Well, she needs to stop. The old biddy's still living in the Victorian era."

Clark grew increasingly wary as Sophie continued to make derogatory remarks and show blatant disrespect towards others. As time passed, she began to understand why Teresa chose to keep her distance from Sophie. The young girl would often voice her complaints, expressing constant dissatisfaction. Sophie lacked drive and enthusiasm, frequently chatting near the water cooler instead of completing assigned tasks. After scanning all the returns and placing them back on the shelves, Clark returned to her station and diligently immersed herself in her work until closing.

* * * * *

IT WAS A QUIET Saturday morning, and the library was closed for the weekend. Charly invited Clark to spend the day with her and the girls—Rachel, Sara, and Carrie.

The previous week, Clark had gone to the diner to meet Rachel and inform her about her decision to move back in with her. Meanwhile, Charly was busy at work and insisted that Clark sit down to update her on the situation with her self-harming.

"How have you been, Clark? You know, with cutting yourself and your panic attacks?" Charly asked, her eyes focused on Clark.

Clark said, feeling much happier these days, "I've been attending therapy regularly and practicing mindfulness, which has helped me stay grounded. It's been six months since I last harmed myself and almost two months since I had a panic attack."

Charly's smile widened, her eyes sparkling with joy. "I'm so glad to hear that. You know everyone was worried about you, especially Vin and Gun."

Clark nodded solemnly. "I know. But I can't let myself feel trapped, as I did at the clubhouse.

A chuckle escaped Charly. "It wasn't the smartest thing for Vin and Gun to do, but they did it out of concern. In the five years I've known them, Vin and Gun have never shown interest in a woman like they do with you, Clark. From planning surprise outings to checking in on your well-being, their actions speak volumes about their genuine care for you."

Clark suddenly felt a rush of heat on her cheeks, and her gaze dropped to the table in a sudden bout of shyness.

Charly reached across the table and put her hand over Clark's. "I've learned that the men of this generation are very different from their parents' generation."

In response, Clark raised her eyes to meet Charly's gaze. "Dom's parents didn't treat him well. His father was abusive, and his mom was negligent. They abandoned him at a young age, and that's how he ended up being adopted by his aunt and uncle. Have you had the chance to meet Sharyn and Deacon yet, Clark?"

Clark shook her head.

"At first, Sharyn didn't think I was good enough for her sons, so she gave me a hard time because she was protective of them."

Clark's eyes widened in disbelief as she gasped, "What! That's awful. You're the best thing that has happened to them," she said in shock.

"That's water under the bridge. Now, she loves me!" Clark laughed at Charly's enthusiasm.

"Did Vin and Gun tell you about their parents?"

Clark nodded. "Yes. Vin and Gun's mothers left them as children, and their fathers are incarcerated for murder."

"That's right. In the early days, the MC was very different from today. Achilles has eliminated practices like drug trafficking and involvement in prostitution that were part of the MC's operations. Although they operate a strip club, they do not force the women to engage in any sexual acts. Any patron who violates the no-touching rule is promptly ejected from the premises and permanently banned from returning."

This was all news to Clark because Vin and Gun were usually secretive about Club business.

"A key difference is that the men today are more inclined to seek long-term relationships. While some marriages, such as Sharyn and Deacon's, have stood the test of time, the newer generation also wants a deeper, more meaningful connection. Well, most of them do!

Sara and Chad are a perfect example of a couple who have been together for over ten years and recently got married. And as you know, they have a son, Nolan."

Charly's expression turned dreamy, prompting a warm smile from Clark.

"Then there is Dom, Jax, and me. We've faced many challenges together, but we've always come out stronger. I've never been happier or more accepted by anyone than with Dom and Jax. They're my life. And the same goes for Jake, too."

Clark felt a twinge of jealousy in her heart. She, too, wished for what Charly had with Dom and Jax. But did Vin and Gun want more than a casual relationship?

"I know that look, Clark. Are you worried about how Vin and Gun truly feel about you?"

Charly's remark reminded her of Gun, who could read her like a book.

"I just don't think our relationship is the same as the one you have with Dom and Jax or what Sara and Chad have."

"Why? Because they haven't said they loved you?"

Clark's eyes flew to meet Charly's gaze. "How did you know?"

"When I finally told Dom and Jax that I loved them, they went quiet and couldn't get away from me fast enough," Charly's laugh bubbled out, causing Clark to furrow her brows.

"Why do you find that amusing? I would be shocked if they responded like that," Clark admitted.

"I was the first woman outside their family to express such feelings. They even sought advice from Sara!"

"I'm aware that Vin and Gun care for me; that much is clear, but I still don't believe our relationship is close to what you, Dom, and Jax have."

"Clark, that's a conversation you need to have with Vin and Gun when you're ready."

✳ ✳ ✳ ✳ ✳

CHARLY AND RACHEL WERE proud of her progress in counseling sessions and improved well-being. They both complimented her on her rosy glow and happier demeanor. It was true.

Clark felt stronger than ever and not so afraid of her panic attacks. By understanding the root causes of her panic attacks, Clark also gained valuable coping skills that gradually alleviated her fears.

All five women were browsing through the colorful array of sexy lingerie inside a boutique. Charly held up a red open-cup bra with a matching crotchless thong, asking, "What do you think of this one?"

Clark laughed at the revealing outfit. "I can imagine what the guys would think," she said. "No need to remove anything because everything's accessible."

Sara's eyes widened with excitement as she marveled at the crotchless thong. "Ooh, I want a pair of those. The black pair looks tempting. I think I'll go for it," she exclaimed, eagerly searching the racks for the perfect one. "Chad's going to have a heart attack when he sees these."

"He's more likely to have a heart attack at the sight of you in them," Carrie said with a chuckle.

After Charly and Sara finished paying for their clothes, Clark and the women left the shop carrying gold and black store bags. Everyone was too focused on the men's reactions to their sexy lingerie to notice the newcomers. Clark almost bumped into Sophie, who had been speaking with a friend outside the shop.

Curiously, Sophie looked at Clark's bag and asked, "Hey, Clark. What's in the bag?"

"Just some clothes." Clark had purchased a lacy babydoll top and shorts, nothing risqué like Charly and Sara's crotchless lingerie.

"Did you buy those clothes for the hot guy who came into the library?" Sophie persisted, nudging her friend.

"No. Just a nightshirt and shorts. For myself to wear," Clark added so that Sophie wouldn't get the wrong impression.

"Can I see what you bought?"

Sophie tried to grab Clark's bag to see the sleepwear. Charly swiftly intervened by placing herself between Sophie and Clark, safeguarding Clark's privacy and thwarting the intrusion.

"Sorry, we're late for our reservation at the restaurant," she tugged on Clark's arm and hurried down the street, with the others following.

"Jesus, Clark!" Sara grumbled, looking annoyed. "Who was that? She was incredibly nosy."

"That's Sophie, a coworker from the library." Clark decided to tell them the truth about Vin. "Vin came into the library last week, and Sophie caught sight of him. Since then, she's been bombarding me with questions about him."

"Oh, my God, that doesn't surprise me at all," Sara remarked drolly. "Vin's pretty easy on the eyes."

"Oh, yes!" gasped Rachel, her eyes lighting up. "It's his mesmerizing baby blue eyes, the charming smile, and the mysterious aura he exudes," she said breathlessly. "And those muscles and tattoos."

"Rachel!" exclaimed Clark. "I didn't know you liked Vin like that!" she teased, eyebrows raised in amusement at Rachel's sudden confession.

"Well, you know …" her roommate and friend blushed profusely, her cheeks turning a deep shade of crimson as she tried to conceal her embarrassment and secret admiration for Vin. "I know he likes you, but a girl can dream, can't she?"

They arrived at Sandgropers, a restaurant inside a high-end shopping mall. Sara explained that the mall, owned by the Iconic Sons Motorcycle Club, exuded an upscale shopping experience. Clark had a hard time reconciling the juxtaposition of a motorcycle club with an upscale shopping environment due to the contrasting nature of the two establishments. The mall boasted an exclusive clothing boutique, a luxury shoe store, a high-end jewelry store, a cutting-edge technology outlet, a chic café, and the renowned Sandgropers restaurant and bar.

Clark felt a deep sense of relief and gratitude when Sara and Charly generously treated her to lunch, knowing she could not cover the expense herself. Noticing the absence of prices on the menu, she inferred that it was probably an expensive meal due to the upscale ambiance of the restaurant. Anticipation built up in Clark as she perused the enticing array of dishes on the menu.

As she settled on the spicy scallops with pumpkin puree, the aroma of the seafood coming from the kitchen tantalized her taste buds. When her meal arrived, Clark forked a juicy scallop smeared with puree into her mouth and chewed it, an explosion of flavor hitting the back of her throat. She closed her eyes and savored the rich combination of buttery scallops and tangy puree, relishing the burst of umami and sweetness on her palate.

Four sets of curious eyes belonging to her friends looked at her when she opened her eyes again.

Charly asked with a playful smile, hiding her amusement, "How is your job going, Clark? Does this coworker, Sophie, bother you?"

"I try to steer clear of her at work because she causes problems. It's mainly due to her confrontational attitude and tendency to avoid work. However, for the most part, she doesn't bother me," she admitted, happy to share it with these four women who had only shown her kindness.

"I can relate to dealing with a difficult coworker because of my experience at the Brothers in Arms Bar and Grill," Charly revealed in a hushed tone, barely audible. Clark had to lean in closer to hear.

Clark was surprised to learn that Charly had worked at the bar and grill. "What happened?" she asked, eager to learn more about her new friend.

"I had a good friend, Jess, who played a crucial role at the bar and grill in my early days. She was my mentor, guiding me through the initial challenges and enlightening me about the unwritten rules in the workplace." Charly laughed at Clark's grimace, "Ah, the guys and their infamous rules, right?"

"They should include those details in the contract before you sign it so you understand what you are agreeing to," Clark joked.

"Jess had an abusive boyfriend, Sol, who used to knock her around a bit. One evening, after a night out at a karaoke bar, Jess and I were on our way home when we unexpectedly came across Sol waiting for us. Jess and I were attacked, which is why Dom insisted that we stay at the clubhouse for our safety. At the clubhouse, I met Jax, and that encounter profoundly impacted my life."

The dreamy look in Charly's eyes almost made Clark wish that things were the same for her. Her choice to stay away didn't diminish her longing for Vin and Gun.

"I knew Jess and other women at the bar and grill had crushes on Dom. What I didn't know was that Jess also liked Jax. Therefore, when both Dom and Jax started showing me some attention, Jess got jealous because she had feelings for both of them. It's understandable because I would feel jealous, too."

As Charly told her story, it struck Clark that their experiences were similar. Like Clark, Charly was pursued by two men from the club. She also faced jealousy issues with a coworker, and it seemed evident that Sophie envied Clark's bond with Vin. This realization sparked her curiosity to hear more about Charly's story.

"Anyway, during our stay at the clubhouse, Jess started acting differently towards me. I realized our friendship was over when she started avoiding me and spending more time with the other women.

She tried to sabotage my job by interfering with my tasks at work. I'd set up the tables at my station each morning, only to find that Jess and another colleague, Maxine, had put it all away again, resulting in a reprimand from Rocky."

Clark asked, "Are you referring to Rocky, the sweet, laid-back guy?"

Clark couldn't imagine the big guy, who loved sharing stories about his daring-do, ever raising his voice.

Someone cleared their throat, and Clark, noticing the sound, glanced over to see Carrie fidgeting. She nervously tucked a strand of hair behind her ear, her hand trembling slightly, and swallowed hard. Her face had a slight blush, her cheeks tinged with pink.

Could the young, sweet twenty-three-year-old harbor feelings for the forty-year-old biker?

"Jess and Maxine even got me arrested once by falsely accusing me of stealing Jess's diamond necklace," Charly continued. "But it was a blatant lie." Charly's eyes welled up with tears as she recalled the painful memory.

Rachel put a comforting hand over Charly's, offering silent support. "It was fitting that Jess ended up in jail after falsely accusing you, Charly. She needed to face the consequences of her actions," Rachel sympathized. "Jess deserved a longer sentence than the three months she got for causing you all that emotional and mental distress. It was as if Jess went from being your best friend to your worst enemy overnight."

Clark was horrified by Charly's mistreatment and had to remind herself that love could drive people to extreme behaviors. If Clark thought she had it hard right now, all she needed to do was remember Charly's story.

After a moment of silence, Clark could sense Charly's distress as she processed the impact of her disclosure.

Clark was blessed with the unconditional love of two parents and a devoted, protective older brother. She vividly recalled the moment Charly confided in her about her baby brother's tragic death at the hands of her stepfather. It appeared that Charly had endured a tough life, facing various hardships. Both Clark and Charly had a shared history of triumphing over tragedy.

＊＊＊＊＊

"THE CAKE STAND WAS about to topple over …" Sara paused in her account of Nolan's upcoming birthday preparations, excitedly describing his chosen theme and the elaborate cake he wanted.

"Chad!" she squealed, instantly scraping her chair back and running towards her newlywed husband. With his broad shoulders and rugged beard, the big man easily caught her in his bear-like grip. Considering the man was almost twice her size, catching a woman leaping into his arms should have been as effortless as plucking a flower.

Next to him, Jax focused his gaze on Charly. Her eyes were still red from her teary confession earlier about Jess and Maxine attempting to have her arrested, and his eyes narrowed as he stalked right up to her. He cradled her in his arms, ignoring her protests that she was okay.

The third man stood alone, his sharp eyes scanning the room as he observed the scene. There was a subtle tension in his posture as he kept a watchful eye on Clark. Her gaze bore into Gun, a mix of longing and apprehension reflected in her eyes. Her heart hammered against her ribs, making it difficult to breathe. She took a few deep breaths to steady her heartbeat. She wasn't concerned about having a panic attack. She was determined to avoid letting her guard down and jeopardizing her mental well-being by maintaining a safe distance from Gun, but it was proving more challenging than she had imagined.

Her heart ached with longing whenever thoughts of Gun and Vin crossed her mind. After feeling the intensity of their kisses, the tenderness in their lovemaking, and their tireless care for her well-being, Clark was certain she wanted to continue a relationship with them. She couldn't understand how being with Gun and Vin, who had provided both physical and emotional support, could potentially damage her recovery progress.

Even though her mom had made the arrangements to see Dr. Martinez, Gun and Vin were instrumental in motivating her to seek counseling for her panic attacks and self-harm. She was actively attending the sessions and making remarkable improvements. Although Dr. Martinez recommended that Clark focus on healing before starting a relationship, the doctor didn't realize that Gun and Vin had already secured a special place in her heart.

Gun took the initiative. Approaching Clark, he pulled up a chair and straddled it. Clark couldn't help but notice the subtle flex of his arms as they casually rested on the chair, hinting at his undeniable strength. A swarm of golden butterflies danced in her stomach, their delicate wings fluttering with excitement, causing a radiant smile to bloom on her lips. Gun's eyes sparkled with warmth as he returned the smile, a rush of exhilaration tingling through her fingertips.

"Hey," he whispered as he leaned closer to Clark. "It's good to see you, Clark. How are you?"

"I've been working on getting stronger every day," Clark replied, feeling happier than she had in a long time.

"I'm pleased to hear that, Red," he said.

Clark loved it when he called her "Red," a term of endearment that never failed to bring a blush to her cheeks and a frisson of excitement.

Gun offered her a ride home, which she readily accepted. With a final wave to her friends, she walked to the waiting vehicle and sank into the plush leather seat. She inhaled the familiar smell of leather and the woodsy scent of the car freshener. Clark pulled on the seatbelt and heard the satisfying click, securing her in place.

* * * * *

THE SCENT OF LEATHER and sandalwood permeated the confines of the car. Inhaling the faint, sweet smell of strawberries emanating from Clark, Gun turned to face her.

"May I?" he asked, gently reaching out and touching the sleeve of her top, seeking permission.

With Clark's consent, Gun pushed the sleeves of her top up, revealing her scars. He examined her arms meticulously, feeling the texture of the silvery lines and gently turning her wrists over.

"Why do you only cut on the top of your arm?"

"I was afraid I'd cut too deep and bleed out. I wasn't feeling suicidal; I was just in pain."

"Most of the scars have faded." Gun couldn't see any recent cuts, proving that Clark was telling the truth.

"I made sure only to make shallow cuts to feel pain without risking serious injury."

"Have you felt the urge to harm yourself recently?"

"No. Dr. Martinez has helped me to work on my self-awareness. She made me realize that I can't change how I think until I understand what's causing me to think the way I do."

"What was that?" Gun asked, gently rolling her sleeves back down.

"I experience "toxic guilt," where I feel guilty even when I haven't done anything wrong. It's like constantly carrying a weight that doesn't belong to me, but it feels impossible to put down."

"Is that why you were having panic attacks?"

"Yes, the burden of emotions became overwhelming, and cutting myself was the only way I knew to stop the panic attacks. It worked for a while. Looking back, I realize how harmful it was, but it was my only escape."

Gun absently watched as Clark fiddled with the cuff of her sleeve. Despite her fragility, she appeared stronger in spirit. Her emotional strength and courageous efforts to conquer her demons filled him with pride.

"I meditate, do a lot of self-talk, set boundaries, stay out of other people's problems, and remind myself that it's not my responsibility. Stepping away from getting involved in others' problems is still a constant battle, but I do it."

Gun couldn't restrain himself from taking her into his arms, not bothering to hold back. "I'm so fucking proud of you, Red," he whispered tenderly.

ELEVEN

Clark used the tip of her shoe to push off and create momentum as she swayed on the porch swing. The glass of sparkling wine she held emitted a gentle fizz. The sun began to descend like a golden orb hanging low in the sky. The front door creaked open, and Corey stepped outside, his aluminum crutches clanging against the metal security door. Clark carefully placed her glass on the small iron table before getting up to help Corey.

"I'm fine, Sparky," he grinned, playfully winking at her as he adjusted his weight on the crutches.

Once Corey settled on the swing, Clark took his crutches and leaned them against the porch rail. Corey then rested his arm on the wooden swing behind Clark's head.

"Last night, huh?"

Clark said, "Carrie and Rachel offered to help me move my things back into the apartment tomorrow morning."

"I'm sorry I won't be able to help you." He indicated the cast on his leg.

She laid a hand on his knee. "Corey, I didn't expect you to help. Don't worry about it," Clark comforted him.

"I hope I get to see your apartment soon. Ensure it has adequate security and is in a safe neighborhood."

"Ever the loyal protector," Clark replied, "Corey, you've always been there for me, guiding me like a true big brother. I hope you know how much I appreciate what you've done for me. You welcomed me with open arms from the moment we met."

Clark leaned against Corey's sturdy shoulder, feeling the reassuring strength beneath her cheek and the warmth seeping through his shirt. Her mind flashed back to when she first peered over the old, rickety fence and saw Damien, Corey, and Archer playing in their large backyard. A smile crept across her face as she fondly recalled the boisterous roughhousing, like when Corey and Damien got into a mud fight and the playful scuffles that filled their childhood days.

"I do, Sparky," he gasped dramatically, rubbing the spot where Clark had playfully pinched him due to his persistent use of her childhood nickname.

In the distance, Clark heard the thunderous roar of a machine growing louder as it approached. Her eyes widened with giddy delight as Vin smoothly maneuvered his motorcycle into the driveway, the engine purring to a stop. Vin lowered the kickstand of his bike, removed his gloves and helmet, and carefully set them on the visor. With anticipation and apprehension, Clark rose slowly from the creaking swing, the cool afternoon breeze ruffling her unrestrained hair.

Bounding up the steps two at a time, Vin engulfed her in a tight hug, practically swallowing her up.

"Hey, Shortcake," he said softly, his eyes flicking to Corey with a hint of curiosity. "Who's this?"

While Vin held on tightly to Clark, she introduced him to Corey. "Corey, this is Vin. Vin, my brother, Corey."

Without releasing her, he extended his hand to shake Corey's. Corey, who couldn't stand without his crutches, begrudgingly shook Vin's hand while eyeing him suspiciously. Corey gruffly demanded, "Who are you?"

"A friend. You got a problem with that?" Being in his arms, Clark felt the tension of Vin's possessiveness seeping into her bones.

"Hold on, guys. Vin, calm down, and Corey, Vin is my *friend*. Let's handle this like adults."

Corey eyed Vin cautiously as he asked, "What kind of friend?" Clark was uncertain whether Corey's guardedness stemmed from Vin's biker identity or his proprietorial move.

"A regular friend. Behave yourself," she warned her brother, opting to keep her romantic involvement with Vin private.

"Can we chat someplace more private?" Vin asked, clasping her hand tightly, leaving her with little choice but to follow his lead.

"Vin, remember Corey's family. Don't start any trouble," Clark reminded him solemnly.

"Let's talk here," Vin suggested, gesturing towards a wrought iron table and chairs placed in the center of the garden. Lawson had lovingly transformed the garden into a serene memorial for his two sons, filled with carefully nurtured evergreen shrubs like holly, boxwood, and junipers. With meticulous care, Lawson shaped the shrubs into a dense hedge, creating a natural privacy barrier around the garden. He had also poured his love into crafting a rustic wooden bench adorned with a heartfelt plaque dedicated to his beloved sons, Damien and Archer.

On quiet evenings, Clark's parents found solace in the garden. They enjoyed a drink as they unwound in the peaceful surroundings, feeling the presence of their sons nearby.

"Are you progressing with Dr. Martinez in your therapy sessions?" inquired Vin, moving his chair closer to Clark.

"Have you spoken to Gun?" How else would he know the name of her psychiatrist?

"Yes, but we always kept a close eye on you."

She retorted, "Vin, I expected you to respect my need for space and privacy."

"Because we care about you and want to help, Gun and I needed to know you're dealing with your issues. You're important to us, and we're proud of you for seeking therapy and working on getting better."

"And I did it all without getting kidnapped," she laughed. "I needed help, but taking that first step wasn't easy. It meant letting go of what I believed was helping me, even though it wasn't."

"Self-harming is not helpful, Shortcake. You still cut yourself?"

Clark spared Vin a smile and explained, "No, I haven't self-harmed since the time before you held me hostage."

"You mean that, babe?"

"Yes, Vin. I'm serious about returning to my normal self again. It's been two months since my last attack."

Vin tenderly kissed her temple and softly whispered, "I'm glad to hear that."

Vin's light touch sent shivers throughout her body, and Clark had to take a deep breath to compose herself. Her feelings of trust and friendship towards Vin and Gun remained unchanged.

The sun disappeared beyond the horizon, and the outside security lights were automatically switched on. Two lone figures, illuminated by the flame of the single-light globe, sat peacefully as they discussed Clark's progress, challenges, and steps toward healing.

✶ ✶ ✶ ✶ ✶

AFTER TAPING THE LAST boxes, Clark set them aside and turned to Rachel and Carrie, who had arrived half an hour ago to help her move. Today was moving day, and Clark was thrilled at the prospect of regaining her independence. While she sincerely appreciated all the help from Connie, Lawson, and Corey, including their assistance with packing and emotional support, she was eager to reclaim her freedom.

Clark cautioned Rachel to handle the box of China dishes carefully, emphasizing that they were fragile heirlooms passed down for generations. Connie's grandmother had given them to her as a wedding gift, and she had passed them on to Clark when she first moved out of home with Archer at seventeen.

Rachel's ensemble featured denim overalls, a vibrant psychedelic top, sturdy brown work boots, and a scarf elegantly knotted over her hair, adding to her distinctive style. Her long, dark plait cascaded down the middle of her back like a silk ribbon, swaying gently with her movements.

In contrast, Carrie exuded elegance in denim shorts, a soft pink T-shirt, and fashionable Cloudswift sneakers. Her shorts accentuated the length of her long, slender legs, creating the illusion that they stretched on endlessly like graceful stilts. Carrie gathered books from the table and carefully placed them in a box.

Corey sat on the porch swing with a box sofa placed in front of him, using it to elevate his leg and ease the discomfort.

"Careful with those books, Carrie. Clark hid Archer's Dorian Gray novel in that stack," his voice resounded beneath the porch. Despite his warning, Carrie brushed it off, tired of his bossy attitude throughout the morning.

The front security door swung open, and Rachel stepped over the stoop with the heavy box in her arms.

"That's heavy, Rachel. Make sure you put that in the back seat. We can't have the dishes breaking from sliding around in the back of your vehicle."

Rachel opened the rear passenger door and set the box of delicate China plates on the back seat. With a loud bang that echoed through the quiet neighborhood, she slammed the door shut and stomped up the porch steps. With her hands firmly planted on her hips, Rachel stood before Corey, her face contorted in a scowl.

"Listen, Mr. Know-it-all, stop telling us how to load those damn boxes into the car. We know what we're doing and don't need your input."

Clark, who had been eavesdropping from behind the security door, was taken aback by her friend's outburst. Rachel, typically known for her permanent smile, sweet temperament, and quirky sense of humor, had a tough side. Clark had to admit that Corey deserved to be scolded by Rachel for his overbearing behavior. She knew it was coming from a good place, but it was annoying.

Instead of reacting defensively, Clark was shocked when Corey's smile widened, and he apologized to Rachel.

"Sorry, Rach. I'm feeling a bit useless just sitting here. I'm trying to help," he explained.

Clark peered through the dark screen when Rachel didn't reply immediately. She watched closely as her friend blushed a pretty shade of pink while swallowing hard. Corey smirked mischievously as he gazed back at her.

"Um, yeah …" she finally stammered. "Well … stop talking and just sit there and look …" Rachel instructed, slamming her mouth shut.

"And look … what?" Corey asked innocently, still grinning.

"Forget it," Rachel growled. "Just sit there." After that, she briskly marched back inside.

Clark quickly retreated to avoid being caught eavesdropping on their conversation.

She couldn't blame Rachel for being a little disconcerted by Corey. Her brother, with his charming smile and easy-going nature, was handsome. Unfortunately, he was also a confirmed bachelor with no plans to settle down soon, preferring the freedom of his independent lifestyle. Rachel, known for her quirky fashion sense and spontaneous adventures, was the complete opposite of Corey, who immersed himself in work with a no-nonsense attitude. However, as the saying goes, opposites attract, and in the case of Rachel and Corey, their differences just might complement each other perfectly.

* * * * *

CLARK AND RACHEL WASTED no time settling back into their familiar routine now that they were living together in the same apartment. Exhausted from a long day at work, Clark flopped down onto the pleather couch, a rush of air accompanying the squeak when her body hit the plush cushion.

Moments later, Rachel entered the apartment after finishing work at Jeb's Diner for the day. She collapsed onto the nearby couch with a tired groan.

Rachel grumbled, closing her eyes in exhaustion. "Oh my God, Clark. Harry was in a right mood today. Twice, I had to take his order back to the kitchen. The first time, it was too cold, and the second time, it was too hot!"

Clark joked, "Was it just right the third time?" she teased.

"Ha, ha. Very funny. What about you? How was your day?"

"You'll never guess. Sophie came right out and asked me to give Vin her number." Clark rummaged through her bag to find the paper containing Sophie's phone number and Facebook account details.

"Oh, my gosh, Clark. What are you going to do?" Rachel had guessed that Clark still harbored romantic feelings for Vin and Gun. Given their complicated history of unresolved feelings and Clark's mental health issues, she appreciated her friend's discretion about the situation because Clark had no idea where she, Vin, and Gun stood.

"I'm going to give it to Vin if I see him," she replied, tongue in cheek.

"Why would you do that?" gasped Rachel, her eyes as big as saucers.

"Because Sophie needs a lesson in respecting other people's boundaries and feelings. She's always hurting the other coworkers' feelings with her unwanted opinions and thinks she can get away with it."

"I wish Charly had been as assertive as you regarding her coworkers who constantly belittled her. They put her through a lot of heartache," Rachel murmured to herself.

"What happened to her friend Jess? Did you mention she went to jail?"

"Yes," Rachel replied quietly.

Clark scrutinized her roommate closely. The haunted expression on Rachel's face alarmed her. "What's wrong, Rachel?"

Rachel explained that Jess had been missing for a while and that there were suspicious circumstances surrounding her disappearance, which led people to believe she had died.

Clark sat agape in horror at the shocking revelation and was eager to hear the rest of the story. Rachel's silence prompted Clark to inquire, "Why is Jess presumed dead?"

Clark watched intently as Rachel took a deep, shuddering breath, her eyes brimming with worry and fear. "Dom and Jax searched everywhere for her right after she was released from prison, but she was nowhere to be found."

"Couldn't she have just moved away to another town?"

"I don't think so. There's much more to the story, but I don't feel it's my place to tell. Charly's the one to ask about the full story."

Clark nodded in understanding, seeing the physical impact on Rachel after sharing only a fraction of the details.

As intriguing as it sounded, it upset Clark to know that Charly's trauma ran much deeper than just losing a friend.

$$* * * * *$$

"RACHEL! YOUR PHONE'S RINGING," Clark shouted from the kitchen; the clinking of delicate China plates echoed in the small room as she carefully put away the last of the dishes.

Clark listened, hearing running water, and realized Rachel was in the shower. She returned to the spacious lounge room, where the bright mid-morning sun filtered through the curtains, and unpacked another box. Rachel's mobile phone rang again, lighting up the screen. Clark frowned when she saw Corey's name on the screen, wondering why he was calling Rachel.

Amused, Clark let Rachel finish her shower before asking about Corey's call, curious about what was going on between them.

Her roommate exited the bathroom, and steam billowed out of the room. Rachel had a fluffy white towel wrapped around her body and a striped beach towel covering her wet hair.

"Why are you looking at me like that?" Rachel asked, frowning at Clark, who sported a knowing grin.

"My brother has been calling you," Clark replied, chuckling at the guilty look on her friend's face. "All right, tell me what's going on?" she demanded.

"It's nothing, really," Rachel said shyly, "Corey came into the diner the other day. We chatted, and he apologized for his behavior when helping you move before asking me out. I said yes."

Clark wasn't surprised by the news, but a seed of doubt crept into her mind. She questioned whether any potential setbacks would affect her and Rachel's relationship, especially if things did not work out between Rachel and her brother. Reflecting on Dr. Martinez's teachings, Clark recalled the advice she had received. Taking a deep breath, Clark reassured herself that she didn't need to intervene. Choosing to allow Rachel and Corey's relationship to develop on its own, Clark accepted that she had no control over it. The decisions made by the two adults would ultimately determine whether it flourished into a beautiful bond or went up in flames.

Clark flashed a warm smile at Rachel. She was pleased with herself for refraining from getting involved and thus sparing herself unnecessary stress.

"Well, you better call him back. He's been blowing up your phone!"

Rachel's face lit up with a massive smile as she quickly grabbed her phone. Rachel had always been a constant source of support and encouragement for Clark, making her truly deserving of all the happiness in the world. From the beginning, Rachel had been Clark's pillar of strength, providing comfort and guidance through every hurdle she faced. The late-night conversations filled with bottles of wine, boxes of tissues, comforting hugs, and sage advice had sustained Clark through her most difficult times. In her mind, by giving Rachel the space to nurture her blossoming relationship with Corey, Clark believed she could express her gratitude for Rachel's kindness and generosity.

TWELVE

On a lazy Sunday afternoon, Clark was lying on the comfortable couch, engrossed in a murder mystery novel. Rachel had gone shopping at a local market earlier with Corey, looking for a birthday gift for her mother. Clark was thrilled for Rachel and Corey as they had spent every day together for the past week. Rachel would excitedly recount every detail of her dinner dates with Corey, from the delicious food to funny conversations. She omitted the romantic details because, to be honest, Clark wasn't interested in hearing about her brother's sex life.

Rachel's display of such animation and excitement was unprecedented. In the past, she had shared stories of her personal life more humorously and sarcastically. In Rachel's experience, the men she dated often boasted about their physical strength but lacked intellectual depth. However, according to Clark's biased opinion, in her brother's case, he was both brawn and brains.

Clark felt a sense of warmth and happiness seeing their relationship blossoming, easing her worries about their compatibility.

A sharp knock at the door made her jump in fright. Wondering who it could be, Clark found the interruption highly unusual on her typically quiet Sunday afternoons, especially when she wasn't expecting any visitors.

A gorgeous man with tousled brown hair stood on the other side of the door. He was wearing a tight black T-shirt and dark blue denim jeans. His black boots shone like polished wood, exuding a faint scent of leather and shoe polish, complementing his attractive attire.

Clark's heart raced as Vin leaned casually against the doorframe. His heartbreakingly beautiful smile captivated her. When she mirrored his charming smile, Clark noticed a slightly glazed look in Vin's bright blue eyes.

"Hey, Shortcake," he greeted cheerfully.

"What brings you here?" Clark's heart pounded with excitement upon seeing Vin. Based on their recent, regular, unplanned interactions, she wondered if Vin and Gun hoped to reconnect with her. If Vin and Gun clarified their intentions, Clark would be only too happy to resume their connection from where they left off.

Clark felt clearer-headed now. Since she started seeing a psychiatrist and taking prescribed medication, she handled situations more rationally. Feeling happier and noticing positive changes in her mental health, she no longer saw her concerns about medication addiction as a problem, realizing that the benefits outweighed the risks.

Having Vin and Gun back in her life noticeably contributed to her happiness. She cherished their company and felt no pressure from them to rekindle their relationship.

Clark felt ready to discuss her romantic feelings with Vin and Gun. She loved them but wasn't yet prepared to tell them. However, they could definitely discuss reigniting their relationship. The only problem was she wanted one of them to initiate the discussion because she felt it would show their interest. Clark was confident she was all in, but she wondered if Vin and Gun felt the same way. Or was it just a friendship now?

"I came to find out what your plans for dinner were."

Clark felt giddy and excited about going to dinner with Vin. "No plans," she replied eagerly.

"You want to go to the bar and grill? Gun will be there?"

"Okay," she smiled happily. "But I need to change first."

Without waiting for his reply, Clark hurried into her bedroom to change. She swapped her shorts and blouse for a long, flowing green dress that accentuated the golden flecks in her eyes.

During the ride across town to the restaurant, Clark's stomach fluttered with butterflies and fireworks. She leaned against Vin's leather jacket, relishing the familiar feel and smell of him. Clark kept her hands still, pressed against his hard abs, but secretly, her fingers tingled with the urge to delve under his shirt and feel the smooth contours of his enviable eight-pack.

A secret thrill coursed through Clark as she spotted Gun waiting outside the bar, puffing on a smoke. The man was a mountain of rugged gorgeousness from the top of his dark blond hair to the tips of his steel-capped boots.

"Red," he said as he enfolded her in a bear hug. "You all right?" he asked, his eyes skimming over her features.

Inside, crowds were seated around the establishment. Sliding across the semi-circular booth, Gun entered from the left, and Vin entered from the right. Dom was the first to approach them, his grin lighting up his face with a mischievous twinkle. Charly was one lucky woman. Dom consistently attracted attention with his ruggedly handsome features. Make that double-lucky, as Jax's charm, warm smile, and confident demeanor effortlessly drew attention wherever he went. In addition to having two attractive boyfriends, Charly also had supportive partners who stood by her no matter what.

"Clark, how are you doing?"

"I'm doing well, thanks, Dom. How's Jake?" Clark asked since she hadn't seen the energetic boy in a while.

"Trouble," he said with a straight face.

"No doubt he takes after his dad."

Dom chuckled, agreeing, "Can't say you're wrong."

The look he sent Vin and Gun threw Clark off. "Is everything okay?" she asked.

"Enjoy your meal, Clark. It's all good. I'll send Stacey over to serve you." He got up and motioned for the same blonde waitress who had served them with a flirtatious smile during their previous visit.

"Hi Vin, Gun," she said seductively. Clark scoffed at the waitress's blatant attempt to flirt. Despite feeling uncomfortable seated between Vin and Gun, a wry smile played on her lips.

Gun looked at Clark curiously and asked, "What's that?"

"Nothing," Clark replied, avoiding eye contact.

"What'll you have?" Gun asked as the aroma of sizzling steaks filled the air.

✶ ✶ ✶ ✶ ✶

VIN WAS KEENLY AWARE that Stacey was trying to get his and Gun's attention. Their brief history made Stacey believe she could ingratiate herself into his life. However, he was focusing on the beautiful woman sitting next to him. She was the only one he was interested in.

As they dined, they shared stories about the chaotic office events involving the new receptionist, Simone, and her blunders. Gun let it be known that she didn't hold a candle to Clark and that her organizational skills far surpassed Simone's lackluster performance. Vin could empathize with Gun's frustration because Simone often came in late, made weak excuses, double-booked appointments, or forgot to type them in altogether. While they discussed this, Vin became increasingly annoyed with Stacey's intermittent interruptions.

"Can I get either of you anything else?" Stacey asked, her hand resting on Vin's shoulder, her eyes darting between him and Gun.

Vin noticed Stacey's fresh coat of lip gloss on her lips. He also registered that the young girl had excluded Clark from the request.

"We're good, thank you, Stacey." He and Gun chuckled at Clark's sarcastic response.

"Behave yourself," Vin warned, enjoying the possessiveness in Clark's remark. He didn't care about Stacey but wouldn't stop his girl from marking her territory.

* * * * *

CLARK THOUGHT ABOUT HER situation with Sophie at the library as the guys griped about their troubles with Simone at the tattoo shop.

"What was that sigh for, Shortcake?"

"Just thinking about work."

"Everything okay?"

"Sophie's being intrusive and keeps asking questions about our relationship. I feel like she's constantly prying into my personal life, making me uncomfortable."

Dr. Martinez had advised her to openly discuss her concerns regarding personal and work issues with Vin and Gun now that they had reconnected. This was key for addressing any challenges effectively and receiving support from trusted friends. Clark needed to understand the value of accepting help from others rather than facing problems alone.

Vin growled, "You need to say something to Mrs. Prentiss. If she doesn't do anything about it, I will," he warned.

A twinkle danced in Clark's eyes as she peered up slyly at Vin. "There is one way you could help that might be effective."

Vin extended his giant arm around the back of the booth seat and leaned in closer to Clark. "Oh yeah? Do tell," he said, with a hint of conspiracy.

While digging into her bag, Clark retrieved the paper with Sophie's number and passed it to Vin.

"You could call her and let her know you're not interested in dating," she suggested.

"What's this?" Vin's brows furrowed deeply as he looked at Clark, reacting to the message. "What the heck?"

"Sophie specifically requested that I pass on a message for you to call her," she said, amused by his irritation.

"Do you find this amusing, Shortcake?" He gently lifted her chin, locking eyes with her. "You're the only one I want," he whispered, his voice brimming with sincerity and longing.

Clark's laughter faded, giving way to an explosion of joy that enveloped her, filling her with delight. Those were the words she'd been waiting for.

"But I do know how to end this ridiculous campaign of hers," Vin volunteered.

Vin then presented his idea, which Clark wholeheartedly approved of. During their private conversation, Gage stopped at their table.

"Well, if it isn't my stalker," she teased with a playful grin.

During his last visit to Clark's parents' house, Vin admitted to keeping an eye on her for her safety. Before she could object, he justified his vigilance by pointing out the potential danger she unknowingly posed to herself by interfering in their altercation with Cork. Preventive measures were necessary to keep her safe.

Gage gave Clark a chin lift and stated, "Making sure you're safe, Clark."

Clark asked, "From myself, you mean?"

"Not touching that one."

Clark reassured, "Gage, it's all good."

Gun cut in, giving Gage a dirty look, and asked, "You want something, bro?"

"Yeah. Kill needs to talk to you."

Gun responded, scowling, "Now? I'm busy."

Gage replied seriously, "It's important."

Gun made eye contact with Vin. "You take her home?" Then he signaled something to Gage, who turned and left.

"I'll see you out, Red," said Gun, taking her hand.

As he escorted her outside, Gun unexpectedly enveloped her in a pair of strong arms, pressing her face against his hard chest. Gun said gently, "Okay, Red. Vin will take you home, and I'll see you soon, yeah?"

His deep brown eyes locked onto hers, their intensity melting her from the inside out. Her lips tingled, her heart racing as she waited with bated breath, feeling the heat of his gaze. Suddenly, he let her go, crushing her hopes of a kiss.

While on their ride back home, Clark contemplated whether Gun's aloof demeanor indicated a sense of disconnection or if he was merely going through the motions out of a sense of obligation.

With precision, Vin parked the motorcycle in the lot in front of her apartment complex. Guiding her to the second floor, he pulled her aside to lean against the railing. "Not ready to say goodnight yet."

Feeling a mix of joy and vulnerability at Vin's desire for more time, she relaxed in his arms. "Is everything all right with Gun? I noticed he seemed distant earlier."

"Yeah. Club business, babe. You know that."

"I do." Clark worried, her lip between her teeth, unsure how to ask about Gun's feelings toward her. Recalling Dr. Martinez's advice to express her feelings, Clark decided that being direct was the best approach. "Does Gun still want me?"

Vin tightened his hold around Clark. "Yeah, Shortcake. He does. Why do you ask?"

"He didn't kiss me." Clark subconsciously licked her lips. Vin's eyes traced the path of her tongue and groaned.

"You want a kiss, babe?" As Vin's head moved closer to hers, she nodded eagerly.

Clark's lips met Vin's, and the taste of scotch and mint lingered on her tongue as they began their familiar dance. Their heavy breaths quickened, and their lips met and parted in a rapid tango, tongues, and saliva mingling in fervor.

Clark's thighs tensed as Vin's hand trailed down her lower back, gently cupping her derriere with a possessive and firm touch. He squeezed and molded Clark's cheeks like sculpting clay, shaping them with ownership and passion. Clark wound her arms around his broad shoulders, lifting herself onto the tips of her toes to draw closer. Vin effortlessly lifted Clark, balancing her on the rails with a steady hand without breaking their connection.

They shared passionate kisses late into the night, punctuated by intimate conversations and tender caresses, rekindling their bond. At one point that night, Rachel emerged from the apartment to investigate the commotion she heard from the hallway. Witnessing Clark and Vin huddled together against the railing, Rachel nervously chuckled at the romantic scene before closing the door again.

＊＊＊＊＊

AS CLARK'S SHIFT AT the library neared its end, she was relieved to escape finally, but not before Sophie delayed her.

Sophie asked eagerly, "Did you give that guy my number?"

"I did."

Sophie inquired, "What kind of friend is he, Clark? He's so freaking hot, and you're …"

"Not?" Clark wasn't surprised by Sophie's thoughtless remark about her appearance.

"You must admit it seems strange that he seems like a bad boy, and you're pretty … unadventurous."

Sophie carried on as if her words were inconsequential, utterly oblivious to the hurt they caused, twirling her hair absentmindedly.

"How did you become friends, anyway? What could you possibly have in common with him?" Sophie prodded.

Sophie's insensitive words caused Clark to stand there, feeling hurt and frustrated. In a bold move, Clark decided it was time to implement Vin's plan. Spotting him waiting by his motorcycle in the dimly lit parking lot, she gestured for Sophie to follow her, the sound of crickets filling the night air.

Sophie chirped away happily, her tone bubbling with excitement as she walked beside Clark toward Vin. He wore jeans, a leather jacket, and aviators. Vin exuded the aura of a classic rebel, with a cigarette dangling from his lips and a nonchalant air about him as if he had not a single worry in the world. Clark could easily discern the thoughts and emotions racing through Sophie's mind at that moment.

"Hey, Shortcake," Vin greeted cheerfully.

He eyed Sophie with a hint of curiosity, subtly studying her with polite interest.

"Vin, this is Sophie. She has been eager to meet you for a while now."

Clark observed the unfolding interaction between Sophie and Vin. She thought it was time the persistent girl got a taste of her own medicine. Clark wanted to see what Vin had to say if Sophie dared to make digs at her.

"What's up?"

Clark suppressed a smile as she observed Sophie's failed attempt at impressing Vin with her flirty grin.

Sophie fluttered her eyelashes coquettishly. "Hi," she said breathlessly. "I saw you come in the other day and can't believe how hot you are!"

"Yeah," Vin replied indifferently. "I've heard that many times before."

"I thought maybe we could be friends," Sophie suggested with a hopeful smile.

Clark bit her tongue, annoyance, and amusement flickering in her eyes.

Clark observed Vin inhale deeply. His expression darkened, revealing his displeasure at Sophie's insinuation. A warm rush of happiness spread through her, causing tiny bubbles of joy to dance in her belly.

"Friend? What the fuck are you talking about?" Vin grumbled, frowning at the pretty brunette.

Sophie balked, realizing she had misinterpreted his irritation. "I thought maybe we could be friends," she said, gesturing towards Clark. "You're friends with Clark?" she said accusingly, her voice tinged with the smell of desperation.

"We're more than friends," Vin emphasized.

Sophie's eyes widened in disbelief, and her jaw dropped at the ludicrous idea. She glared at Clark with resentment. "You didn't tell me."

"Don't fucking look at Clark like that. She doesn't have to tell you shit. You need to mind your own damn business."

"It's okay, Vin. I can speak for myself." Clark laid a hand on his bicep, trying to calm him down.

Vin's ire deflated, replaced by pride and admiration as he looked at her. "I know you can, babe."

Clark arched an eyebrow, a hint of skepticism coloring her expression. "Then let me."

Ignoring Sophie's outrage, Vin cradled Clark and kissed her. "Ready to roll?"

With a final glance at the fuming Sophie, Clark donned the helmet and mounted the back of Vin's motorcycle.

Clark knew her amicable relationship with Sophie was over due to the misunderstanding about her romantic relationship with Vin. The unfortunate incident would resolve Sophie's badgering issue but created a new problem of strained trust between them. She suspected her failure to disclose her relationship with Vin upset Sophie. Clark knew she wouldn't forgive or forget the misunderstanding. She had been humiliated and likely blamed Clark for the situation.

✱ ✱ ✱ ✱ ✱

CLARK WENT INTO THE library's members' computer area to switch off all the computers. It was closing time, and the last patron left just before closing.

She could hear the murmur of voices and knew Sophie was one of the people talking. She was fine with Sophie ignoring her. Not trusting Sophie, Clark was especially wary after overhearing her say untrue things about Clark earlier.

Clark checked the return slot to ensure all the books, especially the rare editions, had been placed back on the shelves. With all her tasks completed, Clark went to say goodbye to Mrs. Prentiss and Teresa, thanking them for their help during her busy day.

Head down, Clark exited through the front entrance of the library. In her haste, she almost collided with Gun, who suddenly appeared in her path.

"Whoa!" she raised her hands instinctively to prevent a collision. "Gun! What are you doing here?"

"I told you I'd see you soon." Clark marveled at Gun's commanding presence. His arms were crossed tightly, his biceps resembling mountains, and a fierce expression was etched on his face. Although it was the usual Gun stance, it failed to capture the depth of the man behind it.

Clark scanned the empty parking lot for his midnight blue motorcycle. "Do you intend to give me a lift home?" she asked expectantly.

"Not yet. Before we go, I need to address something important. Vin tells me you were upset because I didn't kiss you the other day. I intend to remedy that."

Clark felt a surge of desire as he kissed her passionately. She eagerly responded by parting her lips, inviting him in with a soft sigh, and deepening their kiss. The kiss continued endlessly, with both of them unwilling to extinguish the passion that burned between them, each moment only fueling their desire further.

After Gun finally pulled away, Clark fell back to earth with a thud.

Gun chuckled at her dazed expression, his eyes glinting mischievously as they caught the streetlight's reflection.

"I'm taking you to the clubhouse," Gun announced with a sly grin, his tone inviting.

She hesitated, her mind racing with memories of her last experience at the clubhouse, before finally responding, "Um … I don't know, Gun."

Gun asked with concern, "What's the matter?"

"Last time we went there … it didn't end well."

"Don't worry, I'm not kidnapping you. You're free to leave anytime you want to. Unless I can persuade you to stay," he added cheekily.

Vin met Clark at the front of the compound and swooped her up in his arms. "Glad you made it, Shortcake. You staying the night?"

Vin caught Clark off guard with the invitation. Although their relationship seemed to be getting back on track, they hadn't discussed resuming their intimate relationship yet. Furthermore, Clark didn't have any toiletries or spare clothes. She also didn't want to inconvenience Sara by borrowing her clothes again.

Clark blushed and mumbled, "I don't have a change of clothes."

"Oh, babe. What I have in mind doesn't require clothes," Vin said seductively, winking suggestively.

She playfully but firmly stated, "We need to discuss how things will be, Vin. They can't go back to what they were. Until we have that conversation, we should wait."

Gun came up behind her and enveloped her in his big, strong arms, gently nuzzling her neck, a sensitive area. He whispered, "Got it, Red. We'll have that conversation tonight," his voice filled with reassurance and promise.

✶ ✶ ✶ ✶ ✶

THE BROTHERS CONGREGATED AROUND the bar, drinking, while the women sat together on the sofa in the front room.

Gun glanced at Clark, huddled on the sofa with Charly, Sara, and Carrie. The pink and orange sky illuminated the clubhouse grounds outside, creating a vivid backdrop in the window. In the middle of that setting sat four animated women. His lips twitched when they erupted into fits of giggles—something they did often whenever they got together. Seeing Clark effortlessly bond with the other women filled him with pride; her exuberant presence added vibrancy to their group dynamic. This highlighted the significance of her being part of their social circle as they planned to restart their relationship.

Gun couldn't wait to discuss their plans and where they were heading. Their deep connection solidified the idea that their long-awaited reunion was about to happen, marking a significant turning point in their lives. At thirty-five, he was prepared to commit to one woman, seeking a deeper connection beyond casual encounters. He had thoroughly enjoyed his free and carefree time as a single man. Now, he had discovered someone who ignited his heart. She brightened his days and filled his nights with passionate dreams. He was eager to fulfill these dreams with Clark.

Someone elbowed him, and Gun twisted his head around to find Vin smirking.

"What?" he asked, annoyed at being interrupted while watching his woman. Vin briefed Gun about the confrontation that occurred at the library.

"The chick she works with, Sonya ... Sally ... I can't remember her name."

"Sophie," Gun supplied.

"Yeah, Sophie. She found out that Clark and me are together. Got upset at Clark."

"She needs to mind her own business," growled Gun, feeling protective of Clark.

Vin agreed, "That's what I told her."

"Does she know about me and Clark?"

"I highly doubt she's aware," Vin responded thoughtfully.

"I'll discuss this with Clark tonight," Gun stated firmly.

Recalling Charly's experience with bullying from her coworkers at the bar and grill, Gun felt a strong resolve to shield Clark from similar mistreatment.

* * * * *

THE SUN HAD GONE down, and the clubhouse was now shrouded in the glow of the fluorescent lights. As it was past Nolan's bedtime, Sara went to find her son. After a quick goodbye, Carrie left with Sara, leaving Charly and Clark alone. The four women had spent a delightful evening catching up, sipping champagne, and regaling each other with hilarious anecdotes about work, family, and the misadventures of their daily lives.

Charly took the last sip of her champagne before asking, "I hope you don't mind me asking, Clark, but your relationship with Archer, wasn't he technically your brother?"

Perhaps it was the champagne, but Clark chuckled at the memory.

"There had always been chemistry between us since we were around fourteen and sixteen, respectively. Nothing happened between us romantically until I was seventeen, but Archer constantly teased me about the most embarrassing things before we started a relationship. Once, we were at the local pool, and I was excited to wear the first bikini mom had bought me. In front of his friends, Archer made a snide remark about my flat chest. Feeling horrified and humiliated, I ran home crying."

"Oh, Clark. That's terrible," Charly sympathized.

"It was at the time, but with hindsight, I think he might have been either warning his friends to stay away or trying to get my attention."

"So, how did it go from teasing to a relationship?"

"One night, Mom and Dad had gone out for a romantic dinner. Corey had recently moved into his own apartment, and Damien was off with his friends, leaving only Archer and me at home that night. We were watching a classic horror movie. I can't remember its name, but I do recall that it was about a haunted mansion with a vengeful ghost. We both shared a love for watching gory movies filled with blood, guts, and screaming."

Clark smiled at Charly's look of horror. Charly whispered, "I never would have guessed."

"The tension was palpable as the scene unfolded, with the eerie music building up to the inevitable encounter with the masked killer, who was actually a ghost. When it got to the part where the ghost jumped out, Archer leaned over and kissed me. It was my very first kiss, and I remember pushing him away. However, I didn't push him away when he went in for another kiss. Thus began the journey of a beautiful relationship." Clark recounted the memory in a trance-like tone, her eyes shimmering with joy and sorrow.

There was a lull in their conversation as Clark's thoughts traveled back to that fateful night with Archer.

Charly let out an awkward chuckle. "So … how's everything at the library?"

Clark laughed along with Charly, stepping back into the present. She felt comfortable confiding in her. There was an unspoken bond with Charly, a sense of trust that encouraged her to share her deepest secrets without fear of judgment.

"Sophie met Vin the other day," she stated, grimacing.

"The coworker from the mall?"

"Yes, it didn't go well," Clark replied with a frown. "Vin made it clear that we were together."

Charly tried to hide her smile as she asked, "Is it true? Are you two together now?"

"We're working on it," Clark admitted honestly. "We still need to discuss some things, but I'm ready to start again. I've missed Vin and Gun terribly."

"You exude strength, confidence, and joy now," Charly beamed, her face transforming into a vision of beauty.

Expressing her gratitude, Clark replied, "I appreciate your kind words." Knowing that others could see her confidence reflected on the outside was heartening. "I've been curious about something. Where is Jake's mom? You've never mentioned her."

Charly's grin faded, replaced by a somber expression that clouded her features.

Clark rushed to appease Charly, gently touching her arm to offer comfort. "I'm sorry, Charly. You don't have to answer. I'm just being nosy," Clark apologized, her tone filled with regret.

"It's all right, Clark. It happened a while ago. I'm fine." Charly insisted. "The fact is Jake's mom was murdered."

Clark gasped, shocked by the news. "Murdered? Oh, Charly, that's terrible. I can't imagine how Jake must be feeling."

Charly gently squeezed Clark's hand reassuringly. "It's okay. While we weren't close, she was still Jake's mom, which counts for something."

As Charly took a deep, quivering breath, Clark sensed she was about to reveal more.

"Jake was only two at the time. Dom told him that his birth mom is in heaven and that I was an angel who came down to look after him." Charly's face lit up with a glimmer of a smile.

"Kyra, that's Jake's mom, was brutally attacked and killed by Sol, the man who abducted me."

Struggling to conceal her horror, Clark tightly pressed her lips together. She focused on Charly, not wanting to disrupt the tangled web of intrigue.

"After his release from prison, Sol was driven to find Jess and punish her for having him locked up. At that time, Jess had already vanished, and rumors circulating led us to believe she was dead. In a desperate attempt to locate Jess, he abducted me, unaware that I had no clue where she was. He would have killed me too, but I killed him instead."

A heavy silence wrapped around Clark, allowing the gravity of the words to sink in. No wonder Rachel didn't want to say anything after hearing such a shocking revelation. The details of the story, filled with intricate twists and horrifying events, were both complicated and abhorrent.

"I didn't go to prison or anything because it was self-defense." Clark nodded in agreement. Locking Charly up after being abducted would have been a grave injustice, considering the traumatic experience she had endured.

"Shane, the detective who handled my brother's murder years ago, was the one who found me, along with Dom and Jax. Shane has been my savior since I was twelve. Without him, I don't know where I'd be today. During the difficult times of moving between foster homes, Shane and his wife, Tessa, stayed in touch with me. I'll have to introduce you to them."

"Charls?" The softly spoken word was filled with love, concern, and possessiveness.

Clark looked up to see Dom and Jax staring at Charly as if they were prepared to annihilate whatever had upset her, ready to protect her at all costs. Behind them, Vin and Gun stood vigilant, watching Clark intently. Clark's expression softened, and her eyes filled with tender affection. They shifted from a defensive stance to a more relaxed posture.

"Ready to go home, babe?" Jax asked Charly, a secret look transpiring between them.

Clark recognized the familiar longing in Jax and Dom's eyes, a desire to be alone with the woman they both adored.

Her gaze shifted to Vin and Gun, and she noticed a shared spark of mischief in their eyes, prompting her to tilt her head down, concealing a smile of anticipation. Before diving into any intimate moments, they needed to have a conversation.

As Jax assisted Charly into the Jeep, Clark felt a warm hand gently encircling her waist. Gun pulled her close, his eyes gleaming with determination, and guided her towards the darkened back room area where a single flickering candle illuminated a small table.

"What's this?" she asked, looking confused.

"It's called romance, babe," Vin explained, a playful smile tugging at one corner of his mouth.

"You haven't forgotten about the important conversation we need to have first, have you?" Clark reminded him seriously.

"Let's have it then," instructed Gun, gesturing for her to sit on the bed. "Okay, shoot."

Clark gave herself a moment to gather her thoughts before speaking. Closing her eyes briefly, she tried to recall the spiel she'd memorized a hundred times.

"All right. If we do this, you must understand I'm getting the help I need. I'm attending counseling, and I'm on anxiety medication. With that in mind, please do not make decisions about having any sharp implements lying around or keeping me here for my safety. Got that?"

Clark paused to allow her words to sink in. She watched the pair do the ESP thing. Their telepathic connection seemed unchanged.

Gun spoke up. "We can agree to that as long as you promise to talk with us if you're tempted to harm yourself. We're here to support you and want you to feel comfortable sharing your thoughts and feelings. We're here to help."

"I've realized the importance of seeking support from others, and I promise to talk to you if I feel the urge to harm myself."

Vin climbed onto the bed and wrapped his arms around her tightly. He kissed her forehead. "That's my girl."

Judging by the soft look in Vin's gaze, he had something more exciting in mind—a different kind of exchange involving physical touch. Her breath caught at the sound of fabric tearing as he impatiently stripped off his T-shirt, the scent of his cologne mingling with the mustiness of the room as he carelessly discarded it on the floor.

Without waiting for directions, Clark knelt before Vin and confidently stroked his erection through his jeans. She swiftly helped him out of his remaining clothes and tenderly cradled his cock in her palm. Feeling the heat of his manhood, she bent down to take him in her mouth. Vin's chest rose and fell in sync with her movements as she savored the taste of him. His guttural groans and whispered words of encouragement fueled her desire. Vin's hand guided her mouth to take him deeper. Feeling him penetrate the back of her throat, she gagged involuntarily, the bitter taste of bile rising in her mouth as she struggled to catch her breath before resuming.

Prioritizing her pleasure was a ritual for these two men. Vin and Gun always made sure Clark was sexually satisfied before seeking their own gratification. She was grateful for the pleasure they bestowed on her and wanted to reciprocate the gesture.

While one hand held the base of Vin's thick cock, her other hand gently massaged his testicles. Clark felt a surge of heat building in his core, his muscles tensing as he let out a husky growl, signaling his imminent climax. He ejaculated into her mouth. She swallowed the salty essence, the bittersweet taste filling her mouth.

After wiping her lips with the back of her hand, she glanced at Gun, who was sprawled on the bed pleasuring himself. His eyes followed her every move as she moved over his lap, gently taking his hand away and replacing it with her eager lips.

Their figures cast long, flickering shadows in the darkness, illuminated only by a single candle flame. Vin hustled to get her pants off in a surprisingly ungraceful manner as she caressed Gun's cock with unhurried strokes. Clark assisted Vin by turning this way and that, lifting a leg and an arm as he undressed her.

Focused solely on Gun, she continued to pleasure him with deliberate movements of her hands. Gun thrust his hips upwards, making her gag. Clark had difficulty taking his large penis in her mouth, but she did her best to adjust. Within minutes, he tensed up, grunted, and then he, too, ejaculated inside her mouth.

As she reached up, her lips met Gun's, lingering in a silent exchange that allowed him to taste his essence. Smiling, she asked, "You like that?" with a hint of satisfaction and mischief.

"You talking about the blowjob or the kiss?"

"I meant the taste of your semen, Gun," she clarified, a playful glint in her eyes.

"It's an acquired taste. I prefer the taste of your cum, Red," Gun replied, his eyes filled with desire.

Suddenly, Vin moved her naked body to the edge of the bed. He gave Gun a meaningful look, silently communicating his intentions, before bowing his head.

"Yeah, but tonight it's my turn," he declared before swiping his tongue through her folds to sample her juices.

"Oh, my God!" she cried, her body quivering as Vin's tongue hit the right spot.

Within minutes, she was approaching her climax, her breathing hitching and becoming erratic and loud while her body slowly arched.

Clark, already excited from pleasuring them, quickly went over the edge, her legs twitching uncontrollably.

Gun stretched his arm out with a warm smile and said, "Come here." Clark snuggled against him. "It's good to have you back, Red. I missed you," he whispered with longing in his voice.

"Me too," she replied, her eyes shining with affection.

"What about me?" Vin playfully pressed his torso against her back, a hint of jealousy lacing his tone.

Clark turned her head towards Vin, her eyes brimming with joy, a radiant smile on her lips. Tenderly cupping his face, she leaned in and kissed him deeply, expressing her love for him.

THIRTEEN

It was a bustling Friday night at the clubhouse, and Clark was relaxing with Sara and Charly at the bar. Amidst the lively chatter in the background, the women had to raise their voices to be heard. The bubbles tickled Clark's nostrils as she sipped, the liquid flowing down her throat like a sparkling waterfall. The effervescent drink triggered a sense of light-headedness, prompting occasional giggles to bubble up. The women cheered as they clinked their champagne glasses.

Since they reestablished their relationship last week, Clark has discovered the joys of being with Vin and Gun. Their connection was intense and hot as they explored every aspect of their sexual relationship through passionate nighttime lovemaking. More importantly, they got to know and learn about each other.

Clark discovered that Gun shared her love for reading. Vin, on the other hand, was a horror movie enthusiast, while Gun favored action films. Vin was a diehard fan of AC/DC and had Clark in fits of laughter as he belted out his favorite song, *You Shook Me All Night Long*. Clark's ability to sing surprised the men, especially since Charly, who often attended karaoke nights, shared the same talent. They learned that Clark had a half-brother who lived in another state. Vin shared that he was a twin, but sadly, his brother was stillborn. This news saddened Clark, but she could not imagine a different version of Vin.

Every night, they explored new and exciting sexual adventures, discovering positions that heightened their pleasure and deepened their connection. Role-play scenarios and sensual massages became a favorite of hers as she enjoyed the physical intimacy. Gun and Vin introduced Clark to innovative positions such as the Lotus Blossom and Reverse Cowgirl, allowing Clark to enjoy face-to-face interaction and better stimulation of the G-spot.

Jax walked over to the pool table and began racking up the balls. Vin and Gun automatically followed him and gathered around the table. Clark, Charly, and Sara watched from their stools at the bar.

Clark soon learned that her men showed remarkable expertise at the game. She was impressed by Vin and Gun's precise aim and strategic ball placements, admiring how effortlessly they controlled the game with calculated precision. Her eyes followed every smooth stroke of their cues, mesmerized by the fluidity of their actions as they leaned over the table to line up their shots. Unbeknownst to Clark, the seemingly innocuous game of pool was about to captivate her unexpectedly.

"They're good, aren't they?"

Clark suddenly realized Charly was talking to her. "Pardon?"

Chuckling, Charly reiterated, "Impressive, aren't they?"

"Mmm-hmm," she agreed.

As the evening progressed, the clubhouse hummed with animated conversations and the clinking of glasses, creating an infectiously lively atmosphere. Among the familiar faces, Clark's gaze settled on Stacey, the waitress from the bar and grill, who greeted Vin and Gun with a provocative smile as they exchanged a brief conversation.

But what shocked Clark more was Sophie's arrival. She was wearing a revealing outfit: a tight, shimmery dress that barely covered her groin and breasts. Sophie confidently held Stacey's hand as they sashayed towards the pool table, where Vin and Gun stood.

"Isn't that brunette with Stacey, your coworker from the library?" Sara asked, tapping Clark's arm.

Clark nodded grimly, feeling a mix of surprise and concern.

"Why is she here? How did she manage to get in?" Sara said, looking towards the doorway where a prospect was stationed as security tonight.

"They're holding hands. Stacey and Sophie know each other," Clark murmured, closely observing Sophie.

"Well, Stacey can't just bring anyone without permission," Sara grumbled.

Clark clenched her teeth as Sophie leaned in close to Vin. Even from where she sat at the bar, Clark watched Sophie flash one of her megawatt smiles and flirt with Vin. Clark clenched her fists, nails digging into the worn fabric of the stool, fighting the urge to confront Sophie and wipe that smug grin off her face.

Vin looked down when Sophie got close, and frowned. A wave of relief washed over Clark as she observed their interaction, her tension easing slightly. Vin stepped back, deliberately putting space between himself and Sophie. Surprise flickered across Sophie's face. She whispered to Vin, but he shook his head and gestured towards the door.

Excitement bubbled up inside Clark's heart, filling her with hope. Was Vin telling Sophie to leave? She would gladly usher her out of the clubhouse.

But Sophie didn't leave. She stubbornly stayed where she was, leaning confidently against the pool table, exuding self-assurance. Clark noticed that Sophie was receiving admiring glances and subtle smiles from the other men.

Charly smiled at Clark, winking, "Vin doesn't seem interested." Clark responded with an enthusiastic nod, her smile widening to reveal her dimples.

Sara commented, "Doesn't appear as if she wants to leave. And look, she's created a bit of a stir among the guys."

Abruptly, two bikers strode purposefully toward her, their eyes gleaming with unmistakable interest. Their lecherous grins widened as they ogled her almost naked body.

Sophie's head swung around when one of the men spoke to her. She stepped backward as if intimidated by the two men surrounding her.

Sophie said something to Vin, but he and the two men burst into laughter. Clark had no idea what they found amusing, but she didn't care.

As the man reached out to put his arm around her, Sophie deftly slipped out of his grasp and pointed to Vin.

Feeling a surge of protectiveness, Clark pushed off her stool, intending to intervene, but Charly grabbed her elbow.

"No, Clark. You can't get in the middle of it. Stay here and wait it out."

Realizing Charly was right, Clark reluctantly acknowledged the wisdom in her words. She'd been warned enough times by Vin and Gun to stay out of their business.

Sophie made a slight commotion and a small squeak as she was gently but firmly led out of the clubhouse. At the doorway, the two men who had thrown her out confronted the prospect. From their tense postures and furrowed brows, it was clear that they were displeased with the situation.

Clark glanced over at Vin and noticed him whisper something to Gun, causing Gun to throw his head back in hearty laughter.

Clark was annoyed by the sight of Stacey fawning over Gun. Clad in skimpy shorts and a top that left little to the imagination, Stacey boldly pressed her body against Gun, creating a tight knot of unease in Clark's stomach.

Unlike Vin, who had refused Sophie's advances, Gun nonchalantly twirled his cue stick, conversed with Jax, and appeared oblivious to the woman's proximity. Maybe he enjoyed her advances. Intense jealousy gripped Clark as she watched Stacey's bold actions.

Her temper flared even hotter when Stacey slid her hand into the back pocket of Gun's jeans while he passively stood by. Gun remained rooted in place, displaying an air of indifference as if the unfolding events were of no consequence.

"I wouldn't let Stacey go near my man," Sara said casually.

"But he's letting her touch him. Look, he's not doing a single thing to stop her."

"What do you plan to do about it?" challenged Sara.

Clark watched intently as Gun directed his gaze towards Stacey. He said something to her, and the young woman threw back her head and laughed with the grace of a beautiful swan, elegant and poised like a ballet dancer. Consumed by jealousy and anger, Clark's breaths came out heavily as she resolved to play the same game. With determined steps, her heels clicking on the floor, she advanced towards the bar. Her focus zeroed in on Gage as her target.

"Hey, Gage," she said, smiling at the sharp-witted man.

Clark observed the handsome biker engrossed in conversation with another woman, his attention seemingly fixed on her. Unbothered by his distraction, Clark's heart simmered with betrayal and determination. She wanted to get even because she felt betrayed by Gun's actions. She reasoned that if Gun thought it was acceptable for him to entertain the attention of another woman, then she had every right to reciprocate.

"What's up, Clark?" Gage's voice carried a hint of curiosity. He briefly acknowledged Clark with a nod before diverting his attention to the other woman.

Positioning herself strategically, Clark inserted herself between Gage and the disgruntled woman to reclaim Gage's attention.

"I came over to say hello and see what you're doing," she said.

Gage retreated, raising his hands in surrender. "Whoa, sweetheart. What are you doing?"

Clark nervously licked her lips, finding the situation more challenging than anticipated.

"Just talking," she explained sweetly, touching his shoulder.

"Yeah, you can do that without touching me, Clark. This isn't happening." Gage stood up and stepped away, creating some distance.

Clark sighed audibly. "What's your problem?"

Gage was not amused. "They're my problem." He jerked his head at someone behind her.

She whirled around and gave Gun and Vin a fierce glare.

Gun asked Clark, "What's going on, Red?"

"We're just having a conversation," she said, shrugging nonchalantly.

"It looked like you were doing more than talking, Shortcake. Care to explain what's going on?" Vin questioned, his voice taking on a steely and unyielding quality.

Deliberately making eye contact with Gun, she let him see her displeasure.

"Since Stacey was climbing all over you, maybe I was allowed to do the same. It's only fair."

Gun took a deep breath and exhaled slowly, trying to calm himself down.

"Listen up, Shortcake," Vin intervened while Gun cooled down. "You touch no man besides me and Gun; you got that? Any more shenanigans, and I'll spank that tempting ass of yours."

Clark let out a surprised squawk as Vin lifted her over his shoulder without ceremony and swiftly carried her to the bedroom. After being dumped on the bed, Clark quickly sat up, shocked at being manhandled so aggressively.

Gun pinned her with a determined glare. His voice was solemn as he said, "Stay away from Gage. If you go near him like that again, I won't be responsible for my actions."

"So, you better keep Stacey away!" she exclaimed.

"Jealous?"

"No more than you are."

"Fuck me," Gun muttered, running a hand through his hair.

"You allowed her to touch you."

"Who? Stacey? I barely noticed her."

"She had her hand in your back pocket, groping your backside, Gun. Did you see the way you reacted when I was talking to Gage? That's how I felt when Stacey was touching you. Why didn't you stop her?"

"I will in the future," promised Gun, his temper cooling now that he understood why she had approached Gage. "This is not how I want you to handle things in the future. Next time, we'll talk about it."

"Next time, instruct Stacey to stay away from you, just like Gage kept his distance from me," Clark suggested, feeling much calmer now that they were having a rational conversation.

"Good to know. Otherwise, Gage would be one messed-up fucker by now. Understand that you could've gotten him into some deep shit, Red."

Gun's warning left little doubt about what he meant, but Clark didn't want him to blame Gage for her mistake.

"I'll apologize to him then. I don't want you to hurt Gage, Gun. He's done nothing wrong."

"Then don't toy with him. He knows you belong to us."

"Does that mean you belong to me?" Clark asked sassily.

Upon Gun's agreement, she added, "Maybe you should inform Stacey."

"I'm done talking."

Clark let out a high-pitched scream as Gun rolled around with her on the bed. The playful interaction between Clark and Gun began with light tickles and soft nibbles. It then escalated to lively play-fighting, leading to passionate kisses and spirited roughhousing. Vin joined the fun, sparking another round of laughter and screams. The room reverberated with heavy moans, the sound of wet kisses, and whispered commands, drowning out all other noises.

✶ ✶ ✶ ✶ ✶

DURING AN INTERVAL BETWEEN bouts of sex, Gun leaned against the bed headrest, with Clark safely tucked under his arms. Vin was playing with the TV remote. The sound effects from the TV show echoed in the room, and Vin quickly turned the volume down.

Gun asked, "This coworker of yours, does she know about me?" Gun kept his arms around Clark's shoulders as she peered at him, her golden honey eyes shining innocently.

Clark shook her head, her expression troubled, as she chewed on her bottom lip. "I have no intention of telling her about you. She'd be jealous if she learned about you, especially since you fit her 'bad boy' type."

"Will she give you any trouble?" Gun would not tolerate anyone mistreating his woman.

"I know what you're thinking, Gun, but I prefer to handle this alone. Involving you or Vin in this situation might complicate things further. It's best if neither of you picks me up for rides anymore. I'll take the bus home instead."

"Who's this badass girl that's taking on the world, one bitch at a time?" Vin crowed, his eyes sparkling with admiration as he looked down at her.

"The new and improved Clark, ready to take control of her life," she voiced confidently.

Clark squirmed when Vin lowered his head and playfully licked her neck.

Gun watched their playful banter. His heart swelled with immense pride for Clark, his eyes gleaming with respect for her remarkable accomplishments. She had made significant progress from the impulsive person she used to be, who acted quickly without thinking. Given her openness, honesty, and determination to stand on two feet, how could he not wholeheartedly support her?

✳ ✳ ✳ ✳ ✳

CLARK LINED THE BOOKS neatly on the shelves, turning several books so the spines faced outward. Noticing that some fiction books had been mistakenly placed on the wrong shelf, Clark reorganized them and returned them to their proper places.

Her ears perked when she heard low whispers in the aisle behind her. Clark heard Sophie's husky voice ridicule her name and comment negatively about her work. Leaning closer, Clark listened to Sophie criticize her organizational skills and spread false rumors about her performance to Diane, another coworker. It sounded like Sophie was describing her own work standards to the unsuspecting librarian. Hearing words like lazy, incompetent, and flirt made Clark think of Sophie's behavior.

Ever since the night Sophie got thrown out of the clubhouse, her jealousy had escalated, and now she was resorting to spreading malicious and false rumors about Clark. The insults of being called lazy, incompetent, and a flirt paled in comparison to the derogatory terms like 'whore,' 'slut,' and 'STD' that had been circulating.

It was time for her to address the situation with Sophie. The younger woman needed to be corrected, and Clark was the only person who could do so. Sophie's jealousy was unjustified and becoming increasingly problematic. Clark's personal matters were private; Sophie should not meddle in them. They could learn to get along or avoid each other, but speaking disrespectfully about another person was unacceptable.

Clark approached Sophie, who stopped talking when she saw her at the end of the aisle.

"Sophie, we need to talk," Clark said politely, conscious of Diane's watchful gaze.

Sophie visibly swallowed, a sign that she had been caught gossiping. She tucked her hair behind her ear nervously.

"Sure, yeah," she said, her voice sounding croaky.

"Excuse me, Diane," Clark stated firmly, prompting Diane to leave.

She quickly returned to her station, leaving Clark and Sophie alone.

Clark wasted no time in directly confronting Sophie. "Why are you telling lies about me?"

"I ... I didn't!" Sophie denied, her cheeks flushing with embarrassment.

"I overheard you just then telling Diane that you had to finish my tasks because I'm too lazy to do them," Clark accused, effectively cutting off any opportunity for Sophie to continue lying.

"You misheard me," Sophie scoffed. "I said you always finish your tasks on time," blustered Sophie, continuing to lie.

"Sophie, stop lying. Are you spreading lies because you're upset that I didn't tell you about my relationship with Vin?"

"You lied to me!" Sophie whined, her voice getting louder.

"Keep your voice down, Sophie," Clark warned. "You don't want Mrs. Prentiss to scold you again."

"You lied to me," Sophie whispered.

"I didn't exactly lie to you, Sophie. I just didn't tell you. It's not your business who I see."

"But you knew I was interested in Vin. I was humiliated the other day," Sophie sniffled, choking up.

"Look, I'm sorry about that," Clark said gently. "I should have told you the truth; none of this would have happened."

"At the clubhouse, I know you must have played a part in me being thrown out!"

"No, that had nothing to do with me. Why were you even there, Sophie? If Vin has already told you that he and I are more than just friends, why did you flirt with him at the clubhouse?"

Sophie's lips turned down, making her look like a lost child. Clark suppressed a grin, masking her amusement at Sophie's immaturity.

"Are we good now?" Clark asked, seeking confirmation from Sophie that their discussion had been resolved.

"I suppose we are," Sophie replied grudgingly.

"Then, no more gossiping about my work. Understood?"

Clark felt proud of herself for handling the situation with Sophie maturely and calmly. Time would tell if Sophie kept her end of the deal and stopped spreading lies about her. She could focus on her work again without any more stressful confrontations with Sophie.

✶ ✶ ✶ ✶ ✶

CLARK DANCED ANTICIPATORILY TO the door at the sharp tap-tap of Vin's knock, the sound echoing through the deserted hallway. Vin and the others had been on one of their "business trips" for the past two days, and Clark had been lonely during their absence.

Her stomach tightened as Vin, with a seductive smirk playing on his lips, strolled into the apartment. She inhaled the rich sandalwood scent of his cologne, loving the earthy fragrance.

He swept her up in a bear hug, rendering her breathless as a gasp escaped her lips. "Missed you, babe," Vin said. "Did you miss me?"

Clark's voice cracked with emotion. "Yes!" she cried, wrapping her arms tightly around his neck.

"Show me how much," he demanded, carrying her to the bedroom.

✶ ✶ ✶ ✶ ✶

AFTER SOME TIME HAD passed, Clark found herself with her legs coiled around Vin's thighs, feeling his body rocking above hers. Despite their initial urgency in tearing each other's clothes off, Vin intentionally slowed down the pace to prolong their lovemaking.

"Love this, babe," he tenderly kissed the tip of her nose, eliciting a rush of warmth and affection in Clark's heart.

With a contented sigh, Clark closed her eyes. "Me too."

"Want to make this last, but I'm close," he said as his breathing grew ragged.

"Faster!" she gasped urgently.

"Want you to come first," he groaned.

"I'm nearly there."

Unwinding her legs, Clark arched her back and lifted her pelvis to create better friction. She took a deep breath, holding it in as her climax approached. Vin's movements intensified, driving deeper and faster.

Vin slumped on top of Clark. She luxuriated in the rush of warm air caressing her skin and the pulsating rhythm of his quickened heartbeat while her fingers glided through his hair's smooth, silken strands.

Vin gasped, "Jesus! Needed that, babe."

She let out a short scream when Vin rolled them over, placing her on top of him. Clark folded her arms and rested her chin on Vin's chest, looking at a satisfied man.

Vin crossed his arms behind his head in a relaxed pose. Clark admired the way his biceps flexed with the action. Everywhere she touched him, she felt the hardness of his muscles. His solid, powerful build resembled that of a heavyweight wrestler, akin to a monstrous behemoth in strength and size.

When he saw her distracted by his muscles, he teased, "Eyes up here, Shortcake."

"I can't help it. Your physique is spectacular," Clark confessed. "I'm sure you've received countless compliments from women."

"Not touching that one, babe," Vin replied with a grin.

Clark adored everything about Vin, from his compassionate nature to his devilish humor.

"I spoke to Sophie today," she announced proudly. "I told her to stop spreading rumors about me at work."

"What did Sophie say?" Vin rolled to his side, fully attentive to Clark.

"She denied it initially, but I discussed what happened with you last week. She confessed that she was humiliated by the whole incident."

Vin grumbled, "That's her problem. She shouldn't have flirted with me in front of you. It was disrespectful. Nobody disrespects my girl."

Clark tried to squirm away from Vin's firm hold as he gently nuzzled her neck. The scene was filled with laughter as they tumbled on the plush, tousled sheets. Pillows and the duvet slipped from the bed to the floor as they playfully wrestled with each other.

* * * * *

THE RELATIONSHIP BETWEEN THE three of them improved significantly over the next six weeks. This was primarily due to the incredibly satisfying sex, which strengthened their bond. Clark had always regarded sex as a deeply personal and private aspect of her life, keeping it separate from other areas of her relationships and identity. She had never experienced practices like multiple orgasms, double penetration, or dirty talk before.

Clark reveled in sexual activities such as role-playing and bondage. Gun enjoyed it when she explicitly expressed her desires in bed. He would withhold her pleasure if she were unclear about her needs and wants, leading her to beg him to finish what he had started desperately.

Clark, Vin, and Gun lounged on the clubhouse porch at the back, indulging in the crisp taste of cold beer and the fizziness of sparkling wine in the tranquil evening, the air rich with the scent of diesel and earth. The warm, balmy evening blanketed them, painting the sky with a kaleidoscope of colors as the sun dipped below the horizon. A few other men lingered in the yard, maintaining a respectful distance as they observed Vin and Gun enjoying a peaceful moment with Clark.

Gun was complaining about Simone, the tattoo shop receptionist. Her repetitive mistakes and unprofessional behavior were sending him around the bend. Simone was their third receptionist since Clark left.

His exasperation was evident as he said, "The position at the tattoo shop is still available, Red. Simone is a pain in my ass. She can't do a bloody thing right!"

Gun had little patience for mistakes. Unfortunately, Simone frequently arrived late to work, was disorganized, and often misplaced important documents and appointments, such as client files and scheduling details, which drove Vin and Gun crazy.

It was fortuitous that Gun suggested Clark return to work for him and Vin because she'd been considering changing jobs lately. Although Sophie and Clark were civil, Clark craved a little excitement, something the job at the library failed to offer. In contrast, the tattoo shop did offer that excitement. However, Clark had reservations about returning to the tattoo shop because of the previous issues that caused her to leave in the first place.

"Will you always be on my case if I accept the offer?"

"Probably," Gun replied without guile. "You meddle in our business, and yes, I'll bust your ass. You let Vin and me handle any potential trouble. Got it?"

She understood that returning to work at the tattoo shop would require her to step back and allow Vin and Gun to handle any issues that arose. It would be a true test to see if she could apply the conflict resolution strategies she had learned to navigate the challenges ahead.

"I'll think about it," she answered noncommittally, sipping her wine.

"You thinking about quitting your job at the library?" Vin asked.

"Yeah, I've been contemplating it for a couple of weeks now. The routine tasks at the library have started feeling monotonous, and I crave more challenges," Clark explained.

"Don't take too long to think about it, Red. The sooner you can start, the sooner I get my sanity back," Gun joked, giving her a snapshot of his dry humor.

"Understood, sir!" Clark said, saluting her lover with two fingers.

"Want to put you over my knee, Red. Are you ready for that?"

Clark saw the glimmer of desire in Gun's sharp gaze at her sassiness. Having already received a spanking on more than one occasion, Clark recalled the sharp sting of each slap, feeling embarrassed and aroused at the same time. The memory made her shiver.

Noticing her reaction, Gun replied with a sly smile, "Yeah, you're ready." His hand subtly traced a line along her spine.

With a swift and confident motion, Gun lifted Clark smoothly over his shoulder. He carried her towards the bedroom, the muffled sound of their footsteps echoing through the silent hallway.

✶ ✶ ✶ ✶ ✶

CLARK CRINGED AT THE singer's warbling on stage, annihilating one of her favorite songs. Clark felt obligated to be here because Charly insisted everyone participate in a karaoke night. She was seated between Vin and Gun. Charly had also persuaded Sara, Chad, Pen, Dom, and Jax to attend the karaoke night.

Clark smiled, sympathizing with Pen. While everyone else had come with their partners, Pen was dragged into coming without his best friend, Gage. Gage had prior plans, although he wouldn't share them. Clark suspected it was his excuse to get out of coming here tonight.

Charly introduced Jim and Mac, her friends from the karaoke bar, to everyone. Dom and Jax pushed three tables together, creating the largest group in the bar so everyone could sit together.

The atmosphere was lively, and the crowd erupted into applause, cheering the tone-deaf singer's efforts as he exited the stage. Jim then took the stage to sing Slim Dusty's *A Pub With No Beer*. The guys enthusiastically banged their hands on the table and cheered.

Excitedly, Charly leaned in from her spot at the edge of the group and shouted above the merriment. "What are you singing, Clark?"

Clark skimmed the song list at the karaoke bar and chose to sing Hozier's *Take Me To Church*.

Charly exclaimed with delight, "Oh! I love that song!"

Clark asked Charly, "Do you want to sing it together?"

Charly's eyes widened in surprise as she replied, "Sure, let's do it!"

This way, Clark wouldn't have to be on stage alone. The idea of stepping onto the karaoke bar stage with a sea of strangers watching her sing filled Clark with extreme nervousness.

Once on stage, Charly took Clark's hand and squeezed it. Clark took a deep breath, and both women approached the microphone, waiting for the deejay to cue them to start. When the words appeared on the screen, Clark's worries about the crowd faded as she focused on singing the song. Despite a hiccup at the start where she missed her cue, Clark swiftly recovered and joined Charly in singing along.

As Vin had predicted, Charly's talent as a singer was undeniable. Together, they were an unstoppable force, as evidenced by the thunderous cheers and wolf whistles throughout the song.

"Fuck, babe. That was brilliant!" Vin praised Clark, kissing her.

"Thanks, Vin. Are you performing next?"

"Yeah. Jax and I are doing *You Shook Me All Night Long*!" he replied enthusiastically.

Clark couldn't wait to hear them sing. Charly had warned her earlier that Jax was also an AC/DC fan.

As the pair finally took the stage, their presence ignited a frenzy among the crowd, stirring up an electric atmosphere. Their performance captivated the audience more with their infectious enthusiasm and stage presence than with their vocal precision. Their performance set the audience on fire, eliciting a wild and energetic response.

The night was a success, and Clark was pleased she came. She was proud of being brave enough to sing on stage with Charly.

While relaxing in her chair, Clark swayed to the slow rhythm of Mac's rendition of *I Walk The Line* by Johnny Cash. She observed the quiet crowd around her. From the corner of her eye, Clark noticed Pen intently watching someone in the room. Her eyes turned to see who he was staring at.

Two young guys and two women were having a lively conversation at the bar. The two brunettes were flirting with the males, but a third woman stood nearby, looking slightly bored. She was also dressed casually, wearing jeans and a plaid shirt. In contrast, her friends were dressed to the nines in form-fitting, sexy dresses.

The blonde appeared out of place at first, but upon closer inspection, Clark noticed her captivating features, accentuated by her partially hidden face under a blond bob.

Looking back at Pen, Clark could now see that he was watching the blonde. He seemed oblivious to anything but her as she stood at the bar, twirling her bottle, wiping the condensation, and playing with the label on the glass.

Clark observed Pen watching the woman. Pen was usually distant and aloof, maintaining an invisible wall between himself and females. With the brothers, though, he was an entirely different person—cracking jokes, sharing witty remarks, and demonstrating a knack for improvisation, which Clark had witnessed firsthand.

"Mel! Let's go," shouted her friend as she and three others walked towards the exit.

Mel picked up her bottle, drank the last remnants of her drink, and followed her friends out. Clark grinned when she saw Pen's gaze follow the woman until she disappeared through the door. Clark felt disappointed that Pen failed to pursue the woman he had shown an interest in.

FOURTEEN

When Clark entered the shop, she was hit with the familiar smell of disinfectant, tattoo ink, and latex gloves. After a nine-month absence, it was her second day back at Blood Tattoos. Kim and Jacko were thrilled to see her, welcoming her with tight hugs and emphatic requests not to leave again.

Clark soon understood what Vin and Gun had been complaining about when they said Simone's disorganization was causing issues. She had spent most of yesterday refiling invoices and paying outstanding bills accumulated over the past several months. Clark reviewed the appointment schedule and made a few phone calls to clients to reschedule their appointments, ensuring there were no double bookings or missed appointments. After checking the stock in the storeroom, she ordered basic supplies like cleaning products, gloves, and plastic wrap. Vin and Gun handled tattooing machines, inks, and needles.

Clark felt valued by her colleagues because of the compliments she received on her efficient management and smooth transition back into her job. Experiencing a new sensation of being needed and capable of fulfilling her duties successfully was invigorating for Clark.

Vin was already in the office, as evidenced by the glow of light peeking from under the door. He must have heard her arrive as the office door opened, and a tall, handsome man with a broad grin came striding out.

"Morning, Shortcake," Vin greeted happily, planting a quick peck on her lips.

Clark's lips tingled from the soft kiss. Thankfully, they were the only two in the shop, allowing for a private moment. Any minute now, Clark expected to see Kim and Jacko arrive. Impulsively, she reached up and kissed him once more. Clark realized her mistake when Vin interpreted this as a signal to pull her closer and kiss her passionately.

"All right, you two. Enough of that nonsense," joked Jacko as he and Kim entered the shop. A sudden gust of wind rushed in, swirling a pile of dead leaves around the shop.

Kim grimaced in disgust, exclaiming, "Ew!"

"What?" exclaimed Clark, her forehead wrinkling in surprise.

"Not you, Clark. Vin," she said, winking at Clark flirtatiously.

"Yo, enough of that, Kim. This is *my* woman," Vin interrupted, moving away from Clark.

"You two here to canoodle or work?" Jacko griped good-naturedly, throwing Clark a sly sideways glance.

Clark got out a broom and began sweeping up the dead leaves. It was time to get back to work.

✳ ✳ ✳ ✳ ✳

"THE CHICKEN RISOTTO WAS delicious, Rachel. Since you cooked tonight, I'll stack the dishwasher," Clark offered, sliding back her chair and collecting their plates.

After loading the dishwasher with plates, cups, and cutlery, Clark placed the washing tablet in the dishwasher's detergent holder and closed the door. Once the machine was humming away, Clark entered the living room. Rachel was sitting on the couch with her legs tucked under, looking down at her phone with a focused expression while scrolling through messages.

"Rachel, put your phone away. We need to chat," Clark ordered, standing with her hands on her hips.

Her roommate must have been expecting this conversation because she put her phone down with a sigh. Rachel uncrossed her legs, leaned back, and patiently waited for Clark to speak.

Clark sank into the soft cushions on the other side of the comfortable couch, a hopeful smile playing on her lips. "Let's have it. I want to know what's happening with you and my brother," Clark prompted.

Clark leaned back on the other side of the comfortable couch, settling in to hear some good news.

Rachel revealed almost shyly, "I guess it's okay to tell you now. Corey and I are together. We like each other and want to see where this takes us."

"You two are very different. How do you feel about Corey's take-charge personality? He tends to make decisions without consulting you and likes to be in control."

Having personally experienced it, Clark was fully aware of this fact. As she grew older, she craved independence in making decisions by taking control of where she lived and being able to manage her finances, as well as the various responsibilities and activities that grown-ups engage in. Unfortunately, like the big brother he was, Corey liked to dictate her actions without any intended maliciousness and make choices that clashed with her own.

Clark distinctly remembered the day she and Archer decided to reveal their feelings for each other to the family. Corey vehemently opposed their relationship due to their upbringing in the same household. Even though they weren't biologically related, everyone saw them as siblings.

"I haven't seen that side of Corey. He's charming, patient, and funny. And super-hot!" Rachel added with a schoolgirl giggle.

"That's all true, Rach. He's got a lot of love to give. And he's brilliant. I hit the sibling jackpot with Corey."

Clark's heart swelled with joy at Rachel and Corey finding happiness together. She couldn't wait for the day when she could fondly call Rachel her sister.

"I'm meeting your parents for the first time on Saturday," Rachel said worriedly to Clark.

"You've got nothing to worry about, Rach. Mom and Dad are the best parents ever. They'll love you and welcome you with open arms, just like they did with me," said Clark.

"That's what Corey says. It's just meeting them for the first time, you know. I'm nervous about what they'll think of me—my fashion sense, my way of speaking. I don't always have a filter when expressing my thoughts. I'm afraid I'll say something to upset them." Worry etched across her face; Rachel nervously bit her lower lip.

"They won't care about that; they value authenticity over formality. Mom and Dad are incredibly open-minded about many things. They were supportive of Archer's and my relationship despite initial doubts. And remember when Dad surprised me with tickets to that indie music festival in the city?"

"I hope they accept me," she murmured timidly.

Clark patted Rachel on the shoulder. She told her not to fret so much and reassured her that her family was hospitable. If Corey liked Rachel, her parents would love her because they trusted Corey's judgment.

✳ ✳ ✳ ✳ ✳

"HI, CARRIE." CLARK HAD arrived at the clubhouse and wandered to the back to see Carrie sitting at a table in the corner. Nolan and Jake were playing in the gated playground beside the garage, surrounded by tall trees and wildflowers. Sara was working in the office nearby.

Carrie, the tall, slim blonde with piercing blue eyes, returned a warm and welcoming smile. "Hi, Clark. Are you looking for Vin and Gun?"

Vin and Gun were in the next town on what they called "official business." They were expected to arrive in about an hour after completing their business.

"I know they're not here yet. They told me, or more accurately, ordered me to wait here for them," she said, flashing her dimples. "Are you babysitting?" She nodded towards the boys huddled together, looking at the ground. From across the table, Clark couldn't see what the boys were studying because they had their heads together, blocking her view.

"Look what I found!" shouted Jake, running to Carrie, holding something in his palm.

"What is it?" Carrie asked, curious.

Clark was also interested in seeing what the boys had found. When Jake opened his hand, a slimy, brown earthworm squirmed.

"It's a worm," Jake said excitedly, jumping up and down. "I'm gonna put it in my bug catcher."

"What happened to the cockroach?" Clark asked, hoping Jake had let it go by now.

"It died," Jake pouted, looking upset.

Clark and Carrie exchanged a quick, amused glance before turning to Jake with sympathetic expressions.

"I told him that cockroaches don't live long, but he didn't believe me," Nolan interjected, looking at Jake with a knowing look.

"It was only a baby cockroach," the four-year-old protested, folding his arms. He reminded Clark of his dad, Dom.

"That thing was huge," argued Clark, shuddering at the memory.

"Did you know that earthworms breathe through their skin?" Nolan asked Clark.

"No. I didn't," she smiled at the studious-looking young boy wearing black glasses.

"They can breathe underwater, too," he informed her, confirming Nolan's expertise. "And do you know why they come up to the surface when it rains?"

Clark shook her head, completely engrossed in the fascinating facts Nolan shared.

"It's because the rain sounds like predators, so they come up to escape," he explained earnestly.

"Wow! I had no idea," Clark exclaimed, impressed by Sara's son's vast knowledge.

"Dad!" Nolan cried happily. His eyes widened with excitement as he gazed past Clark's head towards the approaching figures.

Excitedly, he ran across the graveled yard and leaped into his dad's arms.

"Hey, Nolan," Chad said with a laugh, ruffling his son's hair.

"Daddy!" Jake giggled, running to Dom, his short legs pumping as fast as they could.

Dom crouched down, lifted his son into his arms, and gave him a big, wet kiss on the cheek.

A tingling sensation, like a trail of tiny electric sparks, started at the base of her spine and slowly traveled up to her scalp. Clark's dimples deepened as she spotted Vin and Gun heading towards her, her heart racing excitedly. She felt the urge to sprint towards them, like Nolan and Jake, but hesitated, fearing it would seem overly sentimental. She remained in her seat, torn between the desire to join them and the need to maintain her composure patiently.

Clark noticed Carrie stiffen in her peripheral vision when Rocky, with his usual nonchalant gait, came ambling down the steps.

This was the second time Clark had observed a change in Carrie's demeanor because of Rocky. After spending some time with Vin and Gun, she intended to focus on uncovering the truth about Carrie's feelings towards the much older biker and the nature of their relationship.

"Shortcake," Vin crooned, sweeping her up in his arms.

"Hi," Clark murmured breathlessly, aware that Gun was approaching them.

She lifted her mouth for a kiss from Gun while still wrapped in Vin's embrace.

"You made me wait forever," she complained, pouting prettily.

Vin seized the moment to kiss her puckered lips.

In his usual straightforward manner, Gun proposed a solution he believed would resolve everything. "Do you need some loving?"

Clark understood his implication perfectly, and her body tingled with anticipation. "I *would like* some loving. Yes."

"I'll make you feel better," Gun promised, nudging her toward the bedroom.

✶ ✶ ✶ ✶ ✶

CLARK ENTERED THE KITCHEN and found her target. Carrie stood at the sink, peeling potatoes with a silver peeler. She was assisting in preparing the potato bake for tonight's dinner. Carrie had her back to Clark as the evening sun went down, casting an almost angelic glow around her. Carrie was taller than Clark and typically wore denim shorts, frilly tops, and sneakers.

"Hey, Carrie. I've been looking everywhere for you," Clark said, automatically grabbing a peeler and picking up a potato to help Carrie.

The younger woman smiled warmly as she continued peeling, her eyes crinkling with gratitude. "Oh, yeah? What did you want to see me for?"

Clark paused, eager to gauge Carrie's reaction, waiting for her to stop peeling and meet her gaze. The tactic worked.

"Rocky?" Clark posed the name as a question to see Carrie's reaction. She didn't have to wait long for the rosy blush in Carrie's cheeks to appear.

"Nothing is going on between Rocky and me," she denied a little too quickly.

"Then why do you get tense whenever he's around or his name is mentioned?"

"No, I do not," Carrie adamantly denied, causing her shoulder-length blonde hair to sway with the denial.

"Carrie!" Clark gently admonished. "You're talking to me, the woman who had a huge crush on her bosses for months and never said anything. I know when someone hides their feelings because I did the same thing."

"Honestly, Clark, it's not like that. I have feelings for Rocky, but we're just friends." The sweet, demure woman lowered her eyes, but Clark caught their sadness. "He'd never be interested in someone like me," she whispered sadly.

Clark didn't know the exact reason why Rocky rejected her. All she knew was that he was missing out on a kind and caring person.

"Men are idiots," Clark chuckled. "Look how long it took Gun and Vin to confess their feelings to me."

"It's not every day that the guys here have romantic relationships with women outside the Club. I guess your situation is different, just like Dom and Jax's situation with Charly."

"Could Rocky not be showing interest because of the age difference?"

Perhaps he thought Carrie was too young for him. It's not that Carrie was immature; in fact, she displayed remarkable maturity for a twenty-three-year-old woman.

"I … perhaps," Carrie stuttered.

Clark caught the hesitation in Carrie's voice, her keen ears picking up on its subtle tremor. Carrie and Rocky had a more profound connection than was initially apparent.

"What are you hiding from me?" Clark persisted, intent on unraveling the truth.

Carrie nervously licked her lips. "Did Charly ever say anything about me?"

Pursing her lips in recollection, Clark recalled the countless times she and Charly had shared stories over coffee. "Nothing bad. She always says positive things about you. Charly holds you in high regard and looks up to you. Why?"

"It was Charly who saved me from an abusive situation," Carrie stated quietly, her eyes downcast and fingers fidgeting, almost hesitant to admit it. "If it weren't for her, I'd still be with one of the men who abused me, trapped in a cycle of fear and pain."

Carrie's disclosure left Clark speechless, and she reached out with her hand in silent support.

"Which man?" Clark felt so angry on behalf of Carrie that she had to remind herself to take deep breaths.

"His name was Bolt, but he's no longer part of the Club. The Club confiscated his vest when they discovered the abuse he was inflicting on me. They only found out because Charly was trying to help me escape from the clubhouse where I was being abused."

Clark was pleased to see a glimmer of a smile as Carrie mentioned Charly's name.

"How did she do that?"

"She woke me up in the early morning, although it was hard to sleep back then. The slightest noise would jolt me awake in terror, fearing that Bolt would hurt me again.

When she realized I was naked, Charly gave me her clothes, and together, we quietly made our way outside without alerting Bolt. Then, I helped her carry a chair over to the back gate for a makeshift ladder since it was locked. Charly climbed over first, then landed in Dom's arms."

When recounting the last part of her traumatic experience, Carrie let out a low chuckle as if remembering something funny from that chaotic moment.

Suddenly, Clark understood why Carrie thought Rocky only wanted to be friends with her. Clark wondered if Rocky's behavior stemmed from concern for Carrie's well-being or their age difference, making it difficult for him to view Carrie romantically.

"Is that why you think Rocky is not interested in a relationship with you? Because of your history with Bolt?"

Carrie nodded glumly.

It was a tragedy that someone as kind-hearted and lovely as Carrie felt this way about herself. Clark had seen how she cared for the boys, helped in the kitchen and with chores, and served diligently at the bar. Carrie performed all these tasks without complaining.

* * * * *

"THEN JAKE SUDDENLY APPEARED with filthy hands and clothes, his bug catcher teeming with about fifty squirming earthworms. He dug up the garden searching for the wriggly little things, creating piles of dirt and holes everywhere."

Charly erupted in laughter at the memory, and Clark joined in. She pictured Jake looking pleased with himself, covered in dirt, his bug catcher in hand, and the earthworms squirming inside.

"He loves those bugs," Clark remarked, remembering Jake's enthusiasm for the creatures at the clubhouse.

"Tell me about it," Charly said, grimacing. "On one occasion, he even caught a redback spider. I was out of my mind, worried that the spider had bitten him, but Jake said he used a stick to catch it."

The two women sat outside a local café, enjoying a hot cappuccino. The chocolatey froth tempted Clark's taste buds. She inhaled the delicious aroma of the Arabian coffee beans. The clock had just struck six in the evening, filling the air with the distant chimes of the nearby church bell. The street exuded a sense of serenity, with the aroma of freshly baked bread wafting from the bakery and a few streetlights illuminating the evening sky. Only a handful of people scurried along, their footsteps echoing softly as they completed their last-minute shopping.

After finishing work for the day, Clark arranged to meet Charly, who was already at the café across the road from Blood Tattoos. Kim and Jacko had gone home, but Gun stayed behind in his office, likely engrossed in his bookkeeping tasks.

Charly said, grinning, "Rachel said that the dinner at your parents' place went well the other night. She was anxious because she wanted to impress your parents. Rachel is usually comfortable talking to anyone. I always see her talking easily with strangers on the street."

"I know," agreed Clark. "She wanted to make a good impression.

I told her not to worry because my parents would love her. Corey has never taken a girlfriend home because he has never been serious about anyone. I'm glad he chose Rachel."

"Me too. Your brother couldn't find a better girlfriend. Rachel is incredibly kind and compassionate. Did you know she volunteers at the homeless shelter next to the Baptist Church? Any man would be lucky to be with her," praised Charly.

Clark chuckled. "Looks like the admiration is mutual, huh? Cause that's what she says about you."

Clark looked up and noticed a black van with tinted windows parked in front of the tattoo shop. Three ominous figures, their faces obscured by dark hoods and their movements silent as shadows, emerged, sending a shiver down Clark's spine. The men moved with calculated precision, slipping silently through the shop's entrance.

"Charly!" Clark gasped, hastily pushing back her chair, her eyes widening with fear as she spoke. "Three guys just went into the tattoo shop where Gun is. They got out of that black van across the street. Take a photo of it and see if you can get the license plate. I don't have a good feeling about this. When you've done that, call Dom and the others and get them down here immediately," Clark instructed urgently.

"What are you going to do?" Charly unzipped her bag to get out her phone and take a photo of the van.

"I'm going to go in and see what's happening."

"No, Clark, you mustn't. It's too dangerous," begged Charly.

Suddenly, a commotion shattered the peaceful evening, with frantic shouts echoing inside the shop. One man opened the door while two others forcefully dragged Gun outside. Gun's face was covered with a hood, and his struggles were in vain as he fought against their grip.

Gun was forced into the van, and the door slammed shut. The driver spun the wheels, leaving skid marks on the road.

"Charly, I need your keys!" demanded Clark.

Clark's body went numb, consumed by the single-minded mission to rescue Gun. She was resolute in pursuing them; nothing could sway her.

"Clark, you can't! Do you even know how to drive?" Charly asked, visibly trembling.

"Yes," Clark responded without thinking. Her sole purpose was to track down Gun. Although she didn't have a driver's license, Clark had keenly observed enough driving to understand the fundamentals. Fueled by her fear for Gun and anxious to chase down the van, she was confident she could manage.

Charly reluctantly passed her keys to Clark, her face contorted with a worried frown.

"I'll call Shane, too. He's the detective who found me when I was abducted," Charly reminded Clark, the words rushing out.

Clutching the keys tightly, Clark dashed towards Charly's car, determined to follow them.

She quickly clicked the seatbelt in and mentally checked off each step: ignition, clutch, handbrake, shift gears, check mirrors. Feeling the engine's power beneath her, Clark cheered as the car slowly moved forward. After checking the side mirror and confirming that there were no approaching vehicles, she accelerated. She pressed her foot down on the accelerator, going faster than the speed limit. Time was of the essence; it was an emergency, and she needed to hurry.

Clark's heart raced as she strained her eyes to spot the elusive black van, adrenaline coursing through her veins. Merging into highway traffic, she realized she had left the town behind. Clark pressed harder on the accelerator to catch up to the van. She cried in relief when she saw it up ahead. The van momentarily disappeared as the road twisted and turned with hills. Afraid of losing sight, Clark frantically checked the speedometer. Her heart pounded as she realized she exceeded the speed limit by almost double. When she spotted the van ahead, Clark eased off the accelerator, worried about having a potential collision or getting stopped by the police.

Clark was grateful that there were a couple of other cars on the highway, allowing her to stay two cars behind the van in pursuit. She had to be careful not to get caught following them; the entire mission could be compromised if she was spotted. Clark's stomach dropped when the van turned left onto a dirt road. She deliberately slowed down, creating a greater distance between them. She figured she could track their movements easily because it was a straight, single dirt road, providing clear visibility and making it easier to follow discreetly. She slowed to a stop until the black shape disappeared. When the van was out of sight, the car crawled forward to continue following them.

After driving another ten miles, Clark finally spotted an old, run-down shack hidden among the overgrown trees. The car remained hidden behind the bushes, so she carefully opened the door and got out for a better view.

The van parked in front of the building, and the door slid open. Two men got out, pulling a now unconscious Gun with them, his feet dragging on the ground, leaving deep grooves in the dirt. Clark's heart was racing way too fast, but she couldn't stop worrying about his condition, uncertain if he was still alive.

Clark waited impatiently until the men shut the door to the shack before she parked Charly's car further into the bushes. Stealthily moving through the shadows outside the building, Clark cautiously crept up to a window on the side of the shack. She could hear raised voices inside but didn't want to peer into the window yet, afraid of being seen.

Cork's voice boomed as he directed accusations at Gun, claiming that Gun had been involved with his "bitch". He held Gun responsible for disrupting his drug connections and orchestrating his expulsion from the Club. Clark seethed with anger at Cork's tirade of vitriol against Gun. Each groan of pain from Gun, accompanied by the sickening sound of Cork's blows, made Clark cringe involuntarily, her heart aching with each distressing noise. But it meant that Gun was still alive.

It seemed like a lifetime before Cork stopped his attack on Gun. Clark had to contain her rage and wait for the right moment to move. She couldn't be seen. Otherwise, they'd both be in trouble. She was here to rescue Gun, and that was her only goal.

Clark waited for over an hour, pressing her ear against the cold, rough siding of the house, straining to catch every sound from within. Murmurs from the three men filled the air, punctuated by the occasional groan from Gun. There was a moment when he remained quiet for an unnervingly long time, leading Clark to fear the worst—that he might be dead. Her shoulders relaxed as Gun's groans broke the silence once more. Clark surmised that he must have lost consciousness during that time.

Her ears perked when she heard the rumble of an engine. From her position behind the siding of the house, Clark watched as the van drove away. Risking a look, she peered through the window, but her heart sank when she saw someone still inside with Gun. He sat in an old, rickety chair, tapping his gun against the side of his head with a menacing grin as he spoke to Gun. The man had removed his ski mask, revealing a scar above his right eyebrow. Clark instantly recognized him as one of the assailants who had attacked Gun and Vin at the tattoo shop.

Her heart clenched as she glanced over, stifling a gasp at the heartbreaking sight of Gun slumped on the floor, his hands tightly bound behind his back. The most harrowing sight was his face, a canvas of bruises and blood, each mark telling a tale of violence and pain. Gun's left eye was swollen shut, a stark reminder of the brutality he had endured.

Clark immediately began searching for a makeshift weapon; she needed something to defend herself with. As she crept around the building's perimeter, she adjusted her eyes to the darkness, listening intently for any signs of movement. Pulling out her phone, Clark switched on the flashlight to illuminate the ground, avoiding any accidental beams of light that could give away her position. She was relieved when she discovered a rusted steel pole among the junk near the back door. Clark lifted the branches and sheets of corrugated iron with great care, straining to extract the pole without making a sound. As she tested it in her hands, she assessed its strength, believing it could be effective if she applied enough force in her strike.

Now, she had to distract the assailant. Walking up the steps to the front porch, she froze when the wood creaked beneath her shoes. After cautiously tapping the far-right window with the steel pole, she swiftly darted to the left side of the house, keeping to the shadows. Heart pounding in her chest, she pressed herself against the corner, each beat a drumming reminder of the lurking danger.

✳ ✳ ✳ ✳ ✳

GUN LIFTED HIS HEAD, groaning in excruciating pain as his headache intensified, pulsating through his skull. His left eye throbbed relentlessly as if protesting its mistreatment, and he was convinced that he had sustained at least a couple of cracked ribs. Cork had relished every brutal blow he landed, enjoying Gun's pained reactions as his body tensed with each strike. His hands were securely bound, rendering him utterly defenseless.

Accusingly, Binge asked, "What the hell was that noise? Was it you, Gun? Playing tricks on me, son?" as he aimed his weapon at him.

With tremendous effort, Gun managed to whisper, "No," his whole body engulfed in pain.

After checking that Gun was still tied up, Binge asked, "Then what was it?" He stood by the window, attempting to look out into the darkness, but could only see his reflection.

"You stay here. Got it? Yeah. You won't go anywhere," he cackled, his words dripping with malice as he pointed out Gun's immobility.

Gun watched as Binge slowly opened the door and peered out. "Who's there?" he shouted. When no one answered, he opened the door wider and stepped onto the porch, his heavy tread leaving a trail of squeaks on the old wooden floor.

Binge returned to grab his phone to use its flashlight. "Can't fucking see two feet in front of me," he complained and left again.

Gun heard the distinct sounds of creaking wood, rustling leaves, and twigs crackling under Binge's solid weight as he moved. The air thickened with an unsettling stillness, shrouded in an eerie silence. Gun strained to listen, trying to identify who could be out there. Maybe it was a hungry animal hunting for food.

Suddenly, Gun heard a thump, an "oomph," and twigs crackling as if someone were running. His senses were acutely attuned, bracing himself for whatever awaited him within its shadowy depths. He couldn't hear Binge anymore and wondered if someone had got to him. Gun tried to sit up, but the sharp pain shooting through his side forced him to remain still.

Then Clark stood in the doorway like an apparition. His heart pounded with joy at the sight of her, but then fear gripped him as he realized the danger she had exposed herself to.

"Clark," he said, groaning at the pain in his injured side.

Clark rushed to his side, her face filled with concern at the sight of his injuries. She attempted to help him up, but he was in too much pain. "Gun, we need to go now! I don't know how long the guy will be out cold. Please, try to get up," Clark pleaded.

Determined not to endanger Clark further, Gun got up with Clark's help despite his excruciating pain. Initially leaning heavily on her for support, Gun straightened up and realized he could move more than anticipated. Limping, he followed her outside.

They walked past Binge's unconscious body, the smell of damp earth in the air, and made their way to the car parked behind the bushes.

"I didn't know you had a license," Gun commented to Clark as she put the key in the ignition.

"I don't," she grinned mischievously at him, momentarily relieving the tension of the dangerous situation.

That was until Gun heard Binge's growl behind them. Suddenly, a gunshot echoed through the air, accompanied by the sharp clang of metal striking metal.

"Hurry, go, Clark!" Gun shouted urgently.

Clark swiftly pressed the accelerator, the tires kicking up a swirling cloud of dust as they raced down the narrow dirt track. Gun's head jerked back as the car accelerated suddenly, another sharp pain shooting through his body, causing him to grit his teeth in agony and curse silently under his breath.

"Sorry, Gun," Clark apologized, her brow furrowed in worry and guilt.

"I'm all right, Red. Just keep driving. Get us as far away from here as possible."

✶ ✶ ✶ ✶ ✶

AFTER CALLING DOM, CHARLY waited for the familiar Jeep to pick her up. The car screeched to a stop at the curb, and Dom and Jax raced towards her. Behind their vehicle, a line of motorcycles was parked.

Vin was the first to reach her, his face twisted with anger and fear.

"Where is she, Charly? Where did Clark go?" he barked, gripping his hair in frustration.

Charly understood his fear and didn't take his gruff tone personally. He was scared for Clark and Gun's safety.

"She headed towards the highway, following the black van."

"Jesus Christ!" he exclaimed, panic evident in his voice. "This can't be happening."

"Vin, we've tracked Charly's car. We're heading there now," Dom informed him as he pulled Charly close. "Charls, go back to the clubhouse with Pen," he instructed her.

"But what about Clark and Gun? I can't just leave without knowing they're safe!"

Jax stepped closer to her. "Babe, go with Pen—trust Dom's plan. We'll find Clark and Gun," he reassured her.

✳ ✳ ✳ ✳ ✳

"WHERE IS CLARK?" VIN asked, his heart pounding with fear for both Clark and Gun.

"About twenty-five miles east of Greenville. It'll probably take us twenty minutes to get there if we hurry," Dom advised as he walked back to the Jeep. "Charly said she contacted Detective Carter so that Jax will give him the location on our way there."

Vin mounted his motorcycle and followed closely behind the vehicle. Resisting the urge to accelerate and risking a dangerous collision required every ounce of strength and self-discipline he possessed. He felt a surge of adrenaline tempting him to throttle up to full speed and leave everything behind in a blur of motion. Unfortunately, Vin didn't have the precise location, which compelled him to maintain a safe distance behind Dom's Jeep.

Dom slowed down his vehicle and indicated to turn left. Consumed by the overpowering urge to grab Clark and Gun, hold them tightly, and never let go, Vin almost missed the pothole before him. He quickly swerved his motorcycle to avoid it.

Up ahead, Vin recognized Charly's car coming towards them. As he trailed behind Dom, a sense of unease crept in as Vin wondered who was behind the wheel of Charly's car. The overwhelming joy that swept through Vin's heart at the sight of Gun and Clark approaching was unlike anything he had ever felt. Vin's heart sank as he noticed the blood and dark bruises marring his brother's face.

As soon as all the vehicles were stopped, Vin jumped off his motorcycle. He deftly kicked the stand to keep it upright and sprinted towards Clark and Gun. Dom and Jax immediately exited their vehicle, followed by Gage, Achilles, Chad, and Rocky.

Vin rounded the car to Gun's side to check on his brother.

"Gun," he croaked, trying to keep his emotions in check. "You all right?"

"I'll survive," he grinned sheepishly. "Thanks to this beautiful woman," he said, nodding towards Clark.

Clark opened the car door and raced towards Vin, burying her head in his chest and hugging him tightly. It was like her adrenaline tanked, and a torrent of tears swept her away. Vin gathered Clark in his arms and cradled her until her sobs subsided. His girl was a heroine. Clark's courageous spirit saved Gun from an unknown fate. The thought deeply unsettled him.

"It was Cork and two other men," Clark revealed when her tears dried up. "One of them is still there, and he has a gun."

"Binge," Gun called from inside the car.

"Dom, did you hear that?"

Dom nodded and opened the Jeep's trunk. He took out several Glock 17 firearms and passed one to each man.

Achilles outlined the plan: divide and conquer, with each group approaching the target from a different angle.

"Clark, you need to get Gun to the hospital immediately," he said urgently.

Vin observed Clark's reaction and was relieved to see her acquiesce.

"Dom and Jax, you go to the right. Vin, you're with me. Chad, Gage, and Rocky, your task is to flank Binge from the rear. Conceal yourselves behind the trees and remain vigilant until you hear my signal before acting. Understood?"

The group dispersed swiftly, each member stealthily moving to their designated positions.

Vin led Achilles to the front of the rundown old shack. They took cover behind a massive oak tree, which provided plenty of protection.

"I can see a silhouette in the window from the light on his screen. He's calling someone, probably reaching out to Cork," Vin informed him.

"All right, I'll text Chad and instruct him to create a distraction from the back. You let Dom know that we'll enter from the front. With caution," he said, emphasizing the last two words.

Vin and Achilles waited impatiently for Chad to distract Binge from the front, diverting his attention before they approached.

A distant bird call echoed as Vin listened, signaling Chad's role in the plan with the distinctive cawing sound of a crow, a prearranged signal for his part in the operation. He saw Binge, looking very twitchy and nervous, crossing the room to peer out the back window. Vin wondered if Binge knew he was trapped.

"Fuck!" he said as the sound of police sirens grew louder.

Achilles released a sharp, two-fingered whistle to signal the others to halt their plan. They couldn't rush into the shack with their guns drawn, especially with the police presence nearby. Within minutes, the others gathered around, the sound of rustling leaves filling the air.

Dom commanded, "Hand over your guns." Since they weren't supposed to own firearms, Dom swiftly returned to his vehicle to conceal them.

Four police cars, their sirens blaring and red and blue lights flashing, converged at the front of the shack, creating a chaotic scene. Vin stepped out from behind the tree with his arms raised in surrender, waiting for Detective Carter to recognize him.

"Vin!" Detective Carter called from inside the police car, "Stay where you are. Don't come out. Where are they?"

"There's only one male. His name is Binge. He's inside, and he's armed. He's also scared shitless!" Vin shouted from the cover of the tree.

The men stayed where they were and left the task of arresting Binge to the police. It took over an hour for Binge, the coward, to come outside after the police negotiator advised him that the situation could only end well if he came out voluntarily and surrendered his weapon.

Binge was taken into police custody, and Detective Shane Carter approached Vin.

"What the hell happened?" Shane asked. "Charly said that Gun was abducted. Where is he?"

"Clark took him to the hospital. She saved him, Shane," Vin said, his throat choking up with emotion.

Detective Carter and the MC had established a truce, primarily due to their shared connection with Charly. Additionally, Shane played a crucial role in rescuing Charly from Sol and was a significant presence during her childhood. In the eyes of the MC, that made Shane a good man in their books. Furthermore, Shane and his wife, Tessa, had made several visits to the lodge, where the MC embraced them as part of the family.

Shane remarked, "It appears the women are the true heroines," injecting a sense of relief into the grim situation.

"You're not wrong," Vin replied, feeling a sense of peace for the first time since learning about the abduction of his best friend.

"What about the other men? Did they get away?" Shane asked, getting out his notebook.

"Yeah," Vin replied, sweeping a hand through his hair and sighing. "Cork and Farmer are the other men, and I have no idea where they are now."

"Would you mind bringing Clark in later so I can get more details from her? I'll also need to talk to everyone here, including you, to gather information about the incident and statements for the police investigation."

✳ ✳ ✳ ✳ ✳

"WHAT DID YOU TELL Shane?" Achilles asked after Shane left.

If one didn't know Achilles, people would find the club president daunting. The hard-nosed man exuded a formidable and fearsome presence, which made him a perfect leader. Vin had known Achilles for most of his life and considered him a brother, friend, and ally.

"Not much. Just their names. He wants us to go into the police station later."

"All of us?" Achilles scowled, showing his frustration. "Shit!" he exclaimed loudly in response to Vin's confirmation.

Achilles looked at Vin gravely. "This stays between us. Those two will probably go underground for a while, but I'll put Cole on it. See if he can get their location. Handling this situation is our responsibility," Achilles said seriously. "They hurt one of our brothers—twice. That's unforgivable."

Vin wholeheartedly agreed with Achilles. This wasn't a job for the police. Vin and the others would have to share some details to make it look like they were cooperating. The only people he wouldn't involve were Clark and Charly. But they didn't know much anyway, as they were not privy to Club business affairs. Whatever information they shared would be minimal.

<h1 style="text-align:center">FIFTEEN</h1>

The overpowering scent of antiseptic in the hospital filled Clark's nostrils. Her trembling hands served as a constant reminder of the day's harrowing events. She couldn't help but entertain the "what ifs" until she forced herself to focus on the present and be grateful that Gun was alive.

The sound of the hospital's emergency sliding doors opening caught Clark's attention, making her look up anxiously. She stood up when she saw Vin and the rest of the MC were safe. Vin held her tightly, and they stayed that way for several minutes, the reality of the situation hitting her hard. Today, Gun could have been killed.

Vin softly inquired about Gun's condition, his cool breath gently stirring strands of her hair. Clark had repeatedly asked the desk clerk when she could see Gun, but no one could tell her.

"I haven't been able to see him or get any information. What about you? Did you get the guy?"

"Binge? Yeah, the police arrested him."

"Who called the police?" Clark asked, her brow creased in confusion.

"Charly. She called Detective Carter. He's like a father figure to her. She trusts him, so we trust him, too," Vin confessed.

Charly rushed through the hospital doors, followed closely by Sara and Carrie. She ran up to Dom and Jax while Sara ran to Chad. Carrie stood back, observing the animated crowd timidly. Occasionally,

Clark's eyes snuck a peek at Rocky. Her worries faded when she caught Rocky's gaze fixated on Carrie, his expression reminiscent of a predator eyeing its prey with intensity and anticipation. A smile tugged at her lips. Perhaps Rocky wasn't as indifferent as he seemed. Clark glanced at Carrie to check her reaction, but the young blonde was engrossed in conversation with Sara and Chad, unaware of his scrutiny.

A young doctor in a white coat came out, looking for Clark. Anxious to find out about Gun's condition, Clark hurriedly approached the doctor, her heart racing with worry.

"Is Gun going to be okay?" Clark asked, biting her bottom lip.

"Yes. He has some broken ribs, a fractured eye socket, and extensive bruising. These things will heal with time," the doctor explained patiently.

"Can we see him now?" Vin asked.

The doctor looked at the crowd gathered and said, "You can only see him briefly. He's heavily sedated to manage his pain and ensure he's comfortable. He won't be conscious for too much longer."

Pausing at the threshold of Gun's room, Clark cautiously peered inside, noticing him lying on the bed with closed eyes and a bandaged chest. His eye was still a deep shade of purple, visibly swollen, with several lacerations around his lips and cheek, painting a vivid picture of his injuries. Gun opened his eyes before she reached him, indicating that he must have sensed her presence.

Clark clasped Gun's hand with both of hers, absorbing his warmth as he reciprocated with a tender squeeze. The rest of the group entered the room with a chorus of cheers and words of encouragement.

"Brother, you had us all worried there, man," Achilles stated, showing a rare glimpse of softness. "What happened?"

Gun appeared drained and weary; his eyes heavy with fatigue.

"Cork, Binge, and Farmer came in when everyone else had gone. I was doing some paperwork when I heard the bell ring. The three of them ambushed me. Binge was brandishing his gun wildly like some crazed maniac."

Clark squeezed Gun's big hand, showing support and love. The realization that she had nearly lost him continued to whirl relentlessly in Clark's mind, fear and relief tugging at her heart.

Clark asked, "What happened to Binge?"

"He's been arrested. Shane arrived just in time to intervene. Otherwise, the fucker would be dead," Dom growled, holding Charly closer to his chest.

His brothers' swift and determined actions showcased the depth of their loyalty and the lengths they were willing to go to bring him back.

"Gun, you must be so proud of Clark," Charly said, wrapping an arm around Clark's waist in admiration.

Gun stated grimly, "Without Red, I shudder to think what would have happened. Cork's intentions were clear—he wanted me dead but in his own time. He had planned to return and complete the job." The weight of his words engulfed the room in solemn silence, with everyone present visibly affected by the gravity of his revelation.

With her eyes shining brightly, Clark whispered, "I'd do anything to keep you safe, Gun. You and Vin are my everything."

Clark realized she had admitted her true feelings for the first time to Vin and Gun. And she did it in front of an audience. It was an impulsive moment that caught her off guard. It just came out. However, she wasn't bothered by the fact that everyone now knew about her feelings because these people cared deeply for her, and she trusted them. To her, they were not just friends but her second family. Like her parents and brother, they had always understood her better than anyone else. If it hadn't been for their support and love, she would probably still be stuck in a cycle of self-harming and depression.

The women gasped and softly sighed, their surprise at Clark's confession palpable. In contrast, the men stayed quiet, mirroring the stunned expressions of the women. Vin and Gun looked as fragile as feathers as if a gentle breeze could easily knock them down.

Charly, with her usual wisdom, declared it was time for everyone to exit the room and let Gun, Vin, and Clark converse in private. Chad complained that he wanted to hear what Gun and Vin had to say, while Rocky wished Clark the best of luck with them.

When everyone left the room, Gun pulled Clark closer and stared into her eyes.

"What's on your mind, Red?" Gun inquired, his tired eyes instantly brightened and sparkled.

"I'm all ears, Shortcake," encouraged Vin, a mischievous smile dancing on his lips, his voice laced with amusement,

"Isn't it obvious? I'm in love with you," she declared joyfully, grateful that the awkwardness had dissolved into relief and acceptance.

Vin came around the bed and took Clark in his arms.

"I don't know about Gun, but I love you, too, Shortcake. I think I have since the day I met you," Vin admitted his love, kissing her with passion and fire and igniting a spark between them.

Clark vaguely registered the sound of a throat clearing loudly, then turned in Vin's arms to see an impatient-looking Gun.

She teased cheekily, "You love me too, right?"

"Yes, Red. I do. Come here," he demanded softly while holding his hand out.

Clark gingerly stepped into his arms, being careful with his injuries, and placed a tender kiss on his forehead.

* * * * *

EIGHT MEN STEALTHILY CREPT between the trees and boulders in the suburb of Greenville, an abandoned town with many derelict buildings that had been vandalized and burned. The clock hands hovered just shy of midnight, creating the perfect cover for their mission as the MC closed in on Cork and Farmer. The two men responsible for the shooting, abduction, and beating of Gun.

Cork held Gun accountable for his expulsion from the Club,

attributing it to Gun's involvement with his woman and interference in his side drug business. He'd not only forfeited his motorcycle but also lost his good standing and the profit he would have made from the Club's bar and garage businesses. Cork's anger towards Gun was irrational, fueled by baseless assumptions and misplaced blame.

Discovering that Cork and Farmer were laying low in Greenville brought back bad memories for the MC, especially Dom and Jax. It was the same town Charly was driven to after being kidnapped by Sol.

The town was practically deserted, inhabited by only a handful of resilient souls eking out their final years. Over the years, the once-thriving town had transformed into a ghost town plagued by rampant violent crime, drug problems, and a severe scarcity of job opportunities and resources.

Nevertheless, the town's isolation and abandoned nature made it an ideal sanctuary for those seeking to hide.

Achilles held his hand in a closed fist, signaling the men to stop in their tracks. The team gathered around, the flashlight illuminating their somber faces.

Achilles reiterated the plan to each man. "Listen up, brothers. This is the house where Cole says they're hiding. We're going to surround the house. Gage and Pen will approach from the left, Rocky and Chad will cover the right side, Dom and Jax will circle the back, and Vin and I will inspect the front and signal you when it's time to act."

Achilles looked at his brothers with a severe expression, emphasizing his seriousness. "Stick together, watch each other's backs, and ensure everyone's safety. Remember, our goal is to ambush and capture Cork and Farmer. No shooting unless it's necessary. Got it?"

Seeing their nods, everyone dispersed toward their allocated location. Each man's hand instinctively gravitated to their holstered gun, feeling the cold metal, and they double-checked the secure fastening of their handcuffs.

Achilles spoke softly into his phone, "Chad, give the signal."

The sound of an owl echoed, disrupting the quiet stillness of the night.

Silently, the men crept towards the rundown house from all sides. The windows had been smashed, and the doors were missing, making entry to the property accessible. Cork and Farmer should have selected a more secure hiding place.

Muffled voices could be heard from the windows and doorways. Achilles forbade anyone from moving until they could locate the men.

"What was that noise?" Farmer whispered loudly.

"It's a fucking owl, you moron," blasted Cork. "Go back to sleep."

Achilles gave the loud whistle to move. Holding the flashlight and leading the way, Vin kicked open the door to the room where the voices came from. A group of eight men suddenly launched a surprise attack on the two men who were sprawled on the ground, taking them by surprise. The sudden burst of light, coupled with the loud noise, startled them. Just as Cork moved for his weapon, Gage sprang into action, swiftly closing the distance and expertly disarming Cork with a well-placed kick. A ring of eight furious men converged around Cork and Farmer, leveling their weapons at the two men.

"Fuck!" shouted Cork, raising his hands in surrender.

"Don't shoot!" cried Famer, cowering into the corner.

Achilles stood in the middle of the room, a rare smile lighting up his usual severe expression.

"Well, if it isn't the two idiots who thought they could hurt one of our brothers."

Cork didn't bother to justify or explain away his actions. Achilles wouldn't accept any excuses, especially not from Cork and Farmer. They would receive their justice according to the Iconic Sons Motorcycle Club traditions. Achilles was adamant there would be no killing, but their actions warranted a severe beating as a form of retribution—an eye for an eye.

Shane inquired about the bruises and bloodied faces of Cork and Farmer when they were finally turned over to the police.

Achilles replied, "Found them that way."

Shane gazed at Achilles with suspicion etched on his face. "So, you're telling me you stumbled upon them, beaten to a pulp? Do you have any idea who could have done this to them?"

"No idea. You'll have to ask them," Achilles shrugged nonchalantly.

"How did you find them?" the astute detective persisted.

"They rocked up on our doorstep with their tails between their legs."

Shane dismissed Achilles's explanation skeptically, unconvinced by the tough man's words.

"Hang around, won't you? I need to ask some more questions." Shane found it suspicious that Achilles was the sole person to see Cork and Farmer and bring them in without assistance.

"Absolutely," Achilles responded confidently, concealing any hint of unease.

"Was anyone else there when these two rocked up on your doorstep?"

With a sly chuckle in response to Shane's sarcastic question, Achilles retorted, "Nope, just me."

✳ ✳ ✳ ✳ ✳

GUN WAS BACK AT the clubhouse recuperating. Clark and the other women took turns nursing him back to health, ensuring he took his medication, and providing round-the-clock care. The main issue emerged when Gun, accustomed to receiving pampered care, began making excessive demands. Sara had taken her aside the night before to air her and the girls' grievances. Clark promised to talk to Gun.

The night was dark as the trio gathered on the back porch, enjoying a late dinner together. Clark and Carrie spent the afternoon preparing a delicious meal, the kitchen filled with the aroma of pulled pork, zucchini, bacon gratin, and potato bake.

Although the others had finished eating, Vin's return was delayed as he was helping Dom and Rocky with kitchen renovations at the bar and grill. Having been closed for the past three days, the restaurant buzzed excitedly as the chef and sous chef, Con and Joel, reveled in installing the new fridge, freezer storage room, and woodfire pizza oven.

"Red, could you please get me another beer?" Gun asked, automatically expecting Clark to get it for him.

"The kitchen is right there," Clark replied, pointing through the doorway towards the kitchen.

"Yeah, but I'm injured," Gun complained, rubbing his chest where his cracked ribs had now healed.

"I've seen you walking around. Get the beer yourself. And while you're at it, could you refill my glass?" she said sweetly, holding up the champagne flute.

"I thought you loved me," Gun grumbled, his lips turned down in displeasure, pretending to be hurt.

"I surely do," she responded, affection and admiration reflected in her eyes.

Gun's face softened as he saw the sparkle and warmth in her eyes, prompting him to rise from his seat slowly. He courteously took her glass as he went to fetch his beer.

Vin's face lit up as he exclaimed happily, "That's my girl!" with a wide smile. "Gun seems to have gotten too comfortable lately. I suspect he secretly enjoys your attention. It's sparking some wild ideas in my head," he added with a suggestive eyebrow raise.

Hearing heavy footsteps behind her, Clark turned around, expecting Gun to pass her the champagne. Instead, he held both hands behind his back.

"Did you forget my drink?" she joked, seeing his serious expression.

"No. I have something more important than champagne and beer," Gun replied mysteriously.

"Oh yeah? What could that be?" she laughed, enjoying their banter.

"This." Gun produced a jacket. He held it up, and Clark read the *Property of Gun & Vin* inscription.

Clark felt tears welling up in her eyes, deeply moved by the significance of the jacket. She had learned from Charly what it meant to the men of the MC to claim a woman as their property. Charly explained that, unlike most MCs, the Iconic Sons MC treated their women with love and respect rather than viewing them as mere possessions. In return, the men asked for respect, loyalty, and obedience. This practice was vital for the safety of the women; the Club faced constant threats from rival groups, resulting in targeted attacks on the women and families of the bikers.

Clark had witnessed such attacks towards Gun and Vin. Even though she hadn't been attacked personally, she knew about Carrie and Charly's traumatic experiences from their past.

Vin took Clark's hand. "Will you accept the jacket, babe?" He swallowed deeply, his hopeful eyes reflecting his emotions.

"Yes. Yes. Yes," she cried joyfully, wrapping her arms around his strong shoulders. "Of course I will."

"Turn around, Red." Gun held out the jacket, and Clark slid her arms through the sleeves, taking in the new leather smell.

A loud chorus of cheers boomed from inside the clubhouse. Friends and family members surrounded Vin, Gun, and Clark, showing their support and love for the trio. The men clapped Vin and Gun in celebration, while the women hugged Clark, symbolizing her inclusion in the family.

"Clark!" Charly's voice was filled with joy as she exclaimed, "I'm thrilled for you! You're officially part of the family now."

"Congratulations, Clark," Carrie said as she stepped forward, giving Clark a tight hug. "You are one lucky woman."

"No, Carrie," Sara corrected. "Those two are the luckiest guys in the world." Sara kissed Clark on the cheek. "Welcome to the Iconic Sons family, Clark."

"Thank you," she whispered, her throat tightening with happiness.

Glancing over at her two lovers, Clark saw the joy on their faces as their brothers showed their support.

Clark, Vin, Gun, and the MC family celebrated long into the night. As she sat on the outside bench chatting with the girls, Clark's fingers absentmindedly traced the crisscross pattern of the new leather jacket, feeling the bumpy texture under her touch. The warm jacket offered her protection against the chilly easterly winds that had blown in.

Clark had spent most of the night away from Vin and Gun. Occasionally, she would glance over, and they would make eye contact. It appeared that the men and women were expected to socialize within their respective groups. Needing to be close to them, Clark excused herself from the women to spend time with Vin and Gun. She approached the two men leaning over a car's hood in the garage. They were admiring the meticulously restored engine by Jax, appreciating its intricate craftsmanship.

She wrapped an arm around each man, offering a warm smile that radiated her affection and need. When she saw the same desire reflected in their eyes, Clark felt a rush of lust and longing and let out a soft sigh.

"Listen, Jax. I think it's time we turn in for the night," Gun said, his voice deeper than usual.

Jax chuckled knowingly, giving them a chin lift before joining Dom and Charly.

Filled with anticipation to finally be alone together, Clark, Vin, and Gun headed upstairs. Clark shut the door with a soft click as it locked in place, then turned to her lovers.

EPILOGUE

Clark leaned back against Vin's chest on the lodge's porch. The sun bathed her in a warm glow on a balmy spring day, filling the air with the sweet scent of blooming flowers. As a gentle breeze whispered through the trees, wisps of Clark's long, red hair danced across her face. Vin gently picked up the tendrils and tucked them behind her ear. She closed her eyes, loving the pressure of his rough fingers, trailing a path down her neck and into the sensitive area between her neck and shoulder. The ticklish sensation elicited bubbles of happiness that escaped her glossy lips.

Across the lawn, Gun was deep in conversation with Dom near the lake's edge. Clark's eyes slowly traveled from the top of Gun's crown to his studded boots, admiring his impressive physique. Regardless of his attire, he always exuded a magnetic charm, which had a lot to do with how he carried himself.

A month ago, Vin and Gun bought a two-story house on the outskirts of the main town. Clark was unaware of their plans, as they usually divided their time between the clubhouse, where they spent time with friends and family, and the apartment she shared with Rachel.

Gun had told her one Sunday morning while they relaxed on the back porch at the clubhouse, sipping on coffee and enjoying the peaceful morning, that he and Vin were taking her for a drive. Clark, delighted at the idea of going for a Sunday drive, couldn't contain her curiosity. She asked Gun where they were going.

"Not far," he said cryptically, his lips twitching when she clicked her tongue.

"Okay, so you're in that kind of mood, are you?" she quipped good-naturedly, poking her tongue out at him.

"Want to put you over my knee, Red," he responded, his voice low and growly.

"It can wait until after our trip," Clark replied cheekily.

Gun bundled her into the Land Cruiser, and they drove for about ten minutes before arriving at a picturesque area that whispered tales of history and beauty. Gun slowed the vehicle down as they entered the street lined with evergreens, their lush branches casting dappled shadows along the sidewalk.

Clark admired the beautiful homes in the neighborhood, but her admiration was cut short when Gun turned into a driveway, drawing her attention to their destination. Clark looked over at him, wondering why they were there.

"Hop out, Red," he said with a big grin.

Confusion clouded Clark's expression as she tried to decipher the reason for their unexpected stop.

"Come on. Let's take a look," Vin urged.

Now she was stumped—look at what? This house?

Clark took her time exiting the vehicle and glancing around at her surroundings. The house was stunning, crafted with red brick walls that exuded a sense of grandeur and elegance reminiscent of the colonial era, with intricate woodwork adorning the windows and a striking gabled roof added to its charm. It featured a large wraparound porch. Situated on a sprawling estate, the house boasted meticulously manicured lawns and gardens blooming with vibrant flowers. Toweringly majestic oak trees stood sentinel around the estate, their branches forming a natural barrier that shielded the house from curious onlookers.

After stepping inside the house, Clark realized that Gun and Vin had bought the home for the three of them—a place they now called home. This marked the beginning of a new chapter filled with dreams for the future.

Clark moving out of the apartment she shared with Rachel and into her new home with Gun and Vin was serendipitous, as Rachel and Corey had discussed moving in together. Their relationship had flourished, and Clark was overjoyed for her brother and friend. Once a confirmed bachelor, Corey was now happily in a relationship with an incredibly cool, quirky, and amazing person.

* * * * *

CLARK, VIN, AND GUN recently celebrated their first year together. In the weeks leading up to the special day, Clark left post-it notes around the house with cryptic messages about the upcoming anniversary celebration. She had casually mentioned how romantic it was that Dom and Jax took Charly to Stars Align, where they had their first date, for their second anniversary. Clark talked about the custom of giving paper gifts for the first anniversary.

Interestingly, while Clark was planning their anniversary gifts, Gun seemed disinterested, and Vin remained indifferent to the approaching celebration.

On the day of their anniversary, Clark surprised Gun with a box set of books by his favorite author, the Mackay Murder Mysteries series. The tough man was left speechless. He showed his appreciation by preparing a gourmet dinner for Clark. On the other hand, Vin received a framed poster of his all-time favorite band, AC/DC, which he proudly displayed above his desk at the tattoo shop. Vin reciprocated more explicitly and pleasurably in the bedroom.

Moreover, that was not the end of it. Together, Gun and Vin unveiled their surprise—a weekend retreat at a picturesque lodge by the tranquil banks of Peekapine Lake. Clark cried all day at the romantic gesture. The lake held sentimental value as the place where they had their first date.

* * * * *

BUT TODAY MARKED A significant milestone for Pen as he officially became a patched Motorcycle Club member, a prestigious achievement that called for a grand celebration.

During the ceremony, Achilles allowed Gage, Pen's best friend, to give him his vest as a symbol of his membership in the MC. A year and a half ago, Gage and Pen were strangers to each other. Their initial encounter occurred amidst a pickpocketing incident that sparked a chain of events, culminating in a meaningful conversation between Gage and Pen.

Gage had been standing outside the crowded bar and grill, leisurely smoking a cigarette as he observed the unfolding events on the street. Pen had rushed by him, chasing a fifteen-year-old teenager down the street. He caught and grappled with the young boy. Believing Pen was assaulting the teenager, Gage raced ahead, prepared to intervene and confront Pen. When Gage caught up, the teenager fled, and Pen stood holding an item.

Gage shouted, "Did you take that phone from him?" ready to tackle the stranger.

Pen responded, "No, this is your phone."

"What the fuck?"

"The boy took your phone while you weren't looking. I saw him and chased after him when I realized you didn't notice."

Since that day, the two were inseparable, and being single, they were now the most sought-after men in the clubhouse. Vin and Gun no longer hold that honor because they belong to her.

With his dirty blonde military-style haircut, piercing green eyes, and neatly trimmed beard, Gage always took pride in his appearance, making him a compelling and popular man among the women at the clubhouse. Despite towering over many guys at six feet two inches tall, Pen's height surpassed even that. Pen's irresistible charm emanated from his luscious black hair, rich chocolate-colored skin, impeccably clean-shaven look, and dark brown eyes. In contrast to his popularity, Pen was reserved and discerning in selecting his companions. There was a competition among the women in the club to see who could win his affection. So far, few have been successful.

* * * * *

IT HAS BEEN OVER a year since Clark last cut herself. She no longer engaged in self-harming behaviors or had panic attacks; however, she remained aware that things could change. At least Clark was prepared for any challenges ahead, knowing she had the unwavering support and love of her family and two best friends, Vin and Gun. Vin and Gun consistently stood by their promises, always ready to listen to her without judgment and offer valuable advice, creating a safe space for Clark to express herself. Clark felt comfortable discussing any topic with them, no matter how trivial, and valued their trust in her ability to make her own decisions. This meant that she no longer needed to see Dr. Martinez regularly, although every once in a while, she would visit the doctor who had changed the course of her mental illness to help keep her on track with her progress.

Clark didn't feel the need to cover up her scars these days. At this point, everyone had seen her scars and paid no attention. Even Nolan wasn't fazed by her scars. Charly smiled, remembering the first time he saw her exposed arms.

> *"Clark, what happened to your arms?" he asked, his innocent eyes brimming with curiosity rather than disgust.*
> *"I used to cut myself, Nolan," Clark told him honestly.*
> *"Why did you do that?"*
> *"Because I used to have panic attacks."*
> *"Do you still have panic attacks?"*

"Not anymore, buddy. I sought help to overcome them. When I sense an attack coming, I practice breathing exercises to stay calm."

Nolan's eyes lit up. "We learn that at school. I'm good at deep breathing exercises. Want to try it with me? Let's do it together, Clark. Breathe in through your nose and out through your mouth. You're doing great."

Clark did the breathing exercise with him.

"Good job, Clark. Do you feel better now?"

"I do, Nolan. Thanks," she chuckled, charmed by his earnestness.

"What are you smiling at?" Vin asked, looking down at her.

"I remember when Nolan first saw my arms and got me to do the breathing exercises with him," explained Clark.

She felt the vibration in his hard abs as he chuckled at the memory. "That was a significant day for you, Shortcake, to have the courage to show your scars to everyone."

"I look at them now and feel like they represent a lifetime ago."

Vin's lips gently met her upturned ones in a tender kiss, her lips tingling in response.

"The scars are your past, and Gun and me are your future."

"I didn't realize you were sentimental," Clark joked, her honey-gold eyes shimmering with love.

"Only when it comes to you, babe."

Clark watched as Gun and Gage approached the porch, their hands waving animatedly as they discussed the restaurant's renovations.

Gun greeted Clark with a smile. "Hi, Red."

He nudged her over, and she gave him a bit of side-eye at his pushiness. At the same time, Clark reveled in his strength as his large body pinned her between him and Vin—her two heroes.

"Okay, I'm off to the restaurant with Rocky for the pizza oven installation," Gage called out as he skipped down the steps, taking two at a time to catch up to Rocky.

Carrie stood forlornly inside the gazebo, her eyes fixed on Rocky's departing figure, causing Clark to feel a tug of empathy. Carrie's situation was one of unrequited love, even though Clark didn't believe Rocky was entirely indifferent to the younger woman.

$$\star\,\star\,\star\,\star\,\star$$

GAGE DROPPED ROCKY OFF at the curb outside the bar and grill so Rocky could unlock the restaurant. He then parked the car a block away. Exiting the Jeep, he pocketed the keys and headed back towards the restaurant. He and Rocky would meet with the electrician to install the new pizza oven as part of the kitchen renovations.

Gage had taken about a dozen steps before he heard a scraping sound behind him. Alarmed, he quickly turned around and saw a young kid, perhaps around sixteen or seventeen, scratching Rocky's Jeep. He had a tool in his hand, etching long horizontal scratches across several door panels.

"Hey!" Gage shouted, running towards the kid. "What the hell are you doing?"

The teenager, clad in faded jeans and a beige hoodie, looked up at Gage's shout, his eyes widening with fear. Suddenly, the boy started running down the busy street, turning sharply into an alleyway. Gage chased after him, his legs and arms powering to close the distance. As he turned the corner, he noticed the kid had a slight head start. He had already reached the end of the alleyway and was effortlessly scaling a wire fence, moving with the agility of a cat climbing a tree.

Reaching the end of the dark alleyway, Gage's nostrils were assaulted by the smell of rotting fish. The teenager was about to turn down the back street in seconds if Gage didn't act quickly. He doubted his ability to scale the fence as quickly as the kid, knowing his heavy boots would slow him down. Once he cleared the fence at the end of the alley, the boy would disappear without a trace.

"Hey, kid!" Gage called out in desperation.

Miraculously, the boy stopped and pivoted towards Gage. "I'm not a kid," he replied, his voice soft and low.

Gage's fingers tightened around the diamonds in the chain wire fence before he demanded, "Then you should know better. Why did you scratch the Jeep?"

The slight figure moved closer to the fence, a smirk playing on his lips as he taunted Gage, secure in the knowledge that Gage couldn't reach him with the fence separating them. Only when the person drew closer did Gage realize it was a young woman, her features coming into focus.

"Because you think it's okay to ghost people. Remember Amber?" she asked, her tone laced with defiance.

"Who the fuck is Amber?" he growled, not sure if she was playing him.

Gage studied her, his eyes taking in her heart-shaped face and rosebud lips hidden under the hoodie. He could now see the curves underneath her sweater. The hourglass figure showed that she was all woman. Gage couldn't see her eye color, but he noticed strands of blonde hair peeking under the hoodie.

"Oh, now you can't remember her," she said, throwing her hands up. "It must have been something special, huh? You're a real charmer, you know that, Rocky?"

"Rocky? I'm not Rocky," he denied.

"Now you want to play the "It wasn't me" game. It's too late, Rocky. Your name is on the license plate; denials won't work."

Even though this woman had just vandalized Rocky's Jeep, Gage couldn't help chuckling. She was spirited.

"I'm telling you the truth. I'm not Rocky. I'm Gage. Rocky's inside the restaurant if you want to meet him," he challenged, amused to see a glimmer of uncertainty in her expression.

Then he said seriously, "Ghosting someone doesn't excuse scratching their vehicle or justify vandalism."

"It's justified when someone borrows five thousand dollars and doesn't repay it! That's a substantial amount to owe someone," she replied passionately, her fists clenched tightly, showing determination.

"Rocky would never borrow money from a woman. He doesn't need to," Gage defended.

Rocky and the MC, who owned several successful businesses in town, were financially secure. So, the woman's claims about Rocky borrowing money from Amber seemed unfounded and illogical.

"Amber's either lied to you, or you have the wrong guy," Gage informed her, and her silence spoke volumes.

"Amber wouldn't lie to me," she whispered uncertainly, her eyes looking anywhere but at Gage.

"Then you have the wrong person," he stated, feeling sorry for her.

Gage doubted Rocky would share the same sentiment once he discovered what happened to his Jeep.

"What's your name?"

She scowled at him. "I'm not telling you that. You'll report me to the police."

"No. I won't involve the police. I give you my word."

The MC only involved the police if they needed their resources. Otherwise, they handled their own business.

"Lori," she revealed, her voice a whisper in the wind.

As if regretting telling Gage her name, the woman turned and fled, vanishing around the corner.

Gage didn't move immediately, testing out the feel and sound of her name.

"Lori," he whispered.

FEARLESS

ICONIC SONS MC: BOOK THREE

Kahlani B. Steele was born and raised in Perth, Western Australia, where she also pursued a degree in Education focusing on Early Childhood Education. Kahlani now resides in a small town called Kalgoorlie. Her passion for reading was ignited at a young age when she fell in love with *Anne of Green Gables* by L. M. Montgomery, a book that sparked her imagination and set her on the path to becoming a writer and educator.

Kahlani B. Steele used a pseudonym under which she published her debut novel, *Resilient*, in 2024. *Courageous* is her second novel, and the latest book in the Iconic Sons MC series.